David served for almost forty years in the army. Firstly in the Infantry, rising quickly up the ranks and, then, transferring to the elite Army Physical Training Corps, (now Royal).

During his time, he experienced many things both on active service and as the Chief Instructor for the Joint Services Mountain Training Center—things that eventually had to be written about in a fictional form but based on factual events.

To Penny
Best wishes
David Baggaley
MBE BEM.

In memory of Captain Robert James Davies. Soldier, teacher, mountaineer, and friend.

David Brown

THE WOLVES OF THE RADFAN

AUSTIN MACAULEY PUBLISHERS™

LONDON • CAMBRIDGE • NEW YORK • SHARJAH

A CIP catalog record for this title is available from the British Library.

ISBN 9781528928458 (Paperback)
ISBN 9781528928465 (Hardback)
ISBN 9781528965491 (ePub e-book)

www.austinmacauley.com

First Published (2019)
Austin Macauley Publishers Ltd
25 Canada Square
Canary Wharf
London
E14 5LQ

My thanks to Major Mark Pritchard RWR for his advice and help. Jane White for encouraging me to keep going. Carole whose courage gave me strength when I most needed it.

Prologue

When you read this, remember 'Look Alike' said, "It never happened," and if Doyle said, "We can't remember," well that's it!"

The Aden campaign was a vicious war promoted by the North Yemen communists who had killed the ruling Iman and deposed his son. Backed by the Egyptian dictator Abdul Gamal Nasser and indirectly the Soviet Union, the Yemen started its expansion south to take the independent Federation of South Arabia which included the Aden Protectorate that Britain was hoping to complete a peaceful hand over to the civil powers in the near future.

For the British the violence started in 1963 and continued through to 1967, this story covers the period I served there with a great Infantry Regiment that was serving a two-year tour of duty from1963 to 1965. The conflict was largely ignored by the British and world press. A world struggling out of the depths of the Second World War and into the horror of nuclear destruction in the cold war had little interest in a declining empires colonial problems and the expansion of communism.

The events I have written about in the book happened in some way or another. The main characters were either involved or I have used them to tell the stories that were related to me. These may have become taller in the telling or I have used my imagination to entertain. Some of the events may not be in chronological order but I have put it down as it flowed from my mind. I have not used my real name or of those who were there with me. However, they may recognize the characters and the part they played.

Compared to today's weapons and equipment, the soldier of the time was not very well armed or protected. There was no body armor, rifles that were only semi-automatic, no night vision aids, primitive communications systems, and a webbing equipment to carry everything bordering on sadistic.

The casualties for this conflict will never be truly known especially on the NLF, FLOSY or the general Dissidents' side. The innocent as usual suffered the most and those numbers arc impossible to assess. Officially, British military casualties numbered 92 killed and 510 wounded plus 17 civilians killed and 81 wounded. Of the enemy, 382 killed and 1,714 wounded. I believe the enemy and innocents' numbers were much greater than this for the following reasons. None of the rubble of the destroyed villages was searched by the authorities to my knowledge. After a firefight, the tribesmen were very good at removing their dead and wounded. And the ease of movement over the border meant that they could be buried out of sight of the British. Despite the difficulties of flying in such terrain, the RAF would have killed or wounded many more during up country action with the attacks on enemy positions with the amazing Hunter aircraft flown by brave and talented pilots.

– David Brown

"Remember those that serve."

Chapter 1
Starlight and Bullets

David 'Bomber' Brown looked again at the star-filled sky, without any artificial light, pollution for hundreds of miles; the night sky could be seen in all its splendor.

Lying on the cold, hard ground at four in the morning at almost six thousand feet, he could ignore the discomfort and only wonder at the beauty of the universe.

Six months ago, he had been sitting in a Bury St. Edmunds pub, The One Bull, listening to the latest pop sensation, *the Beatles*. The jukebox seemed to have an endless supply of records and people fed the greedy chrome monster with coins to keep the music flowing. The busty barmaid worked tirelessly pulling pints for the squaddies from the training depot, who seemed to have an incurable thirst.

Having finished his two years training at the Infantry Junior Leaders Regiment Oswestry at the age of seventeen, he had moved to the Regimental Depot in Bury St. Edmunds in Suffolk. There, he had, with several others, completed six weeks' preparation training followed by a few days' leave before flying out to join his Regiment which had been deployed on a two-year tour of the British Protectorate of Aden.

The Regiment had already been in action against the so-called Red Wolves of the Radfan as the Qotaibi tribes men liked to call themselves. With the rest of the Brigade, they had pushed the Wolves out of the up country area known as the Radfan, freeing up the ancient trade route which ran from the coast all the way to Mecca.

The Wolves had taken advantage of the 1962 Revolution in North Yemen when the communist backed group supported by Egypt, which in turn was supported by the Soviet Block. The Wolves true to form backed themselves while playing the game with the communists hoping to gain more than anyone else in the deal but who would eventually find themselves being absorbed in the big game of communist expansion.

The barmaids, *Beetles* and beer were now a distant memory and the reality of soldiering in a combat zone was coming nearer every second to Bomber.

The shooting was more intense now and getting close. Bomber thought he could hear people struggling up the steep stone-covered path that led from North to South Yemen.

Six hours ago, his section of eight men had moved from the top of the rocky ridge, which was the dividing line between the two countries, to about half a mile down the slope to provide cover for the withdrawal of the PO (Political Officer) and his four local tribes men from their incursion into the north.

The remainder of the Platoon had taken up a defensive position just on the reverse slope of the ridge staying inside South Yemen.

Anyone coming over the ridge would be silhouetted against the night sky and would be an easy target for the riflemen.

Doyle, the section commander, a grizzled Irishman from Londonderry Northern Ireland, was now talking, telling them not to get triggered happy and to remember the first ones to appear would be the PO and his tribesmen and not to open fire until he gave the order or fired first. Bullets were now cracking overhead and Bomber was aware his only real protection was the darkness that covered him like a blanket.

Bomber knew that it would be a close quarter firefight as the effective field of vision would be less than thirty meters. He pulled the butt of his SLR tightly into his shoulder, caressing his cheek against the smooth wooden stock and waited.

Suddenly from the shadows, a large shape appeared, staggering and clearly exhausted the PO slumped to the ground. He had been carrying one of his local tribesman who must have been wounded earlier on. Just behind came two more dragging between them the forth tribesman who was hopping on one leg.

The chasing group was close now and shots were ricocheting off the hard ground around the section. Not that the chasing group would have been able to see what it was shooting at, but they were using the line of the track as a shooting alley hoping to hit the PO and his men.

Bomber felt his heart pounding and he gripped his rifle tighter, checking once again that the safety catch was off to allow the rifle to fire.

It was clear to Bomber that without help, the PO and his group would be caught and overwhelmed if they did not get immediate assistance.

Suddenly Doyle was giving orders, "Carter, Graham, Moose, Black, get down there and get them up to the platoon, NOW!"

The four raced out. Moose, as his nickname implied, was a big man, six foot four, of solid muscle. He plucked the wounded tribesman from the political officer and threw him up onto his shoulder in a fireman carry. With the other hand, he helped the political officer up and they set off at a lope up the hill.

Meanwhile, Carter and Graham had the other wounded tribesman between them and were moving fast after Moose. Black, who was bringing up the rear, urging the other two to greater speed, suddenly cried out and jumped forward, shouting, "Shit, shit! They shot me in the arse!" But he kept running.
Whoever was leading the pursuing group had sensed that they almost had their quarry and was shouting to urge his men on, but was obviously unaware the PO had help.

Doyle knew that they would be lucky to stop the chasing group with just the four of them and began issuing orders in a hushed voice.

McBride, who had the light machine gun, (LMG), a left over from the Second World War but an effective and deadly weapon for all that, was moved further out to the left with Davis acting as his number two. This would allow them to take the enemy more from the flank, creating maximum damage.

Doyle slid closer to Brown and hissed, "Bomber, when I open fire, you start on the right and work into the middle. I will deal with the rest of the bastards!"

Now Bomber could see the shadows moving and the shape of men pushing themselves hard up the slope. Stabs of flames came from the shapes and the whine of rounds hitting the rocks or cracking through the air was making Bomber press himself into the ground.

Despite the fact Bomber had never shot at another human being or been under enemy fire before, he now felt unusual calm. Using the sights of his rifle would be pointless in the dark at a range of less than thirty yards. The best way was to keep both eyes open and sight along the long barrel. Taking deep breaths and exhaling slowly, Bomber felt himself surrender to his long, hard days of training.

"Fire!" roared Doyle.

Bomber reacted! Bang! His rifle sounded like a cannon in his ears. The right-hand man fell and he repeated it twice more at the shadows. He never even registered the thump of the recoil in his shoulder or even thinking to wait between shots to see if he had hit the enemy. At less than fifteen yards, it was automatic and on target.

Sliding his legs right brought his aim to the left to assist Doyle but no help was needed. The LMG had ripped through the group like a Regimental Sergeant Major through a platoon of raw recruits.

Bomber could not see how many bodies lay in front of them on the track but the shock to the chasing group must have been as if hell had descended on them. The survivors of the devastating fire had fled back down the track, prevented from going right by the steep uphill slope and the gorge on the left; going back the way they had come was their only option.

"Bomber with me," Doyle's rasping accent cut through the air like a rusty knife and Bomber automatically reacted. Jumping to his feet, he followed Doyle who was already several yards ahead of him.

Together they moved forward over the bodies. Bomber tried not to look at them as he went forward. One or two were moving, shaking as if cold and moaning. Doyle did not stop but jogged and hunched over for twenty or more yards. Holding up his hand, Doyle stopped and crouched down, cocking his head to one side with his mouth open to amplify any sound. Bomber imitated him, trying to catch the sounds from further down the track.

The enemy had stopped some twenty-five yard further on in a dip. Someone was trying to rally them.

"Sounds like there must be at least twenty of the wee shits still in one piece. Can't have them coming back now that we have lost the element of surprise," Doyle whispered into Bombers ear. "We'll give them a grenade each, then stand up and empty a full mag into them, then leg it up the hill, okay!"

Bomber acknowledged and, pulling a thirty-six grenade from his pouch, waited for Doyle to throw.

The thirty-six grenade fitted the hand perfectly, so-called due to the body of the grenade being serrated into thirty-six sections, although Bomber had never counted the sections to see if it was so. At the base of the grenade was a plug that unscrewed to allow the fitting of the fuse. The fuse fitted into these was a four-second-one and made the total weight of the grenade at just under two pounds. Designed and used in the First World War, it was still in use with the British Army.

A nudge from Doyle and they pulled the pins, lobbing the grenades into the dark shadow of the dip where the enemy seemed to be roused to a state ready to charge back up the hill.

On throwing the grenades, they both dropped flat to the ground and heard shouts of surprise and almost instantly, a double *cuurumph* as the grenades exploded. Doyle and Bomber jumped to their feet and rapid-fired into the dip where the shouting of a second ago had turned to screams of pain.

As their SLRs clicked on empty, the pair turned and jogged back up hill, reloading as they went.

A shouted challenge from McBride, who was still manning, the LMG was quickly answered by Doyle.

Davis had been checking the bodies and collecting the weapons. He was treading carefully amongst the dead, pulling weapons from them and swearing about the smell and mess. Bomber tried not to look and thanked God it was dark.

"No time for that," snapped Doyle. "Let's go, diamond formation on me."

Doyle took point. Davis left Bomber right and McBride at the back in the standard nighttime patrol formation of a diamond which allowed each man in the event of an enemy contact to face outwards and fire without hitting his own team.

Ten minutes later, they almost walked into a patrol sent from the platoon position to back them up.

The patrol was led by the Platoon Sergeant, called Coker, a tough eighteen-year serviceman who hailed from Suffolk and who had seen action in Korea.

The patrol moved past by a few yards and took up fire positions, while Doyle briefed Coker. After they had spoken, they moved together back to the Platoon position on the reverse of the slope.

Once the platoon was together, a fast patrol pace was set back towards the Company Base. Before reaching the huge dirt airstrip that ran west to east in front of the base, they met the support group who was to provide cover while they crossed the open flat area that bordered the airstrip.

Finally, they were back within the safety of the base and being ushered into the cookhouse tent to consume sandwiches and mugs of hot tea laced with the CQMS's (Company Quarter Master Sergeant) issued rum.

A debrief was conducted by the Company Commander, a slightly portly man who, if had been wearing civvies, could have been taken for a school master, but on closer inspection, one could see the scar tissue on the face from his time as an army boxer and a hardness about the eyes that made him look like a dangerous man to cross. He also spoke perfect Arabic which made him popular with the locals he had to deal with.

The Second in Command, a Captain sat ready to take notes, who, after a recent bout of Malaria, looked like a skeleton with clothes on.

The debrief over the Company Commander dismissed the platoon with words of praise for the night's action and said that a twin pin, a two-engine light aircraft, would arrive at first light to casevac the two wounded tribesmen to hospital in Aden.

Bomber felt that he had hardly slept at all when he and the rest of the section were woken, being told to parade at the dining tent. Black had not actually been shot in the rear, as he had put it, but had several pieces of rock splinters as the result of a round hitting the ground close to him, pluck from his butt by the duty medic who told him to soldier on, a subject that he would moan about for days to anyone who would listen, as he thought he deserved at least five days' rest and recuperation in Aden.

Assembled in the dining tent was the Company Commander who looked angry, his normally placid demeanor changed to a scowl. The Platoon Commander and Sergeant stood a little to one side with their eyes firmly on the ceiling. Doyle marched the section in and was told to stand everyone at ease.

After a minute or two, a short, stocky man showed up dressed in the typical outfit that the political officers chose to wear, a mix between uniform and Arab clothing giving them a Lawrence-of-Arabia look.

He walked in with an air of authority which the Company Commander seemed to reluctantly defer to.

Without introducing himself, he spoke directly to the section.

"You," he almost shouted, "will forget about tonight! It never happened! You never crossed the border! There was not any firefight or casualties! Have I made myself clear enough?" He paused and stared at each one in turn.

Now when you have been threatened and given the stare of death by endless Sergeant Majors, who with one word could make your life hell on earth, being harangued by a pompous man in fancy dress was bound to bring about a few smirks and titters.

It started with Black who managed to choke back a full-blown laugh with a strangled giggle. McBride was the main culprit. He started the chain reaction by nudging Davis on his left and soon, everyone but Doyle was fighting back the laughter. Bomber felt lightheaded and almost hysterical, wanting to cackle like some demented parrot.

The Lawrence lookalike was almost ready to explode when Doyle, in his harsh Londonderry accent, cut through the noise.

"Shut the fuck up, you brainless idiots, and listen to the Officer." That said, he turned to the 'lookalike' and said, "I'm sorry, sir. The lack of sleep has that effect but rest assured, none of us can remember a thing about the last twenty-four hours."

A look of almost confusion seemed to pass over lookalike's face which then changed to one of anger but before he could reply, the flap to the dining tent was pulled open and in came the man who had started the night events.

Without looking at the other officers, he snatched Doyle by the hand, pumping it up and down and said, "Thank God you were there. If you had not moved down the slope, they would have had our heads on a pole by now."

Moving along the line, shaking hands and thanking everyone, he finished at Moose and gave him a bear hug and almost Jigged around the tent. As they were both of a similar size, a full jig would have wrecked the place.

By this time, everyone but the lookalike was grinning like Cheshire cats. A loud 'major' issued forth from 'lookalike' and our Bull Dog Drummond, as we later came to call him, released Moose and said, "I guess the boss has told you that none of this happened but nevertheless, you all have my and my men's thanks." With that, he strode out into the sunlight.

Chapter 2
Base Camp and the Pig

The Radfan covered an area of some four hundred square miles. At an altitude of six thousand feet, it could be either extremely hot or freezing cold. Dry, barren, and sparsely populated, it was ideal for guerrilla warfare. Despite the harshness of the mountainous terrain, small communities flourished, growing crops, grazing sheep and goats, trading along the ancient road that traversed the region all the way to Mecca, the passing traffic providing a much-needed income. This was what the lads called up country as opposed to the coastal area of Aden.

The camp, airfield, and radar site was situated in a key position. It dominated the area and prevented the north-backed 'Wolves' from taking over and spreading the communist control over the local people. Over the border, the Recce Platoon lads told stories of ex and not-so-ex British soldiers working with the tribesman still loyal to the murdered Iman son. Bomber thought the Recce lads would have liked nothing better than to go over the border and joined them, a sentiment shared by many in the Regiment who thought it better to be on the offensive rather than on the defensive all the time.

After breakfast and the ritual of the camp Sergeant Major's parade, the platoon was stood down to clean the platoon weapons and to sleep. Not that sleep came easy to Bomber or any of the section. So they sat talking in low voices and relived the night's action. Except for Doyle and McBride, no one else had been in a close quarter firefight. Now that there was time to reflect, the mind games started.

Davis, who had had the unpleasant task of checking the bodies, could not help but describe the effect of the 7.62 rounds on the bodies. "Bloody LMG cut two of them in half, guts and shit everywhere there was."

"Bollocks," Black shot back. "It was darker than a train tunnel you could not have seen sod all!"

"Is that so," Davis replied with something of a sneer. "It was me that had to collect the weapons and I was standing up to my neck in shit and guts, so fuck you. You was up the fucking hill and it was left to the four of us to save the day or night if you like." As Davis got excited, his Welsh accent became more pronounced.

Before anyone could reply, Doyle appeared in the ditch as it was known. The ditch was the gap between the double sandbagged walls that went completely around their sleeping tent. The ditch had an overlapping entrance at each end.

"Just been having a word with the Recce boys. They have been on the ridge scanning the action sight." The Recce or Reconnaissance Platoon were the unit's eyes and ears and normally spent time ahead of the regiment, but because of the multi tasks they did in Aden, they had been nicknamed the 'Raider Platoon'.

"They said that we got five of the rag heads on the first contact and another five at the second."

"Excuse me, Paddy," Davis butted in with an element of sarcasm in his voice, "if no one was allowed over the border, how do they know?"

Doyle gave his how-would-you-like-me-to-put-my-fist-down-your-throat stare and Davis shrank back trying to blend in with the sandbags.

"Because you Welsh tart." Paddy was now squatting down and leaning forward to give his words more effect and Bomber being the closest could smell the rum that had been consumed by Paddy with his mate in the Recce Platoon.

"That fucking wee shit that told us nothing happened last night was with them and they drove hell for leather in their fancy new Land Rovers to the site to check the bodies before the North Yemen mob could get to them and take them away." Paddy paused then continued in an even lower voice.

"And guess what?" No one answered. "They had up-to-date weapons and two of the dead looked to be Egyptians." Paddy looked at each of his captive audience as if waiting for an answer.

Bomber broke the silence. "Paddy is the Egyptian army over the border or just their special forces, guys?"

"So one of you has a brain that works," he replied. "The truth is it's probably just the specials that have been there since the beginning but for them to accompany the North Yemen on a hot pursuit means something's up!"

"Now not a word of this to anyone but if we go out tonight, I want you all on the ball, so get some sleep."

With that, he turned and left the ditch.

Bomber woke from his nightmarish dream where he had been firing at shadowy figures that no matter how much he shot at them still continued to race towards him.

After a showered, he made his way to the cook house for dinner, the details of last night's action was the talk of the camp – wild stories of hundreds of dissidents being killed, of Doyle fighting hand-to-hand while screaming wild Irish curses. Doyle and Bomber chasing those left alive completely back to Mecca were commonplace.

So much for it never happening, thought Bomber. I wonder who is fueling this crap. In the dining tent, it was partly explained when he saw Davis holding court in a corner with about a dozen or so listeners. With a mug of tea in one hand, Davis Welsh lilt added an almost poetic tone as he embroidered the story of the action.

During dinner, Bomber and the others were pestered for details but wary of the warning they had been given by 'Lookalike', they kept quiet. A much quieter Davis sat with the rest of the section, having been given a severe 'kept your mouth shut' by McBride.

After dinner, Bomber sat near the main Sanger sipping on a mug of tea. As the last of the days' sun drenched the mountaintops with an almost alpine glow, Bomber studied the camp and the way it had been built.

To just describe the camp as a Company Base dismissed the work and attention which had gone into making it a stronghold that commanded a large area between two South Yemen villages full of friendlies and the dirt runway capable of taking the RAF huge flying box called a Beverly and the old DC 3s of the Aden airways. The runway and the planes flew in and out where the lifeline for both the villages and the camp make the runway unusable and the camp and villages would slowly be strangled. To prevent this happening, the runway had not been fenced in but was a free fire zone area and any intruders would be shot on sight.

Built on a gently rising hill, the position was fortified with a perimeter wall of rocks, scoured from the surrounding area, some four to five feet high and three feet thick. Bomber marveled at the skill, man hours, and sheer hard work required to build such a wall. Outside of this was several barbwire entanglements with antipersonnel personnel mines sown between each.

At the summit of the hill was a large sandbagged post known as top Sanger. Approximately twelve feet by twelve, complete with the new GPMGs, (General Purpose Machine Gun), these new belt-fed gun had a much greater effective range and a heavier weight of fire than the old LMG and was now becoming standard issue to all infantry units.

Below and to one side in a separate Sanger stood two 120 mm Wombat antitank guns. These guns were recoilless, so they were very light and easy to handle. In fact they could be loaded onto the back of a long wheel based Land Rover and fired while still on it.

Lower down the slope in the deepest open topped Sanger was a section of 81 mm mortars replacing the old three-inch mortars and these could be fired out to six thousand yards. The combined effect of these weapons was one of awe. The noise and explosive power of the Wombats could only be described as mind-blowing, robbing you of the power to think. That is assuming you survived the round exploding.

The mortars could blanket an area with rounds so fast that it was frightening just to watch. Being on the receiving end would be horrific and fatal, in that order.

Situated at various points around the camp were the platoon defensive positions which gave wide fields of fire covering the complete perimeter and beyond, should the enemy be bold enough to attack the camp.

A Camp Commandant looked after the base which left the Company Commander free to run all the operations outside of the perimeter. Beneath him was a Sergeant Major and a team of soldiers ranging from cooks, pioneers, and store men who maintained the accommodation. This was made up of a series of one hundred and sixty pounder tents for sleeping up to eight men each. As there were just over two hundred men in the camp, there were a lot of one hundred and sixty pounders.

Three larger marquees made up the cookhouse, dining area and headquarters; all of these had sandbag walls built around them for protection from small arms fire and mortar attacks.

The only semi-permanent buildings were the shower block constructed of wood and corrugated iron sheets and thunder alley, two toilets blocks, one for the officers and one for everyone else known as the OR's SH (other ranks' shit house). Both the shower and toilet blocks were surrounded by very high sandbag walls as they were situated at the lowest point of the camp on the more exposed north side.

The toilets consisted of a very deep hole blasted into the rock-hard ground. In the OR's SH there was six back-to-back thunder boxes placed over the top. Each thunder box had a wooden hinged lid. Lime dust would be shoveled into the hole daily to kill the smell and prevent infection, which it failed to do certainly for the former.

Bomber quickly pulled up his trousers and left the OR's SH with just minutes to spare as at eight fifteen, the place would be out of bounds and the Camp Sergeant Major would go in and have his solitary daily constitutional.

He was known to all the soldiers as 'The Pig' which he did in truth resemble, but mostly it was for his treatment of those under his control.

After his visit to the OR's SH at eight fifteen, he would have a camp parade for all the soldiers with no exceptions regardless, even if you had been on patrol all night.

He took great delight in finding fault, giving out demeaning tasks to be completed in an impossibly short time for which another punishment would be added for failing to complete the first task.

Most of the infantry company had protection from his more sadistic tendencies but some of his own soldiers were not so lucky.

One particular individual was a Pioneer Corporal who for some reason was being driven to the edge of suicide by 'The Pig's' constant harassment and some of the lads had decided that enough was enough.

At eight fifteen the next morning, Bomber was waiting with a growing crowd for the Pig to enter the OR's SH for his solitary routine. Once he was in, a figure was seen to enter by the other entrance and after a few seconds came racing out, disappearing up the hill to blend in with the assembled throng.

By which time a large audience had assembled on the pretext of getting ready for the parade. A second later, there was a large 'thump' of a muffled explosion and a number of thunder box seat rose into the air above the sandbagged wall to a ragged chorus of cheers!

Then the Pig appeared staggering from behind the sandbag wall severely hampered by his trousers still being around his ankles and covered in a very unpleasant-looking muck. Looking up at the assembled group, he waved a fist and shouted, "You bastards! I know it was you lot," and then collapsed on the ground.

Two medics appeared almost as if cued to do so, put him on a stretcher and jogged off to the medical tent.

Some hours later, a twin pin aircraft, a two-engine Sky Van, a miniature version of the Beverly, landed and took the Pig off into the blue sky to the cheers of the camp staff. The same plane disembarked a replacement Camp Sergeant Major, a tall, ramrod straight man who looked like he had 'seen it, done it' who at the next morning parade made an announcement which went as follows, "Good morning, I am Sergeant Major Jones and when I go for a shit, eleven of you fuckers are coming with me!"

He smiled at the roar of laughter and proved to be an ideal camp beast, firm, fair, and friendly without tolerating any slackness.

He also instigated that those who had been out on night patrol or guard duties did not need to attend morning parade.

The investigating was short and sharp, and was put down to a buildup of methane gas which was ignited by the Pig lighting a cigarette. The next day, pinned to the entrance of the OR's SH appeared a handwritten sign saying: 'No smoking. It could be dangerous, especially to Pigs!'

The Pig was never seen again!

Chapter 3
Monkey Business and Hell Drivers

Life had settled into a series of guard duties, endless patrols, and nighttime ambushes. To the south of the camp a long, high ridge separated the main camp from an RAF radar site. The radar covered a huge area of sky going well out into the Gulf of Aden and was an important link in the whole area's air defense.

The site itself was guarded by a team from the RAF Regiment but to protect the site from any attack, the ridge that separated the camp and radar site had to be dominated, denying the dissidents any chance of using it to attack the radar installation.

It was on a moonless night that Bomber, now promoted to section second in command, found himself with half of the platoon huddle in the two large Sangers perched on the ridge.

Shifting from an uncomfortably crouched position to a crossed leg sitting one, Bomber stared down the ridge, fighting the boredom and sleep which threatened to overwhelm him.

Trick such as counting out how many rocks he could see down the slope had worn thin over an hour ago. The comforting shape of a GPMG manned by Moose was next to him and at about two o'clock in the morning, Moose nudged Bomber, pointing out shadows that were moving steadily towards them.

Pulling the alarm cord to the next Sanger manned by the Sgt. Coker, a two-tug acknowledgment signaled that Coker was aware and Bomber could hear him talking on the radio ordering a mortar strike by the camp 81 mm mortars.

Bomber could now see many shadows crawling up the slope and there was something strange about the way they moved. Pulling the butt of his SLR into his shoulder, he felt the same calm that had come over him as before. This feeling was bolstering by the shape of Moose sighting down the barrel of the wicked-looking GPMG with a two-hundred round belt of ammunition ready loaded, one in five of the rounds being a tracer which would burn bright, making it easy to follow the fall of the rounds.

Several long tugs of the alarm cord signaled Coker was about to send up a flare to light up the area which would be followed by a two-inch parachute illumination round from the platoon mortar.

The flare soared up and everyone waited for Coker to shout fire but all that came was a great roar of laughter as Baboons raced in all directions.

Bomber felt a wave of relief as the laughter swept over all of them but one person was not laughing but slumped in the bottom of the Sanger, Terry looked all in.

Crouching down next to Terry, Bomber asked, "What's wrong, mate?"

Terry shook his head, "I've had enough of this," he muttered. "Wife and two-year-old son at home, thought we were about to be taken out just then and it just a bunch of fucking apes!" He shook his head as if to clear it.

"I was in the truck that hit a mine that killed Chalky on the push into the Radfan."

Again, Terry shook his head but carried on, "Me and Chalky went through training together, dated girls together. Shit, he was my best man!"

Bomber had not been with the Regiment when the push into the Radfan was made and did not know what to say.

His two years at the Infantry Junior Leaders Regiment and continuation training plus his junior NCO's (Non Commissioned Officers) course had not prepared him as a trick cyclist.

"Okay, mate," Bomber said gently. "Why don't you get your head down for a bit?"

Terry nodded and curled on his side, hugging his knees.
Moose gave Bomber a nudge and whispered, "That's been on the cards for some time, bloody medics just kept giving him tablets and telling him to soldier on. The death of Chalky really did it for him."

Bomber nodded and made a mental note to talk to Coker in the morning.

The early dawn light slowly drove the shadows away and then in a great burst of brilliance, the sun rose above the horizon. Bomber felt the chill of the night leave his body as the sun engulfed him in its warm embrace, banishing the cold and fears of the night.

Bomber watched the relief guard from one Platoon make the steep slog up the slope toward the ridge to take over the Sanger's.

A short discussion between Coker and one Platoon Commander ended with some laughter and Bomber guessed it concerned the Baboons.

Although the return route was in sight of the camp sentries and that the relief guard had traveled the route on the way to the ridge, Coker insisted on good patrol drills for the return. Being tired was not any excuse for complacency, which has been the death of many a good man Coker would often quote and it was something Bomber would remember.

On arrival at camp, weapons were unloaded and equipment stowed safely in the tents. Some of the other guys going for breakfast started making monkey noises as they passed. *How the hell did they know already?* Bomber thought, and he guessed they would be the butt of many a monkey joke over the next few days. *Best let it flow like water off a duck's back and join in the laughter,* thought Bomber.

The big dirt airstrip had to be checked every day for any mines that might have been laid during the night. It was too big to be done on foot with conventional mine detectors, so a unique system had been devised.

Two three-ton trucks, the drivers cab fitted with armor-plating and sandbags for the driver to sit on, were driven up and down the runway at maximum speed. The drivers who were strapped in tight and wore a motor cycle helmet, earplugs, and goggles would ensure that every inch of the runway was driven over. Any mines that had been laid would be set off by the weight of the vehicle passing over it.

Bomber watched the speeding trucks one morning, marveling at the devil take the hindmost attitude of the drivers as they thundered along the airstrip. The cook Sgt. was a florid-faced man of about thirty who had lost count of how many times he had been rotated at the camp. Regaled Bomber with the story of seeing one mine explode by this method. "The explosion blew the wheel off. It must have flown twenty feet up in the air. The truck carried on for about twenty more yards before crashing on its side. The driver was unhurt, thanks to the added protection to the cab, except for a loss of hearing for a few days."

Bomber admired the courage of the drivers who had been nicknamed 'Hell Drivers', all volunteers. They were regarded as almost supermen by everyone in the camp. This small unassuming group of humble men rarely spoke about their job but in good squaddie tradition never refused a beer when offered.

Most of the mines being used by the dissidents were British mines left over from the fiasco of the Suez campaign and passed by the Egyptians to the dissidents. Who said that Egyptians didn't have a good sense of humor?

Chapter 4
Rockets and Beyond

It was five days later when Doyle marched the section to the dining tent where the PO, Bull Dog Drummond and the Platoon Commander appeared. Between them, they briefed everyone on a mission to take place in two days. Rumor had it, the PO had asked for Doyle and his section and no one else for the job.

Bomber listened to the briefing getting drawn in by the PO's enthusiasm about dealing the dissidents, a powerful blow. *On the offensive at last*, thought Bomber.

The section and a team of the PO's own tribe's men were to ambush a dissident group equipped with an ASU 85 armored vehicle. Intelligent reports indicated that they were planning to attack one of the friendly villages, who would not stand a chance against an ASU 85 mm powerful gun.

The plan was for the tribesmen to do most of the shooting but our section would take out the ASU 85.

The PO explained that the ASU was a Soviet-built tank without a turret, light enough to be transported by air and was probably supplied by the Egyptians. Even though it was obsolete by the British Army standards if left to operate in the border area, it could dramatically change the balance of power between the rival tribes either side of the border.

Detailed planning would take place between the PO and Doyle who had just returned from a mysterious forty-eight-hour trip to Regimental Head Quarters, (RHQ), in Aden. Meanwhile, Bomber was to draw out the platoon three-point-five-inch antitank rocket launcher and fire a few rockets to sharpen up his aim.

Later, Bomber went and found the platoon Sgt. who was sitting outside of his tent at a makeshift table consisting of two old ammunition boxes. There, he briefed him on the Terry incident. Coker promised to speak to the Platoon Commander and see what could be done. Before Bomber left, Coker warned him to be careful as the Platoon Commander rightly considered this a full Platoon task but the PO wanted to keep it lightweight and fast moving. This was fine, provided everything worked as planned but it didn't leave any wriggle room for the unknown. And once the shootings started, most plans went to hell, so be careful.

The three-point-five rocket launcher was a beefed up version of the Second World War Bazooka and was capable of knocking out most tanks in current use. The trick was to ensure a hit on the side of the tank avoiding the heavier sloping frontal armor. It had a range of up to nine hundred and sixty yards but for antitank-use, it was best between one hundred and two hundred yards.

Anyone not practiced in using the launcher often ended up putting the rocket into the ground some fifty yards or less in front of the firing position. The reason for this was that the rocket did not reach flight speed until it had almost reached the end of the tube. So anyone unprepared for the weight of the rocket as it traveled through the tube would involuntary let it tip down as it traveled to the front of the tube. Then much to their surprise and shock, it would hit the ground and explode a short distance in front of them – not good if an enemy tank was heading towards you.

Bomber was the acknowledged expert in the platoon with a hundred percent hit rate on the range up to two hundred yards and about sixty percent up to three hundred yards. Over this to many variables came in as to the flight of the rocket, wind, humidity and altitude and Bomber knew that hitting a range target was a lot different to hitting the real thing.

After range practice, Doyle organized the section with Bomber as the rocket man. Davis as his loader between them, they would carry six rockets. Both swopped their SLRs for the nine-millimeter Sterling sub machinegun with the butts folded for ease of carrying. Moose and Black were with the GPMG and as many two-hundred round belts of ammunition as they could carry.

McBride would take an LMG, his personal favorite weapon, to give extra firepower if they needed it. The rest carrying SLRs with five full mag's of twenty rounds and an extra bandolier of fifty rounds. Plus another two hundred round belt for the GPMG, add the weight of this to the water some dry rations and normal kit, gave each man a heavy load to carry.

The next morning was spent in briefings, going over the location of the ambush site, rehearsing the ambush drills and final checks of weapons and equipment.

The afternoon was to be spent sleeping. To avoid detection, they would leave camp after dark, meeting up with the PO and his team who would lead them to the ambush site.

Just before retiring, Doyle took McBride and Bomber to one side. Doyle looked tense and, checking no one was in ear-wigging distance, spoke about his summons to RHQ. "It's like this," he said in an unusual subdued voice. "I am being promoted to Sgt., providing I can stay off the booze."

Doyle paused and looked nervously at both of them. "As you know, I have been there twice before and lost it due to the drink." He coughed and struggled to get a cigarette out of a pack of Camel. McBride reached out and flipped his Zippo lighter for him. With shaking hands, Doyle lit up, nodded his thanks and said, "See what a state I'm in. Not had a drink in forty eight hours and I need help!"

It was the first time Bomber had seen the normally-hard-as-nails-no-emotion McBride look compassionate.

He placed his hand on Doyle's shoulder saying, "Paddy, you can rely on us. We will take it in turns in camp to be with you twenty-four hours a day. I will check you before we go out, make sure no rum has slipped itself in to a spare water bottle."

Paddy smiled and said, "Thanks, Mac and you, Dave. I will not forget this and I have some good news for you two as well."

Bomber thought it was funny at times like this that things were stripped away and real names suddenly became the norm.

"What's that then?" McBride asked.

"Well, while I was in the RHQ, I did some ferreting with the Chief Clerk and if I get this promotion, you, Mac, will get the section commanders' slot. You, Dave, will get the vacant section commanders' slot of three section in two platoon."

"That could be the kiss of death for you, Dave," said McBride, and Bomber noticed he didn't smile when he said it.

"Why what's the problem there?" Bomber asked with that sinking feeling you get when you know there isn't going to be a good answer to the question.

"Well," said Doyle, drawing out the well-then, pausing for thought, "three section was made up of all Irishmen, two brothers with two related cousins, two Armagh oinks, a Londonderry shit called Kelly as section commander who did not know his backside from his elbow and Campbell as his number two.

"Both Kelly and Campbell were killed on the initial push up into the Radfan. Kelly managed to get crushed by a three-ton truck and Campbell to suspicious friendly fire!"

"Since then, no NCO has lasted more than a month without asking to be posted or going sick," McBride chipped in.

"They just need the right man to lead them, someone who they can respect," Doyle sounded upbeat now. "With the last action and this one coming up, you, Bomber, will have that respect. They need someone who is not full of piss and wind, which Kelly had in bucket's load." Doyle sat back as if exhausted by his speech.

Bomber noticed Doyle's hands had stopped shaking. "Paddy, I have never known you to bullshit me and I know that when we are on an op, you don't need the drink. So I am with Mac. Twenty-four hours a day we will help you, providing we get through this next job in one piece."

"No worries. We just have to sit and watch you fire a rocket and the PO and his boys shoot the living daylights out a bunch of ragheads."

Sounds far too easy, the little voice said in Bomber's head.

At twenty-three hundred hours, they arrived at the RV. Bomber had signaled some two hundred yards early to Doyle that the PO was ahead. Not that they could see or hear them but on the soft breeze blowing towards them, Bomber could detect the smell of the rancid tobacco the tribesmen smoked. Twenty odd tribe's men could put up a real smoke screen.

Bomber had never smoked and could detect the stench of the tobacco on the men's clothing at about fifty feet, one of the reasons that Doyle made him point man on patrols as most of the Arabs were addicted chain-smokers.

Most of the lads did not like being on point but for Bomber, it was different. It seemed to bring his senses alive, smell, sound, sight and that indefinable that made the goose bumps rise when you thought danger was near.

The PO and his team quickly took the lead setting a fast pace, too fast for good patrolling but the PO had said that they needed to be in position earlier than planned.

Four hours later, they arrived at the ambush position. A rough track cut diagonally up a slope from north to south. On the west side a boulder and shale-covered slope rose gentle to the night sky. On the east, a narrow but deep *wadi* separated the ambush group who occupied a slope covered in large weather-shattered rocks about the size of a small suitcase. Bomber was impressed the PO had selected such a perfect ambush position.

It was an ideal site to take out anyone moving up the track which the ASU 85 would have to do at a grindingly slow pace. The PO split his men into three groups, the largest in the middle as the killer group and the others were placed out to the left and right as cut-offs, about two hundred yards out to kill anyone who survived the initial contact and tried to escape either back down the track or up to higher ground.

Doyle and the section occupied ground some hundred and fifty feet above the ambush group to provide additional fire, should it be needed and to protect Bomber and Davis. Bomber was allowed to choose his own position for the rocket launcher and looked for a position that gave him a clear field of fire. One of the drawbacks with the rocket launcher was the back blast from the rocket as it flew out of the tube. The best position for firing it for Bomber was the kneeling position which needed a clear area behind. No boulders, slope not rising to steep and no one in the back blast area.

Bomber found his position about twenty yards right of the killer group. Bomber and Davis reasoned that they could get two rockets away before they would have to change fire positions as the flash and smoke from the rocket would betray their position to the dissidents.

Another location was found fifteen yards further right and slightly higher with plenty of cover for them to move to.

Here, they deposited three of the rockets as a backup fire point if it was needed.

At the first position, they assembled the launcher which, when being carried, was in two halves that clipped together making a long tube. Bomber checked the sights and Davis loaded a rocket into the back of the launcher while it rested on Bomber's shoulder. The two wires coming from the back of the rocket Davis left free and would not connect them to the two spring connector until seconds before firing to avoid any accidental discharge of the rocket.

Settling down to wait, Bomber took the opportunity to drink some water and eat a handful of hard tack biscuits. When they had finished, they piled a few rocks on top of each other to give some cover from small arms fire and as dawn slowly began to lighten the sky, they settled down to wait for the enemy to arrive.

About an hour after dawn, the low rumble of a diesel engine could be heard from further down the mountain. At this altitude in clear air with little wind sound traveled a long way. Another hour and the dust cloud from the ASU as it rumbled at a walking pace up the mountain could be clearly seen, but what was disturbing was that through his binoculars, Bomber could see that the number tribesmen walking alongside the ASU was far greater than predicted. Bomber handed the bingos to Davis who whistled quietly through his teeth in a manner that unsettled Bomber.

"Fuck me sideways," Davis hissed. "We could be in the shit here. There's hundreds of the buggers."

A slight exaggeration, thought Bomber, but there was a hell of a lot more than had been indicated at the briefing. Perhaps Blaze was right and the whole platoon should have been involved.

The PO's tribesmen numbered two dozen, armed with the .303 Lee Enfield rifle, a bolt action extremely accurate weapon which the tribesmen loved. However, at the relatively short range, the ambush would take place at it was clear they did not have the firepower. Even with the two LMGs, they could not take out that many dissidents in the first contact.

Next minute, Bomber watched the PO snake his way from boulder to boulder to reach Doyle. Suddenly from being spectators, the section would be adding its firepower to the ambush, and being higher up than the PO's group, they would be able to shoot over the top, putting a massive amount of fire into the enemy from their automatic and semiautomatic weapons.

Crouching between the boulders, Bomber gently placed the launcher on to his shoulder and looked through the sight at his chosen point of aim, imagining the ASU driving into the kill zone. Bomber tapped the top of the launcher with his left hand and Davis attached the two wires at the back. When Bomber squeezed the trigger, a current of electricity would flow through the wires to the rocket, igniting the propellant.

No one in the ambush would open fire until Bomber launched the rocket. The range would be about one hundred and thirty yards, ideal for the task.

By now, Bomber could clearly see the ASU 85 with its wicked-looking long barrel gun. To make the ASU air-portable, the vehicle was without a turret meaning the gun was fixed pointing forward with a small fifteen degree movement left or right but able to elevate as normal. So for the ASU to engage the ambush group, it would have to turn on its tracks and point the whole vehicle at them, which would give Davis time to reload a second rocket and for Bomber to fire.

The main problem would be dealing with the large 12.6 mm heavy machinegun mounted on the top of the ASU. Fortunately, to fire, the gunner had to expose his head and torso and the PO had already given two of his best marksmen the job of taking him out, should the rocket not do the job.

Now the ASU was nearly in the kill zone and unlike the previous contact, Bomber felt tense and unsure as he realized a lot rested on him hitting with the first shot. Bomber felt very exposed kneeling in what seemed like full view of the enemy, but he knew in the poor early morning light and through the dust the ASU churned up, they would be very hard to spot. Taking deep breaths to calm himself, he felt the tension easing as he concentrated on his aiming point. The ASU was moving at a steady walking pace with about twenty dissidents in the front and several on either side, with maybe a hundred more behind, all bunched up. They were talking and some laughing, probably about the devastation they would be inflicting on the villages over the border, but all that was about to change.

Bomber focused on the aiming mark he had visualized on the side of the vehicle. A trickle of sweat ran down his nose and he had an itch in the center of his back.

Whoosh! The rocket left the launcher, flying across the deep *wadi*. It slammed into the side of the ASU and exploded with a roar and at the same time the ambush group open fired. The firing stopped almost as soon as it started. A mighty explosion ripped through the air. The shockwave knocked Bomber backwards, landing on Davis several feet from the firing point. The second rocket that Davis was trying to load was torn from his hands.

Sitting up, Bomber watched in a daze as Davis on all fours searched around on the ground for his field hat. Bomber wondered why he was bothering looking for his hat, then he turned and looked at the remains of the ASU or rather the shallow crater with a track and some twisted steel. The gun lay some twenty yards away from the crater, leaning at an angle against the mountainside. Of the dissidents, there was nothing recognizable. Scattered around were twisted bundles. It was not until Bomber managed to adjust his vision, which seemed to be going in and out of focus, he noticed an arm or a leg in the bundles scattered about.

Mostly, these were of the group walking behind the ASU, of those who had been walking in front and along the side, the vehicle there appeared to be nothing.

Just in front of their firing position was a naked torso. The arms and legs had been torn off by the force of the explosion. Bomber could not help but notice how skinny the torso was. Perhaps it was one of the tribesmen who was walking beside the ASU, or had been inside the vehicle.

Normally, the ASU would carry about thirty, eighty-five-millimeter shells, but the crew must have loaded extra filling all the spare space in the hull with them and any other explosives they thought they might need.

The thin armor on the side of the ASU would have parted like butter when a hot knife slices through it. The squash head high explosive rocket complete with its still-burning rocket motor had ignited, one or more shells setting off an instant super chain reaction.

Bomber sat staring at the scene of devastation, then realized Davis was shaking him and shouting at him but he could not seem to react or hear him, all he could register was that Davis' face was covered in blood with a steady flow of it coming from a wide gash on his forehead. Slowly, in what seemed an age, Bomber managed to get to his feet and began to hear sounds.

Some of the PO's team was still firing its rifles at the bundles on the ground. Others were lying in shock on the ground. Two of these proved to be dead with shrapnel buried in their heads. A few others had minor wounds from the exploding shells but nothing life-threatening.

Bomber could see the PO waving his arms to regain control of his men making. Some attended their wounded while others went with him to check on the dissidents.

Davis shook Bomber again and Bomber focused on him. "Shit, you are covered in blood and stuff!"

"So are you. Are you okay?" Bomber countered

"Sure fine. Apart from my hat being blown off and a ringing in my ears, I seem to be in one piece."

"You are bleeding from your forehead."

Davis pulled out a field dressing and, after tearing of the wrapper, jammed it in place under the brim of his field hat.

Again Bomber turned to where the ASU and a hundred plus tribesmen had been a short time ago.

"What the hell happened?"

"I'll tell you what happened. You just took out the whole fucking raiding group with one rocket." Davis shouted and started laughing in an odd panicky way.

Through the ringing in his ears and the shouts of the tribesmen, they could hear Doyle's voice shouting, "Up here, you two at the double."

Bomber looked around for his SMG which he had put behind one of the boulders, and to his relief it was still there. The rocket launcher was lying a few feet away and Bomber noticed several gouges along the tube and when he tried to disassemble it, the clamps were buckled and jammed. Swearing, he put it on his shoulder and headed uphill. Davis had detoured to collect the three rockets from the backup position.

Suddenly, rifle and LMG fire was coming from the downhill, right-hand, cut-off group and Bomber could see dissidents running, trying to escape.

"So we didn't get them all," said Davis, staring down the mountain.

"Quite a lot seem to have escape. Hope they don't decide to rally and come back at us as I think I've had enough for one day."

The climb up to Doyle and the rest of the section seemed to take forever and Bomber felt bruised and battered. As he got closer, he could see stunned looks on some faces and stupid-looking grins on others.

Doyle grabbed him by the shoulders and said, "Holy mother of God, you are both covered in blood and what's this?" Doyle pulled a piece of bloody bone that had stuck itself into one of Bomber's ammunition pouches, then casually tossed it to one side.

"Well done both of you. Once the PO's finished down there, we are off."

After about an hour, the PO was back and leading his men up the mountain towards them. They had made improvised stretchers with the dead men's rifles to carry the bodies.

Davis and Bomber had taken the time to try and clean off the blood and debris from themselves. All the time Bomber struggled to come to terms with what had happened. Davis had figured that the dissident who had been on the side of the ASU facing them had been blown clear across the *wadi* disintegrating as they went, covering them and everything else with blood and other bits.

Bomber felt sick and had to fight the urge to laugh and cry at the same time. The march back to camp seemed to take twice as long as the march out. Bomber all the time fought to keep his mind on being alert and good patrolling drills and not the sight of the torso that kept breaking into his thoughts. His body felt as if he had been beaten to a pulp by some giant boxer.

Back in camp, hot tea and sandwiches helped to restore the section's sense of a job well done and Davis and Bomber soon became the object of curious glances from everyone.

Doyle ordered both of them to go and shower and change and to be in the dining tent in thirty minutes for a full debrief.

The shower felt glorious and it was as if all the day's events were being washed away with the blood but the little voice in his head kept telling him how easy killing was.

After a shower, clean clothes, and another mug of tea, they both walked back to the dining tent. Bomber felt his legs weighed a ton and he had a splitting headache. Davis had a fresh bandage on his forehead and was walking with his head down. Bomber was sure he could see tears on his cheeks or was it just sweat?

Entering the dining tent, they took seats with the rest of the team. Sitting at the front was the PO, a bandage covering his left ear and head. The Company Commander, Platoon Commander, and the Company Second in Command sat to one side.

The PO started talking but Bomber hardly heard any of it but was jerked back to reality when he heard his name mentioned and realized everyone was staring at him.

Davis nudged him and said in a stage whisper, "Tell them what the fuck happened!"

Suddenly, Bomber felt he wanted to tell them about the naked torso that landed just in front of them and was responsible for them being covered in blood. Instead, he managed to relate the sequence of events as best as he could in a low voice and why such a huge explosion had occurred, all the while wondering why they were all looking at him so intently.

The Company Commander cleared his throat, saying, "A job well done but as before, no mention of this operation is to be made outside of this tent and the Second in Command has prepared some papers for you all to sign."

With that, he stood up and nodded to Doyle who stood and said, "Attention."

Bomber stood with the rest looking straight ahead, dazed and wishing if they could just go and curl up on his bed and sleep.

The papers for signing were full of all sorts of dire consequences, should anyone mention what had happened and that they were fully bound by the official secrets' act until death removed them from the world.

Bomber felt he would be very happy never even thinking about it again, let alone talking about it.

Back in the ditch of their tent, the section cleaned weapons and talked quietly about what had happened. Doyle for once tolerated the talk knowing they needed to get it out of their system and to try and make sense on how the vehicle had exploded like a mini volcano.

The next day, standing orders included a paragraph on headdress stating, "That while field hats" – or as the boys called them, hats floppy – "could be used for patrols and when moving from one location to another, steel helmets were to be carried and worn in ambush position, guard duties, and any other static location." It went on to state, "Steel helmets were to be worn whenever there was a danger of enemy mortar fire or when traveling where there was a danger of contact with mines."

"Well, that just about covers everything," said Doyle with more than a touch of sarcasm. "There's more bloody British mines being planted by fucking tribesmen here than we ever laid in Egypt."

Advice a bit late for our friendly tribesmen, not that they would have worn them even if they had had them but as far as we were concerned, it was just another piece of kit to have to carry, little knowing that for some it would be a lifesaver.

Chapter 5
Dammed

It was a few days later that things changed for Bomber. Doyle had stayed off the rum and looked like and acted as a new man especially when he appeared wearing a third stripe on his arm. As acting Sgt., he was moved to a new platoon. McBride got his second stripe and took over the section and Bomber was to be made acting CPL (Corporal) and sent to three section two platoon.

Three section had earned its nickname 'The Dammed' after a series of events occurring before Bomber had joined the Regiment. Most of the members of three section had joined the Regiment during the time it had been stationed in Palace Barracks Belfast.

Three section had built a reputation of a hard playing, hard drinking group who would fight anyone for any reason and if no one was available, they would fight each other.

Bomber found himself standing to attention in front of two Platoon's Commander, a full Lieutenant who had joined the Company only six weeks ago but had previously completed a tour of duty with the Trucial Oman Scouts which had been raised in 1951 by the British to defend the seven emirate states of Trucial which was just East of Aden. Rumor control had that he had seen some action while serving there.

The Platoon Commander was a little under six foot tall and athletic in build and went by the name of R Blaze or so the nametag on his shirt stated.

His Platoon Sgt. was also present, Sgt. Chester, who had the nickname 'Perfection' which was not used within earshot of him. His face was covered by an elaborate red mustache which went from one ear to the other, joining the little circular band of red hair that made him look, without a hat on, like the local friar.

"Well," said Blaze, as he looked at Bomber up and down. Bomber knew he was not physically what most would think of as a tough infantry man. Just making five foot eight inches in height and of a slight but athletic physique with brown hair, blue eyes, and a boyish complexion he knew he looked more like a choir boy, which he had been early in his life.

Bomber knew his greatest assets were that he had fast reactions and could think on his feet. He could also run or march all day, every day, with a full load when others dropped by the way side. This ability he put down to his childhood when he had to walk everywhere and being at a school that put a lot of emphasis on sport for all. He read every book he could on military campaigns and was fascinated by the way commanders thought of the men under their command.

"Well," said Blaze again, "Let's have a little walk, shall we?" With that, they set off around the camp perimeter with Bomber walking along side and 'Perfection' just behind, listening to all that was said.

"Now," said Blaze, "three section have had a bad time, losing Kelly was bad enough but Campbell a few days later seem to take the spirit out of them." Blaze stopped walking and looked hard at Bomber, then carried on walking and talking. "We have had several replacements NCOs but to be quite frank, none have been up to the job. I think part of the problem is the replacements have been… um… shall we say, a little scared of three section."

A sort of grunting noise came from Perfection, which could have meant agreement or the opposite.

Blaze stopped again, this time staring out over the camp perimeter and turned to 'Perfection', saying, "I think that sums it up, don't you Sgt. Chester?"

"Yes sir. Sums it up nicely."

Blaze carried on. "So when the Company Commander said that you were available to take over three section, I asked Sgt. Chester to speak to Doyle about you. Doyle thinks you have potential, says you stay calm when the shit hits the fan, sort of thing. However, he is, shall we say, a bit of a missing link, so we will take what he says with a pinch of salt."

Bomber felt a little resentful on Doyle's behalf. Whatever his faults, he was a top soldier.

"So," he exclaimed, "what makes you think you can turn three section around?" Blaze suddenly demanded.

"I don't think that, sir," countered Bomber, "but the Company Commander must think I can or he would never have given me the section."

"Mmm," came from Blaze. "Best go meet your section then," and he pointed down the slope over the wall at six men filling sandbags at a navies on strike rate.

Bomber saluted and climbed over the perimeter wall, taking his time to walk towards the section. As he looked at the group, he tried to remember who was who from Doyle and McBride's descriptions. Two who looked very much alike facially but not in physiques must be the brothers. They had their shirts off and were smoking, ignoring Bomber. Two others both with ginger hair, who he guessed to be the cousins loosely related to the brothers, had a half-filled sandbag held open for another shovel of sand which seemed to Bomber to be a longtime coming. *Perhaps the bag would rot before it is filled*, mused Bomber.

A tall, skinny one seemed to be asleep on a pile of empty bags while the other stood throwing stones into the barbwire-fenced area. Bomber found out later that he was seeing if he could explode an anti-personal mine.

Bomber stopped by the group, peeled off his shirt and said, "I suppose we have to get this lot filled and up to the wall, do we?"

"We stay on this shit until the job is done," said the older of the two brothers.

"Right then, best get to it," said Bomber and grabbed a spare shovel and quickly filled the opened sandbag being held by a stunned-looking ginger-nut cousin. Tying the bag's neck, Bomber swung it on to his shoulder and indicated to an already filled one at Ginger's feet, "Put that one up here," he said, indicating his other shoulder.

"I want two more ready for me when I get back," Bomber barked in a firm but not unfriendly voice. "If you think you can manage it, that is," and set off climbing up to the wall.

"What the fuck's going on?" asked Patrick, the younger of the two brothers. "Who does he think he is?"

"I think he is our new Section Commander," said Sean, the older brother. "That crazy fucking rocket man of that Londonderry bastard Doyle."

"I bet he won't do more than two carries," Downey, the skinny one, said.

"You're on," said Sean. "A fiver says he will do four carries."

"Taken," said Downey.

The cousins had two bags ready for Bomber by the time he had returned and quickly loaded him up. As Bomber trudged back up the slope, he played a mental game of how many carries he would do before one or more of them would join in. *That's if they have any pride left*, he thought.

He knew he could have given an order but he wanted willing men who did not have to be threatened. Going back down, Bomber could see that all were filling sandbags. Not rushing but no one was sitting idle.

On getting back after the third load, Downey spoke up.

"Ah, Corporal, I was thinking should you not take a rest now and have a drink of water, this heat is awful bad for dehydration."

"I'm fine. Just keep filling those bags. I'll stop when we have the first hundred bags up there." Bomber pretended not to notice the look of surprise on their faces and set off back up with two more bags.

Downey handed the fiver to Sean, shaking his head as he did so and said, "Can I win it back if I carry more bags up than him?"

"Sure," said Sean, "but it's another fiver if you don't."

"You are on," Downey replied and kicking sand at one of the cousins, snapped, "Come on, you lazy bastard. Fill some fucking bags for me." And the game was on.

With all six working, they had the hundred up in under an hour but there was still plenty of bags and sand left.

"How do you think all this sand got here and the bags?" Jos Rafferty, the stockier one of the two ginger-head cousins, said. Without waiting for an answer, he carried on. "They fucking well truck it all the way up that bloody thing they call a road from Aden."

He paused and looked at the empty bags and then said, "You would have thought they would have filled them up down there where they have tons of cheap labor."

"Why would they waste money doing that when they have idiots like us to do the hard graft?" Sean said and started to laugh.

"Aye," bellowed Patrick, "leave it to the Dammed."

Now they were all laughing including Bomber. As the laughter died down, Bomber looked at them all and said, "Well, I don't feel like coming back tomorrow to finish this lot, so why don't we get on and finish it now and sod tomorrow?"

"I'm up for it," Downey said, thinking of his fiver.

"Let's show those bastards what the Dammed can do," Sean spoke so gently that they all turned to him be sure that he had spoken. Then they were all at it, filling bags, carrying, then holding a bag to be filled, rotating jobs so that everyone had a chance to get a breather.

As they worked steadily diminishing the pile of empty bags at the bottom to a large-filled pile at the top, Bomber felt his first brush with the Dammed had worked out all right.

Standing near the Wombat position, Blaze and Perfection could see what had been achieved in a few short hours.

"I think three section should go back to regular duties tomorrow, Sgt."

"Yes sir," answered Perfection, making a mental note to collect his bottle of whiskey from the CSM (Company Sergeant Major) who had had a bet that Bomber would not last the day without getting into a fight with one of the Dammed.

Bomber stowed his equipment in the section tent, then headed for the shower block. After a good soaking and fresh clothing, he joined the rest of the section sitting in the dining tent waiting for dinner to be served. The dining tent was a large marquee with six-foot long trestle tables and benches to sit on. During the day, the sides of the marquee were rolled up to let in the air and light. The cookhouse and serving area was separated by about twenty feet from the marquee. The air above was patrolled by a squadron of shit hawks (Red Kites) who were ready to swoop down at amazing speed to swipe the food from the plate of the unwary. So a hunched-over posture was needed to protect the plate of food when negotiating this space.

Bomber sat by Sean and decided it was time to find out a bit more about the Dammed.

"So how come we are called the 'Dammed?'" Bomber used the 'we' to re-enforce the fact that they were now a team.

Sean looked hard into Bomber's eyes as if trying to decide if this was a genuine question or he was taking the piss.

After a second or two, Sean spoke in a quiet voice. His Northern Irish accent seemed to be softer than normal. "It started on the first push up the main road to the Radfan, not that you would have called it a road. That was last June. One of the trucks with our kit on had got stuck and we all set too pushing it out. Just as we got it free, it rolled back and Kelly was stood right by the rear wheels. Crushed his chest and killed him instantly."

Sean paused and looked down at the table and lowered his voice even more and Bomber had to lean forward to catch the words. "I was not the best of friends with Kelly. He was pretty useless except on the parade ground, but no way would I have wished that to happen to him."

He stopped there as if to regain his breath and thoughts. "Three days later, we came under fire from a cave high up on the mountain. Rifle fire and automatic fire from a machinegun. Campbell who was acting Section Commander ordered us to take cover on the left side of a *wadi* and to return fire." Again a pause as Sean looked at the others as if wanting confirmation of what was to come.

"Well, there was a lot of fire going over our heads from the rest of the company, too much perhaps, but the next thing is we are ordered to make our way up the slope to the ridge. Which we did in about half an hour and by this time the shooting had died down from both sides."

Everyone was nodding their heads by now at Sean's version of events.

"Just the odd burst from the Dissident's machinegun answered by several of our own, when suddenly Campbell falls and when I got to him, I found he had been shot. Bullets went in the middle of his back and out near his throat."

Sean looked saddened and sat very still for a moment. "He was a good lad, Campbell, someone you could rely on. Of course they blamed one of us but as we were spread out in extended line and could not see the Dissident position; we were not firing. The angle of the wound suggested."

"It came from below," Bomber butted in.

"Got it in one," agreed Sean.

"There was an enquiry of course, but no one was interested, far too much going on," Sean finished looking down at the table.

"Then there was the fucking helicopter incident," Patrick declared. "Whole bloody Company to be picked up and lifted up to the top of some *jebal*. In come the choppers, a couple of twin rotor jobs, half a dozen Navy Whirlwinds and some RAF jobs from Khormaksar." Patrick paused and scratched his head.

"Everyone gets on board and lifts off and away, except our piece of shit gets a foot or so off the ground and sinks back down. We look at the load master as the engine dies and he says overheated engine you have to get off."

"So now the Quarter Master, who is the rear party Commander, orders us to climb aboard the supply trucks which were just leaving."

Both cousins shifted on the bench and chorus. "Fucking bastard smiled when he said it to."

Patrick carried on. "Well, it took us two days of stop, start and get off and walk. It was 110 degrees and dark when we got there and the Platoon Commander was not best pleased we had not been put on another chopper."

"That wasn't Blaze then?" asked Bomber

"No, Pinter," said Sean. "Good bloke, looked after everyone well. No one dared call us the Dammed in his hearing. But he died that night, fell down the side of an escapement while going round checking the sentries in the dark."

"And we got the blame for that, the curse of the Dammed they called it." Jos shook his head as spoke.

At that, the cook banged a pan and shouted, "Come and fill your boots." And they silently went and collected their dinner.

Chapter 6
Good Preparations Prevent
Piss Poor Performance

Bomber pulled his blanket tighter to ward off the morning chill and rolled onto his side on the flimsy camp bed. He must have been dreaming; he thought he had been in his old school, St. Georges in Cambridge, a rundown Victorian building where those not considered worthy of doing the eleven plus exam were shunted to grind out the time until their fifteenth birthday. Then out to fill jobs as butcher boys, toolmakers' apprentice, or shop assistance. Not for Bomber, he knew what he was going to do. Having been in the Army Cadet Force, he was set on the army. His head master, a veteran of the Desert Rats who had fought in North Africa and Italy during the Second World War, had done his best to talk him out of it but Bomber was determined.

Bomber could sense rather than see that the sky was beginning to get light. Forcing himself to abandon the blanket, he set about getting washed, shaved and dressed. Then he gave those of the section not up some not too gentle encouragement to get moving, smiling at the moans and groans and comments that it was still the middle of the night. After breakfast, they formed up by the mortar pits and waited for Perfection to arrive.

"Okay," bellowed Perfection. "There are some Beverlys coming in with loads of weapons and ammunition and guess which lucky platoon gets to unload it?"

"Could it be us, Sgt.?" piped up Downey.

"Never one for keeping his mouth shut the prick," said Sean quietly to Bomber.

"You got it in one Downey and I want you all at the airfield in twenty minutes in fatigue order plus haversack ration and personnel weapons," barked Perfection.

Bomber studied his haversack ration while they waited for the planes to arrive, with four slices of bread with the edges curling up in the heat held some Spam which looked and tasted like lint, a small packet of custard creams and a shriveled up orange.

"No chance of winning any prizes with this stuff," chuckled Sean and tossed his orange up into the air and then, as it came down, headed it at Patrick who caught it and threw it back.

"Hard as a cricket ball," Sean muttered, rubbing the red weal mark on his forehead where he had headed the orange.

The platoon stood in section groups at the edge of the runway. Six trucks were also parked ready to be loaded. A few minutes later, they could hear the drone of the planes.

Bomber was amazed at how the things could fly. A giant box with wings stuck on it and four very large engines, a long tail boom which could accommodate thirty-six fully armed troops sitting in bucket seats and another ninety-four in the box. It was the least streamlined of any flying machine he had ever seen.

The Beverly had come into service in the early fifties and was designed to be a rugged to go anywhere, a heavy-lift aircraft able to take off with a full load of forty-four thousand pounds in less than eight hundred yards and amazingly land on a dirt runway, stopping in just over three hundred yards. It had one drawback in that it was relatively slow, with a maximum speed of two hundred and thirty-eight miles an hour. That's with a strong tail wind according to one of the load masters on Bomber's first flight in one.

The planes landed in clouds of dust and taxied to where the trucks were waiting. Slowly, the huge doors at the rear of the planes opened and Bomber could clearly see along with everyone else that the planes were stacked full of boxes and that unloading by hand onto the trucks would be a long, hard slog.

"Let's get started," yelled Perfection, "two and three section to the left and the rest onto the right-hand plane."

The RAF load masters had already released the cargo nets at the rear and started directing the unloading. The truck drivers had reversed up to the cargo bays and Bomber and his section formed a chain to pass the boxes onto the back of the trucks while the others worked in the cargo hold.

Bomber noticed that the first thing that came off was boxes of point 303 Lee Enfield rifles with nineteen forty-four stenciled on the side after this came boxes of LMGs, again with the same year on the boxes. This was followed by several boxes of two-inch mortars, three point five rocket launchers and hand grenades. By this time, two of the three vehicles were full and now they were filling the third one with what seemed like endless boxes of ammunition.

Bomber paused as the drivers declared a full load and drove off. Looking up at the large tail booms above, he reflected on his experience of flying in the tail booms. He definitely had not enjoyed the experience. Sitting in the uncomfortable seat facing backwards and looking through the tiny porthole, it was disconcerting feeling it flex as if it was not properly attached to the rest of the plane.

Bomber remembered thinking that if this thing goes down, they had no chance of getting out worse. What if the boom flexed so hard that it snapped off and they would all be trapped in the seats as it plunged towards the unforgiving ground below? Shuddering at the thought, he was pulled back to reality by the load master declaring a smoke break but to have it away from the plane.

Now they had time, the guys started to speculate about what was going on. "Why," speculated Sean, "was all this hardware being given to our so-called friendly tribesmen?"

"Well, I think the PO is planning a big raid over the border and is taking all the tribes men he can with him," stated Jos, the more serious of the two cousins.

"Wrong," came a voice from behind them that Bomber recognized as Perfection.

"You may have noticed that all the camp sappers and Pioneer Platoon boys have been shipped to the village. Now what do you think they are doing?"

He looked slowly round the group and this time it was Jamie, the other cousin, who spoke up.

"Would they be building defensive positions, Sergeant?"

"Smart boy," said Perfection. Jamie grinned and sat up straight as if to say I'm in the Sgt.'s good book.

"Yes, there is going to be a raid or more like a full scale attack but not on us. Word has it, the Qotaibi have taken real offense at the destruction of their ASU 85 and the loss of so many men and are going to make an example of the village, in fact wipe it out."

"Will we be involved, Sergeant?" asked Bomber

"I know how you like to blow things apart, Brown. But no, we have been told we will take no part in the fighting unless things start to go badly wrong. This is the sneaky beakies' show. The PO's wcrc often referred to as sneaky beakies, and let's hope they get it right or it could be Dien Bien Phu all over again."

Bomber remembered reading the account of this when at IJLB. Dien Bien Phu was a battle in the French Indochina War of 1946 to 1954, when the French fortified a position inviting the Viet Minh to sacrifice themselves on the French guns. It turned into a disaster for the French, resulting in the complete withdrawal of the French from that part of the world.

Just then, the three trucks returned and after a further hour of hard work, the last of the munitions was off loaded. As everyone made their way back to camp, the Beverleys made a short run and then up and away like two giant Bumble Bees.

Back in camp, they were informed by the Platoon Commander that in an hour they would receive a briefing on the situation.

The whole Company including the support weapons teams of the mortars and Wombats and the elusive Recce (Raider) Platoon were crammed into the dining tent. The Company Sgt. Major called the Company to attention as the Company Commander and his Second in Command entered.

A large blackboard had been placed on a stand high enough so that everyone could see.

The Company Commander had the CSM stand the Company at ease. Then he began.

"Intelligence sources indicate that a large force, mostly Qotaibi possible with some special force support, that is Egyptian, from North of the border is on its way to obliterate the village at the West end of the runway, in retaliation for their recent losses in men and armor."

He paused and indicated the route that the dissidents were likely to take. "They are also keen to re-establish their control of this end of the Dhala Road which must not be allowed under any circumstances." He thumped the table in front of him to emphasize the point.

"As you may be aware, the village has been fortified and supplied with a large quantity of weapons and ammunition. It has also received an increase in fighting men from two other local tribes who have no love for the Qotaibi, or the Red Wolves as they like to call themselves."

The Company Commander paused as the PO we called 'Lookalike' entered the tent and nodded to the Company Commander.

"We will not be directly involved unless things start to go in favor of the dissidents and I will cover that in a minute. We will deploy as follows. One platoon will be at immediate readiness in camp with three of the runway-armored trucks to deploy as ordered.

"Two platoon will be on the ridge manning the radar site Sangers." A low groan came from some of two platoon members as they considered this to be the shitty end of the stick.

"Trust us to get that job, beginning to think that the Company Commander does not like us," complained Sean to Bomber.

"Three platoon will be held in reserve ready to deploy if necessary." Smiles lit up the faces of some of three Platoon thinking they will be able to crash out on their camp beds for the next forty-eight hours.

"The support weapons will be ready to provide DFs (defensive fire) on the allocated DFs plus as ordered by the Recce Platoon FCO (Fire Control Officer).

The Recce platoon will proceed to OPs (observation points) Alpha, Bravo, and Charlie at last light tonight." As he said this, he pointed out the location on the sketch map on the board.

Bomber thought that puts them very close to any action near the village and could see that they would dominate the high points close to the village which he presumed the dissidents would want to control – so much for not being directly involved.

Since the Regiment's deployment to Aden, the Recce Platoon, normally about thirty men strong, had been beefed up to fifty men. All the regular platoons had been plundered of its most experienced men to achieve this, leaving some platoon under strength.

The Company Commander continued, raising his voice to ensure it carried to everyone.

"Now the PO has just indicated to me that the attack is expected to happen tomorrow night but we will be ready as of last light tonight. I know this will put a lot of strain on those of you deploying outside of the camp but we must not be caught napping. There will be a Platoon Commanders meeting in thirty minutes. Meanwhile Platoon Sgt.'s are to prepare everything required. We have five hours to last light Sgt. Major, carry on." With that, he strode out of the tent followed by the Second in Command, the Platoon Commanders and 'Lookalike'.

The Company Sgt. Major called the Platoon Sgt. to him and after a few quiet words, he too left the tent.

Outside, the platoon followed Perfection and headed straight for the ammunition bunker to collected extra ammunition on top of the normal hundred and fifty rounds per man. In all, each man had two hundred and fifty rounds for the SLRs, two hundred extra rounds for the GPMGs and LMGs. Two, two-inch mortar rounds, two thirty-six grenades, a smoke grenade and just when Bomber thought that they could not carry anymore, Perfection said, "I think we will have half a dozen 3.5 rockets and Cpl. Brown, your section can take the rocket launcher."

"Fucking hell," said Jos, "I know they treat us like donkeys but I never thought I would actually be loaded up like one."

"You are lucky," chimed in the ammunition bunker Cpl. "You should see what the Recce lads have taken must have about two camel loads each," he said, laughing.

In addition to the ammunition and weapons, each man had his two water bottles totaling four pints and a *chuggle* bag of water. The chuggle was a canvas bag soaked in water to expand the weave to make it waterproof, and then filled with eight pints of water. Plus two twenty-four hour ration packs and a mini solid fuel cooker, a wool sweater and a great coat whose design had not changed since the First World War. It was large and bulky taking up most of the interior of the large pack but its redeeming feature was that it was very warm. At this time of year, early December, temperatures at six thousand feet at night could easily drop to freezing, so no one grumbled too much about, including the great coat.

After all the other extras had been included, each section was inspected by the Pl Sgt. and Perfection lived up to his name. He checked every weapon, the packing of all the small pouches and the large packs.

Once he had done that, they all shouldered their kit as they would when they left camp and Perfection made all jump up and down then jog, more like stagger with the load, in a circle. Any item that came loose was re-secured, some items redistributed for others to carry.

"I will not have anything falling off or coming loose when we leave camp. It's a short but hard slog up to the ridge and I want it done in one push." Perfection suddenly called the platoon to attention as the Platoon Commander appeared.

Lt. Blaze had everyone gather to him in a half circle with those in front sitting and others kneeling behind. He drew a line in the dirt and then positioned four stones at intervals along the line.

"Okay lads. This is how it is. Our mission is to hold the radar ridge." He looked at everyone and then repeated the mission.

"This is how we will do it, HQ section in the middle Sanger, one section left and two in the right hand one. Now as you know normally from these three positions, we can cover the approaches to the radar site and back to the camp but it leaves us blind to the gap at the end of the ridge which normally is not a consideration. However, if any of the dissident tries to sweep southeast and approach the village from the rear, we will need eyes and firepower there." He paused and looked at Bomber. "Three section will cover this point from the old Sangers above the gap. They are not brilliant but you can do some rebuilding tonight and you are to draw up a spare two-inch mortar and a dozen para illuminating bombs to take with you!"

Shit, thought Bomber. *We can hardly walk with what we already have!*

"Now no one is to open fire without my order unless you are in danger of being overrun but that hopefully will not arise. Are there any questions?" No one spoke for a moment. Then Bomber raised his hand.

"Yes Cpl. Brown," Blaze asked with a slight raise of his voice as if to say, 'You need to ask a question.'

"The Sangers we will occupy are unsighted from your position, sir. What action should I take if we need support?"

"If that case arises, either myself or the Pl Sgt. will take one section forward to where the ridge starts to drop and will give you covering fire from there, okay?"

"Yes sir."

"Right, we have two hours before we depart. There is a meal in the dining tent in thirty minutes after that. I suggest you get what rest you can. We will leave at nineteen hundred hours, so section commanders synchronize your watches," he paused, looking at his watch. "It will be seventeen hundred hours in, three, two, one. Now."

During the meal, some wry comments were made at three section by other members of the platoon.

"Stuck the right toe rags at the Devil's gap, no wonder they call you the Dammed," goaded Ridley, the overweight second in command of one section.

John, who had a notoriously short fuse, fired back, "I heard that it was to be given to one section but Perfection told Blaze a fat knacker like you couldn't walk that far."

Plenty of the lads liked that and laugh openly at Ridley.
Ridley stood having been hit where he was most sensitive but before he could retaliate, Sean spoke in a clear, firm voice, "Sit down, you fucker, or I will tell how you slid your way out of Op Nutcracker."

Ridley's face went bright red and started to stutter but Morton, his section Cpl., put a hand on him and pulled him down to his seat.

After a few seconds' silence, with every one now looking at Ridley, the talk changed and a good humor banter continued. More than a few quietly asking Sean about Nutcracker and Ridley but he would not be drawn.

Bomber made a mental note to question Sean on Op Nutcracker and Ridley once they were on their own.

Chapter 7
Red Wolves Shoot Out

At nineteen hundred hours on the dot, the Platoon shuffled out of the camp. Once clear of the camp and on open ground, the platoon spread out into Platoon diamond formation and started the climb up to the ridge summit.

Bomber found with a little practice he could almost walk instead of shuffle. The extra load of the two-inch mortar and the bombs had been difficult to pack into the fifty-seven pattern webbing equipment. Any sudden movement turning left or right seemed to unbalance the large pack and almost cause an uncontrolled crab like sideways stagger. The shoulder straps and belt rubbed without mercy and Bomber would dearly have like to strangle whoever had designed the equipment and torture the fools who had agreed to buy it for the army by making them wear it for all eternity.

Bomber had watched the Recce boys depart fifteen minutes before them. Their loads seemed even bigger. However, they had loaded all their equipment on to man pack frames, aluminum oblong frames that you could strap all sorts of stuff to and then carry it like a rucksack. Bomber knew from the briefing that they had a much longer trek to their locations and would be in the thick of it when the shooting kicked off. For some strange reason, he felt a little envious of them.

After an hour of nonstop uphill shuffling, Bomber could see the lead section of the Platoon topping the ridge. Despite the cold, he was bathed in sweat, as he neared the top a breeze made the sweat turn cold against his skin and he gave an involuntary shiver.

As each section broke off to its allocated position, Blaze found Bomber and indicated him to follow. Moving along the side of the ridge to avoid being silhouetted against the night sky,

Blaze led them down to the gap Sangers some three hundred yards away from the main Platoon position.

"Okay," whispered Blaze in Bomber's ear, "Get sorted and remember, radio check on the hour every hour," then silently disappeared into the darkness.

Bomber mouthed a silent okay to the shadows and then set about inspecting the Sangers. There were four, one the furthest forward which Bomber guessed had a good position covering the gap but was clearly even in the dark the most exposed. This was in good order, built about three feet thick and four feet high, with just the rocks that had been lying on the ground. Bomber wondered who and how long it had taken them to build the Sangers. The height was just right for the kneeling fire position. It could easily accommodate the whole section but Bomber dismissed the idea and put the GPMG and the rocket launcher in with the McNaulty brothers and Donnie Downey.

One other was to the rear approximately fifteen yards and slightly higher up the slope. He was also in similar order but could only accommodate up to four. In here went John Deegan, and the two cousins Jos Rafferty and Jamie McElroy plus the two-inch mortar and all its bombs. As Jamie carefully separated the para illuminating from the high explosive, Bomber took the flare pistol and flares from Jos. McElroy also had the LMG, so all the spare magazines for this were collected and put in with him.

Having explained arcs of fire to them and reaffirming that McElroy was in charge Bomber made his way back to the main Sanger unraveling the alarm cord as he went. The section radio was in with him, so the only communication between the two Sangers was the alarm cord or shouting.

The other two Sangers were spaced left and right by about fifteen yards and were smaller than the one Bomber had occupied.

Bomber spoke to Sean, "As we haven't enough guys to fill those two, it worries me in case anyone gets in them and takes us on the flank."

"Why not stick a grenade in each and we can use a pull cord to pull out the pin and blow anyone in there to hell?"

The way the answer rolled off Sean's tongue, Bomber guessed he had done this before, so asked him to fix it.

With Patrick manning the GPMG and watching toward the gap which in the dark was invisible unless they sent up a flare, Donnie built a rock cupboard inside the Sanger wall and fired up a hexi cooker to make a brew. The rock cupboard would mask any light from the cooker. The hexi cooker was really just little cakes of firelighters which sat in a folding tin cooker about the size of a large tobacco tin on which a mess tin could be perched – crude and smelly but silent and effective.

Now that he had settled in, Bomber began to feel the cold of the night and noticed the others already had their great coats on. Shrugging into his and sipping on a mug of hot tea from Donnie, he slowly began to warm up.

Looking up at the night sky, he again wondered at the millions of stars that seem to form an umbrella of light over them. It was to be a moonless period and the stars shone with a greater brightness for it. Bomber guessed that was why the dissidents had chosen this time to attack the village, a moonless period they could approach the village unseen.

Staring down toward the gap, it looked like a black bottomless pit, the starlight failing to penetrate into the lowest point of the ridge. Bomber guessed that it was less than three hundred yards, but in the morning he would make out a range card to help if they had to do any nighttime shooting.

The A40 radio crackled into life for the on-the-hour radio check, Bomber answered and all then was silent. The A40 was a small but heavy section radio with a very limited range. The platoon commander had two A41 radios, one on the platoon frequency and the other on the company frequency. The A41 was standard issue to the infantry. It was about the size of a very large box of cornflakes and in its basic state of radio, battery, antenna, and headset weight in at about thirteen pounds. More than half of this was the battery. In theory with its ten-foot whip antenna, it had a range of ten thousand yards but the ten-foot antenna gave away the position when it was waving about saying, ooeee here I am. So normally a four-foot antenna would be fitted reducing the range to six thousand yards. Being high on a ridge was an advantage for range and with a clear line of sight to the main camp, it ensured good communications.

Settling down to one-hour stags at the GPMG position allowed them to get some sleep and stopped them getting to bleary-eyed staring into the darkness for over long periods, which could cause you to think the shadows were moving.

Dawn seemed to arrive quickly and all the Platoon had been stood too for an hour prior to this. In the morning light, Bomber could see that both positions look directly into the gap and anyone in the gap could look directly back at them.

They had carried up some long strips of hessian cloth which was the same color as the ground and this they used to create overhead cover which served several purposes. Firstly it kept the baking sun off them. Secondly it made them keep their heads down and observe solely through the gun slits and thirdly helped camouflage the position from anyone looking in their direction.

Now it was daylight, Bomber could study the ground in front of them, to the left, south, just about visible in the distance he could see the tops of the radar antenna of the RAF site. Directly in front, towards west, was the gap really a large notch in the ridge with a trail going through it. Beyond this, the ground rose up as a continuation of the ridge. To the right, north, the ground sloped down until it met the plain which had some fields with crops growing on them, adding a splash of green and yellow and beyond that was the end of the runway.

North West just beyond the end of the runway was the village that was preparing itself for the battle. Although scanning the village with his binoculars, Bomber could see very little activity.

Beyond the village, the land rose sharply and from the briefing he knew that the Recce Platoon were in three OPs watching the village and would undoubtedly have to stop the dissidents taking that high ground. Again scanning carefully along that ground, he tried to spot the OPs but to no avail, which did not surprise him, given the Recce Platoon's skill at seeing but not being seen.

Sean suggested that they put out some markers to aid night shooting. As they had not thought to bring anything with them to do this they improvised. Taking pages from his field notebook, they used condensed milk from the ration pack to stick the white pages to flat rocks. Then between them they guessed the distances to various points towards the slope. As they did not want to draw attention to the position, it was agreed that one of them would crawl out and place the markers and then crawl back.

Of course no one was keen to do all that crawling over the sharp rocky ground, so they drew lots and Patrick lost much to his displeasure and comments that the draw had been rigged.

Having set the stones with the white paper facing the Sanger at the agreed points, Patrick started to crawl back. Suddenly Sean was alerted by the alarm cord being pulled three times. Bomber and Sean scanned the area and could see coming into the gap about a dozen armed tribesmen. Patrick must have heard them as he froze and pressed himself flat to the ground. Dressed in their garb of head scarves wrapped like a turban around their heads, loose trousers and shirts with thick wool jackets of brown, they blended into the landscape with ease. They walked with the confidence of men who knew this was their patch and had little fear of any enemy here.

Bomber immediately radioed in the contact and looking through the binoculars he could see that the tribesmen were carrying Lee Enfield 303 rifles. This would normally suggest that they were friendly tribesman but Bomber had come to realize that nothing could be taken for granted. They could just as easily be turncoats.

Blaze instructed them to let them pass and to remain hidden and Bomber assumed this was some of the local re-enforcements going to the village. Watching them leave the gap, they did head for the village. Sean continued to watch them over the sights of the GMPG until they were out of sight.

After indicating to Patrick by tossing a stone near him that it was all clear, he fast crawled back to them.

"Fuck me," said Patrick. "I felt as exposed as a naked bishop at a WI meeting out there."

"Not to worry they were friendlies, now could you just pop back out there and move that left-hand marker another three feet left," said Sean with a straight face.

Patrick looked first to Sean and then to Bomber who nodded and said, "Afraid so mate it needs shifting."

Patrick looked outraged and started to curse, saying, "It's exactly where you said it should be to the fucking inch. I don't see why I have to crawl out there again to put it right." He stopped abruptly as all three of them started laughing and shoving him between them.

"Got you," said Sean, laughing uncontrollably.

"You bastards winding me up when I have been laying out there half expecting to get a bullet in my backside."

"Here," said Donnie, pushing a mug of his seemingly endless supply of tea into his hand. "Get your laughing tackle round this and relax I'm just going to get some grub heated up while it's all quiet."

Sean and Bomber discussed the markers and then placed marker on the gun slits of the wall of the Sanger so that at night they could line up the GPMG and know exactly where the GPMG's kill zone would be.

The day passed slowly and each tried to get as much sleep as possible. Bomber's mind wandered back in time to when he was a child in Cambridge, wearing secondhand clothes, always cold in the winter and hungry. Once what was on the table was eaten, that was it, no extras in the larder and no money for popping to the corner shop for biscuits. Not that they were any different from anyone else in the street of two up two down, scullery and toilet in the back yard Victorian houses.

An hour before sunset, they all stood too and watched the shadows lengthen until the darkness covered them like a velvet hood reducing their visual world to the small area in front of their position and the solar system straight up.

After a further hour they stood down. Then they took turns in pairs watching and waiting while the other two rested, brewed up and munched hard tack biscuits.

It was about twenty minutes to midnight when Blaze informed them over the radio to stand too. He had been informed by HQ via one of the Recce OP's that things were about to start. Bomber wondered how close the Recce lads were to the enemy and how it must feel to be so isolated in their location with the ragheads all around them. *Cool heads and a lot of confidence in their ability to deal with the situation,* he guessed.

Staring out into the darkness, the minutes passed slowly and Bomber felt tense willing something to happen. Suddenly flares went up into the sky from the north end of the village. These were quickly followed by parachute flares fired from two-inch mortars which cast a glow over the whole area, creating an effect similar to an old black and white movie.

Bomber could not see any dissident near the village but did not really expect to be in the dark at that distance even with the binoculars. Then the air was torn apart as it seemed every gun in the village roared out, the crack of dozens of rifle shots, the wicked rattle of multiple LMGs and the heavy grind of a .5 machinegun. Stabs of flame and the hosepipe lines of tracer rounds cut through the air like a deadly firework display.

"That's odd. I don't remember unloading any .5 browning machineguns," said Bomber to no one in particular.

"One of the truck drivers told me he and the PO collected four of them from the FRA (Federal Regular Army) and a shed full of ammo for them," said Donnie.

The point-five-inch Browning machinegun (.5 BMG) was a heavy caliber machinegun and, when mounted on a tripod, was a serious piece of hardware. Capable of punching through thick stonewalls and half-inch steel plate, it could tear a man in half if one heavy round struck him. It could also reach out easily to a range of two thousand yards or more.

By now, a furious firefight was in progress and the dissidents were returning a heavy volume of fire. Mostly it appeared to be directed at the largest building at the north end of the village.

Parachute flares continued to light the scene and through the binoculars, Bomber thought he could just make out some figures trying to get closer to the village, but could not be sure, so he handed the binoculars to Sean, asking him to check.

After a few seconds, Sean confirmed that it was figures moving towards the village. Bomber passed the information on to Blaze who acknowledged and Bomber assumed he passed it to the Company Head Quarters, as a short time later tracer rounds from the village streaked out in that direction.

Now the defenders started using the two-inch high explosive mortar bombs which came thick and fast. The attackers seemed to slacken their fire and after about another twenty minutes, the firing ceased.

"What do you think, have they had enough already?" questioned Patrick.

"Can't see them giving in that easily," replied Donnie.

Things stayed quiet for another thirty minutes, then the unmistakable thud, thud, thud of a Soviet 12.6 mm heavy machinegun started hurling rounds at the village the flash of its tracer rounds could be followed quiet easily. Then it was joined by two more from well spread out positions, all three guns zeroing in to the same building which the attackers must have considered key to the village's defense.

The villagers replied by sending up countless parachute flares and returning fire in the direction of the 12.6 machineguns.

"I bet the bastards are using the fire from those guns to flank the village and get to the high ground where the Recce lads are," Sean said with conviction and Bomber silently thought he was right.

The dissident had positioned the 12.6 mm machineguns out of range of the two-inch mortars, so at the moment it was a duel between the heavy machineguns but the villagers were about to add something extra.

"Hey," shouted Donnie over the noise and pointed, "someone's got your job, Rocket man."

They all watched as several 3.5-inch rockets went streaking from the village presumably at dissidents trying to infiltrate under cover of the machinegun fire. Bomber estimated that at least five launchers were in action.

It was frustrating having to just watch the firefight and not being a part of it, and what's more? It was making it difficult to concentrate on watching the gap.

Despite initially dismissing the idea of putting a trip flare at the gap in case an animal set it off, Bomber decided that with all the noise and distractions he should now do so. Taking the three from the second Sanger as protection, Bomber made his way down to the gap and set up the flares, stretching the wires across the width of the track at different intervals. Anyone coming through the gap would set of a flare and be an easy target for the GPMG.

By the time they had made it back to the rest of the section, the firing from the village was beginning to slacken until it was just a few rifle shots or an occasional burst from a machinegun.

A lull of about two hours occurred, then suddenly the night's silence was once again ripped apart, but this time it was from one of the Recce OPs. Two GPMGs and half a dozen rifles were pouring a concentrated cone of metal to a point Bomber estimated as about two hundred and fifty yards down the slope.

"Our mortars have opened up," said Patrick, and sure enough the unmistakable crump of heavy mortars firing could be heard followed a short time later by multiple explosions in front of the OP position.

"Bloody hell, they must be desperate having the drop shorts come in that close to their own position." Donnie had to shout to be heard.

After a few seconds, the mortars stopped and so did the firing from the OP.

"What do you reckon?" said Sean, not really expecting an answer. "Either the mortars stopped the buggers or the OP has been overrun."

As if to answer him, one of the GPMGs from the OP started firing short controlled burst down the hillside and they could see tracers bouncing off the rocks up into the night sky.

Now fire was coming from all directions, one of the other OPs started firing and as if on cue, it seemed that every weapon in the village started firing in all directions with the answering thump, thump, thump of the dissidents 12.6 mm mg's was matched by the lighter weapons of the dissidents who now appeared to have ringed the place.

Now the main camp 81 mm mortars began firing at the dissidents 12.6 mm machinegun positions and they all jumped when with a thunderous roar the 120 mm Wombats fired four rounds at the location of the 12.6 machineguns.

"Jesus Christ," exclaimed Patrick, "if that's not got the buggers, nothing will!"

One by one, the 12.6 machineguns fell silent. With the loss of the heavy machineguns, the fire from around the village began to slacken and Bomber guessed they were withdrawing.

Slowly but surely, the firing ceased completely. Only then did Bomber notice the first traces of dawn beginning to lighten the eastern sky.

There was no point in standing too, as everyone was already at their posts. Bomber told Donnie to get a brew and some breakfast going. Once it was fully lit, Bomber surveyed the village and beyond to the OPs.

After a while, he could see figures emerging from the village and searching the ground working outwards especially towards the dissidents' 12.6 mm machinegun positions.

Suddenly shots rent the air and Bomber could make out figures dancing around and shooting into the sky.

"Guess the mortars and Wombats hit the mark and took out the guns," said Sean.

"I think you could be right," Bomber agreed. "I wonder if there are any body remains there too?"

Patrick gave Bomber a sideways look and said, "Bit bloody morbid, aren't you? And just before we have breakfast."

"No, no. I just thought they might be able to tell if they were all Qoitabi or some of those Egyptians special forces that keep getting mentioned."

Just then, they were interrupted by the other Sanger alerting them to the Platoon Commander making his way to them.

Blaze squeezed himself in and asked how everyone was. All nodded and answered they were okay and Blaze gratefully accepted a mug of fresh brewed tea from Donnie.

"Well," started Blaze. "Last night was a little exciting for the village. It appears the dissidents almost got into the place but were beaten back with a lot of casualties. It appears more dissidents turned up than was expected."

Seems we continuously underestimate how many men they can muster for this sort of action, thought Bomber. *Perhaps we are not giving enough credit to the dissidents' determination to beat us.*

Blaze gulped some tea down, smacked his lips, and continued, "Put the wind up the senior PO who started asking for mortar support and the reserve platoon to be deployed. Company Commander kept a cool head as usual, told him to sit tight, put down some DFs and told the Recce lads to join in which did the job."

Again he paused and drank more tea, commenting, "I wish my lads could make a brew as good as this." He smacked his lips again in an appreciative way. "Only one problem now, some of the dissidents didn't all get away in the night. Some are holed up in the odd *wadi* and such. The locals aren't too keen to try and winkle them out but we can't leave them where they are to cause more mischief tonight."

Bomber was waiting for the punch line and did not think it was one any of them would like.

"So the Company Commander has tasked us to clear our side of the ridge between here and the runway as far as the village.

OP Charlie reckons a few of them may have holed up in the small *wadi* near the end of the fields where the irrigation ditches are."

"So here's what we will do, leave all unnecessary kit in the Sanger, two of the HQ section will man this position.

I will bring the other two sections down and head into the gap. You will provide cover, once we are on the flat and in cover, you come down and leap frog through."

"Okay sir, how long before we move?" said Bomber.

"Thirty minutes," and with that he left.

Bomber was already thinking what to take with them. "Patrick, call the others down here and we better get a shift on."

"Sean, I think we should take the 3.5 and six rockets just in case they are holed up in one of those little caves down there."

"Good thinking. It beats trying to chuck grenades in."

The others arrived and Bomber quickly briefed everyone on what was happening and what to take. Priority was ammunition and water as much as could be carried without it slowing anyone down.

Bomber watched as Blaze and the other two sections reached the gap. Then they turned right, north, and down to the flat ground. Once they had taken up fire positions, Bomber ordered everyone down to the gap in staggered single file.

On reaching Blaze's position, they changed formation to extended line and moved on another two hundred yards and took up fire positions. Although the terrain was relatively flat, small broken rock outcrops made good cover not just for them to use but could also be places where the enemy could have taken cover. Blaze was relentless at keeping everyone moving. Leap frogging through, they carried on until they were roughly one hundred yards from the *wadi*.

Now Blaze signaled for one section to crawl to the rim and give it the mark-one eyeball treatment. After a few minutes, the section commander signaled all clear and both two and three section entered the *wadi*. It was an old watercourse which wound it tortuous way back towards the high ground, a continuation of the ridge they had left. It varied in depth from ten to thirty feet and was a perfect hiding place. One section took the lead leap frogging in pairs quickly from cover to cover. Suddenly they stopped and Blaze went forward to see what was happening.

After a quick chat with the section commander, Blaze signaled to Bomber to come forward.

Bomber made his way forward wondering what was in store for them that one section could not deal with.

Blaze pointed at a bend where several dark holes punctured the wall and said, "We think there is someone in the left hand of those caves. I am going to call out and tell them to come out if that fails, you are to put a rocket right into the entrance. Can you do that?"

Bomber studied the ground for a moment. "I would have to fire from over there sir," he said, pointing to a place near a large boulder. "Can't do it from here because of the back blast and I would not be able to put it into the entrance only the side."

"Okay, we will cover you. Get the 3.5 and make your way there."

"One other thing, sir. I will have to fire from the standing position which will leave me exposed so as soon as I fire, I will drop flat by the boulder."

"Sounds like a plan to me. Let's do it."

Bomber went back to three section, briefed them and then loaded the launcher himself, telling Patrick to bring two spare rockets as far as the point section than to wait there.

With his rifle slung on his back and the rocket launcher cradled in his arms, he looked to Blaze for the signal to go.

Blaze's parting words were, "Wait for my signal to fire and don't miss."

Don't miss, don't miss kept repeating in Bomber's mind as he set off feeling exposed and vulnerable, crawling flat along the side of the *wadi* like a lizard who knew the falcon had him in his sight. Resisting the urge to hurry and make a noise, he carefully leopard-crawled to the boulder.

After what seemed hours but in reality was a few minutes, he was at the large boulder which must have fallen recently from the wall above, as most of the *wadi* bed was washed clear of such rocks.

Looking back to Blaze's position, he almost jumped when Blaze shouted in what sounded like very good Arabic. What he said Bomber was not sure, but he repeated it twice more to no effect. For a second or two, nothing happened. Then Bomber thought he could see some movement near the entrance. Then a burst of automatic fire came from the left-hand cave spraying the area towards Blaze but with none of it going near Bomber who lay still and muttered a silent prayer that he would not be spotted and riddled with bullets before he could launch the rocket.

Next he saw Blaze give him the signal, standing up, carefully. Trying not to make any noise, he shouldered the launcher aimed at the cave entrance which was less than eighty yards' distance and fired. Bomber thought he heard a shout from the cave but had dropped flat and covered his head with his arms. The rocket exploded almost at the same instance he hit the ground. He felt the heat of the blast, dirt and dust billowed out from the cave covering him.

If anyone survived, they were going to be as mad as hell and blast the area with everything they had, Bomber thought and he tried to wriggle in closer to the boulder whilst slipping his SLR off of his back.

After a few moments, Blaze did his Arabic thing again. This time from the right-hand cave came an answer and then two weapons were thrown clear of the entrance shortly followed by two dissidents with their hands raised. As they walked forward, one turned his head and shouted towards the center cave. A reply followed and another weapon was tossed out and a third dissident followed.

They were dressed in the normal garb and they could have easily passed as locals to Bomber but the locals somehow seemed to know the difference.

Blaze ordered them to come forward until they were passed the bend and two-section position. With one section taking over searching the prisoners, Blaze questioned them to ascertain if anyone else was in the caves. They replied pointing to the cave hit by the rocket.

Bomber and three section were ordered to go and confirm the caves were in fact clear. Working right to left, they checked the caves which were fairly shallow, going in no more than ten or fifteen feet.

At the left-hand cave, the remains of the two dissidents were pulled out. The smell was overpowering and Donnie and Jos vomited and Bomber felt himself wanting to join them but needed to get things done quickly. Later he could feel as sick as he wanted.

Flies arrived in their thousands and settled on the corpses. "Where the hell do they come from?" said Sean. "Not a one to be seen for hours. Then some blood, guts and shit, then there they are in the millions, the fucking bastards."

Blaze had brought the prisoners up to the corpses and instructed them to wrap them in the blankets discovered in the right-hand cave and to carry them to two section who were to stay and guard the prisoners

"This will be a bit of a feather in the bosses and our caps." Jos smiled at everyone when he said it.

Everyone looked a bit lost at his words and he explained, "How many times do we get prisoners? Hardly ever so. This is good and the PO will grill them for every bit of information he can screw out of them."

"Yep, got it and we did it." Patrick declared, "Could've earned us some brownie points with the boss and get us of point for a while."

Just then, Perfection called in the section commanders for a briefing.

Blaze gave the prisoners to four of one section to guard having made a radio call to base to send a vehicle to collect them. The prisoners looked dejected and sat cross-legged with their heads bowed.

Two section were to lead on up the *wadi* to the end, which wasn't much more than two hundred yards. Then three section would leap frog through breaking right to follow the dry irrigation ditches back towards the fields and the village.

Donnie was not impressed that half of one section would get a ride back to base and an early tea, while he would get the job of clearing the irrigation ditches.

"So bloody typical, those lazy bastards from one section getting the cushy jobs again."

"Well, you could look at it this way, Donnie," said Bomber who was getting tired of his moaning. "If the boss wants a job doing properly, he is not going to give it to those wankers so it has to be the Dammed."

"So we are not only the Dammed but the best dammed section," Jos mused.

"Keep it down you lot," Perfection had moved up behind them.

How did he get that close to us without us noticing, Bomber thought and made a mental note to ensure even in a platoon location he would have someone facing to the rear.

"Give me the 3.5 and the rockets. I will have someone from one section carry it and if it is needed again, I'll send it forward."

The clearing of the rest by two section went without incident, and soon Bomber was in the lead looking at the start of the irrigation ditches. The ditches were designed to collect the run off from the *wadi* when it rained and channel it down a series of ditches which got smaller and smaller as they approached the fields where it was channeled off to each field to ensure all were irrigated. The ditches had been dug by hand out of the hard, packed earth. Bomber imagined the time and effort that had been taken to do this with crude picks and shovels and wondered if they had originally been dug generations or even hundreds of years ago.

The first of the ditches were deep enough to hide a small man standing and about five feet wide to cope with the volume of water at the start of the rain.

Bomber did not have a clue about the best way to clear the ditches other than get in and walk them.

After a quick discussion with Sean, who had become his number two without any formal agreement, they decided that for the deep ditches four of them would work in pairs leapt frogging through inside the ditch while the others would take a side each and remain on top looking in as cover.

After about three hundred yards of this, Bomber felt hot and drained and wondered why the ditches did not go in a straight line. Being above and able to see, Donnie could have told him that the builders had followed the line of least resistance going around the hard rock out crops that interrupted the areas of good soil.

Sean raised his hand and Bomber stopped. Sean pointed and Bomber squinted to see what he was pointing at. Going closer, he could just make out the thin line of a wire placed about a foot off the ground.

If there was a trip wire, then someone placed it for a purpose probably to cover their position for just such a situation as this. Looking up, Bomber could see Donnie and indicated for him to scout ahead from above. After a few minutes, he came back and said he thought he could see a body in the ditch but no movement.

Moving forward, Bomber tracked the wire which led to a hand grenade wedge between two rocks big enough to hold it in place if the pin was pulled. Going back to the other side of the ditch, he found the end of the wire attached to a curved knife thrust into the hard ground. Releasing the knife took the pressure off the grenade's pin and Sean was able to splay the ends of the pin so that it could not come out.

Carefully, they moved round the bend with Donnie providing top cover. Lying against the side of the ditch was a figure with a Soviet AK47 rifle on his lap, the AK47 being a mass produced favorite of the Eastern Block. Two bandoliers holding spare magazine crossed his chest and his headscarf had been wrapped across his face, hiding his features with just a slit for the eyes. These were closed and Bomber thought that he could be asleep but by carefully watching him for several minutes, he realized he did not have any rise and fall of his chest and was dead. Moving closer, Bomber could see a dark stain on the ground around the body but could not see any wound. Then Bomber noticed the ground seem to move and he tossed a stone and thousands of bloated flies, that had been feeding on the blood, took to the air confirming that death had indeed passed this way.

Sean, satisfied the dissident was dead, took the rifle and passed it up to Donnie. As he did so, the body slid sideways and rolled onto its front. Bomber held his breath both from the smell and in case the body was booby-trapped with another grenade. Bomber silently cursed himself for the error. They could both see that the dark stain had come from the back of the man, and from the jagged shape of the tear in the clothing, they surmised it must have been caused by shrapnel from an exploding mortar round.

Signaling to Blaze who had moved forward to find out what was happening, he ordered Bomber to check the ditch further on for any other trip wire with grenades. There was one more. Sean made it safe. Meanwhile, Blaze had used the radio to call for a vehicle to collect the body. Then two section were pushed through to carry on the clearing.

Another two hours and they had reached the fields with no further discoveries. Blaze ordered sentries out and for everyone to take a break. Bomber suddenly realized he was hungry and was surprised to see how late in the day it was.

Sharing some ration pack biscuits and tinned cheese, they talked about the body, the consensus being that he had been wounded by the mortar fire and slowly bled to death. He was then left there by his comrades who could no longer carry him and get away themselves. The grenades had been rigged to get anyone stumbling across him.

However, they considered that this was unusual for them to leave one of their own behind unless they had been split up and only one or two others had been with him.

Bomber could not get over how peaceful he looked sitting there unlike the previous victims of bullets, bombs and rockets he had seen. He sent a silent prayer to God to preserve them through whatever was to come next and wondered if he would be able to cope. Inside his head, he knew he would at the time it happened but afterwards it might be different.

The break was interrupted by the arrival of two of the airfield trucks and Blaze ordered all on board. The unlucky four from one section had the job of loading the bodies onto their truck and riding back to base with them.

Chapter 8
Camels, Mines, Old Men
and Promises

After the excitement of the Red Wolves shoot out, life settled down to a series of routine patrols and ambush duties. It appeared to Bomber and the lads that the Wolves had decided to leave them alone while they licked their wounds. With just a month left of the tour up country, the Company Commander was determined to prevent any infiltration and mine laying in his area of responsibility.

Bomber looked up at the sky and watched a dozen kites circling overhead. They seemed to float easily in the hot air that had sucked the life out of the patrol. Three and two section commanded by Perfection had been on patrol since first light and it was now close to midday. They had not seen a soul all morning but now plodding towards them was the camel man and his son.

They were regulars passing daily through the area with three camels laden with fodder that they cut from various so-called wet *wadis*. This they took to the villages to feed livestock.

Perfection stopped them for a chat in broken English and Arabic, and in the past they had always been friendly enough but today Bomber noticed that the old man seemed sullen and angry. The son, tall and thin and probably no older than fifteen, seemed nervous and could not look Bomber in the eye when Bomber handed him the ritual compo ration sweet.

None of this had escaped Perfection who ordered Bomber and his section to give the camel loads the onceover. It only took a few minutes to find the three British mark seven land mines hidden in the loads. These mines weighed thirty pounds apiece, twenty of which was high explosive. One of these could blow the track off of any known tank in the world, should it run over it. A truck that was unprotected would be scrap metal and the people onboard blown to hell. As the mines were produced, the old man became hysterical wailing and waving his arms around. Bomber spoke to the son who could speak a little squaddie English. It took him several minutes to work out that the dissidents had arrived two nights earlier at their house which was just this side of the border. The rest of the family was being held hostage against them delivering the mines to a house on the Dhala Road.

Perfection made a radio call to base who told him to wait there; someone was coming out to see them. Bomber hoped he had got the right story from the boy and what he thought he had been told was correct. Settling down to wait, Perfection took time to explain to the old man and his son that they would be helped, but either they did not understand or were not convinced.

Donnie as always produced the makings from his pouches and got a brew going while half the team spread out in all round defense; the rest followed Donnie's example. Bomber was always amazed at them wherever they were. You could always rely on the British squaddie to produce a brew when there was a break in the work or action.

An hour later, three ramshackle vehicles turned up. A truck looked just like any of the others that plied the trade routes. The cab had more decorations than a South American dictator. The sides had been painted many colors over the years that had faded into a dull blur of some pattern long forgotten.

The two others were the Indian version of a jeep and looked as if someone had taken sledgehammers to the body work. They were so dented that there was not a straight line to be seen.

From these emerged the PO we called Bulldog Drummond and about fifteen of his tame tribesmen. The PO sat with the old man and his son. A long and sometimes heated discussion took place.

Perfection had ordered Bomber to get some tea over to them to help the negotiations and it seemed to help calm the old man.

After about an hour, the PO came and spoke to Perfection who got onto base using the radio after which he called both Bomber and the sections to him and briefed them on what was to happen.

"Apparently, the old man is a respected fella in these parts, so they have agreed that the PO will deal with the dissidents holding the old man's family. Meanwhile we will take the detonators out of the mines and let the old man proceed with his son.

"The truck and ten of the tribesmen are going ahead to the house that the old man is to deliver the mines to and stake it out. Once he has delivered them and is clear, the tribesmen will move in and take out those in the house."

Perfection paused and lowered his voice.

"The old man has agreed to this, provided that some of us accompany the PO on the rescue mission. It could be. He does not trust the tribesmen, so wants us there as insurance. The Company Commander has given the 'okay', so it will be as many as we can fit into those jeeps with the tribesmen. The Platoon Commander is to follow us up and meet us somewhere near the house but I don't think he will get there in time seeing as he has to get back to base from his patrol first."

The selection turned out to be Perfection, Bomber and three others, Sean, Patrick, and Jos. The rest of the patrol would return to base under the command of two section commander. As Perfection was about to board the jeeps, the old man caught hold of him by both hands, looked him in the eyes, and spoke slowly and clearly with the PO translating.

"I am trusting you with the lives of my wife, daughter, and two young sons. They are my life my whole reason for living. I have agreed to the plan because I do not want people killed by these bombs I have been forced to carry. God go with you and protect you and my family!"

While he spoke, tears ran down his craggy sun and wind-burnt face, his son openly weeping. Bomber felt himself welling up with emotion.

Perfection must have felt the same, for he held out his arms and hugged the old man and said, "You have my word. I will protect your family and kill the scum."

"That's some statement. Never seen Perfection like this before. Guess we will be doing this and not Bulldog." Sean, spoke quietly into Bomber's ear to avoid Perfection hearing.

With that, they climbed into the battered jeeps and drove off. It took three pain-filled hours of being jolted about in the jeeps which lacked padding of any sort to protect the buttocks. Bomber guessed the shock absorbers had died a long time ago.

Pulling up in a dip by some small humpback mounds, the PO, one of the older tribes man, Perfection and Bomber went forward crawling slowly to the top of one of the humps.

About quarter of a mile ahead, they could make out the house in the failing light. Like most of the local buildings, it was mud built with a flat roof. It probably had four large rooms and the roof had a lean too, covering half of it.

Two rough outbuildings and a corral made of thorn bushes stood to one side. In front of the house, a woman could be seen stirring a pot on an open fire. Three dissidents sat with their backs to the wall of the house watching the woman. Bomber refocused his binoculars and studied them. They each had the headscarf wrapped around their head and wool jackets. Two bandoliers of spare magazines crossed their chests. An AK 47 was held in their laps. All were smoking the foul-smelling cigarettes and Bomber wondered how and where they got them from?

After another minute, the woman took bowls and filled them from the pot and with some flatbread carried it to the dissidents. She then filled three more and took them to the smaller and sturdier-looking of the two outbuildings. Having put down the bowls, she lifted a wooden bar. She opened the door then stooped and picked up the bowls and went in.

"Well, we now know where the children are," said Perfection.

The woman came out leaving the door open, collected another bowl of food and some bread, then returned to the outhouse. One of the men followed her and after she went inside, he placed the bar back on the door.

"Okay, this is what we will do," Perfection stated without consulting the PO.

"Hold on, this is my show," interrupted the PO.

"I am sorry sir, but I gave my word to the old man, a sworn oath if you like."

The old tribesman looked at the PO and nodded saying something in Arabic. The PO paused for a second and made a grunting noise of consent to the tribesman.

"Okay Sgt., your lead. If I think your plan is workable, tell me what you are thinking."

Back behind the mound out of sight while two of the tribesmen kept watch, Bomber could not believe how hungry he was. Munching on biscuits and a tin of cold beans, he reflected on the plan and its simplicity, boldness, and brutality. Now he just wanted to get his head down for a couple of hours.

At one o'clock after a sleepless rest, Perfection had them all checking their kit twice over – no rattles, faces blackened with cam cream, weapons checked and a round up the spout ready to fire. A tap on Perfection's shoulder from the PO signaled that he was moving off with his men just leaving two behind with the jeeps. The PO held out his hand and Perfection shook it. Then they were gone. That simple action between them summed up to Bomber the respect and trust they had for each other.

Having waited forty minutes, Perfection signaled time to move. In a five-man diamond formation, they set off angling away to the right before swinging back towards the house coming in from the right flank.

The PO and his men had gone left flanking and would guard the rear of the house to prevent anyone escaping. Perfection had surmised that the dissident would just have one person on guard by the outhouse where the family was held. The other two would be in the house sleeping.

Perfection's plan was simple. They would approach the outbuilding. Perfection would scan for the sentry with his binoculars and try and determine if the sentry was alert or as he suspected asleep at his post, which he guessed would be outside of the building containing the family.

If he was asleep, Perfection would just walk up and ram his bayonet, which was already fixed to his SLR, into his skull, killing him instantly. Then he, Sean, and Jos would go into the house and deal with the other two. Bomber and Patrick would guard the family and if anything went wrong in the house, they would get the family out and back to the vehicles while the PO moved in with his men.

Bomber crouched by Perfection who studied the buildings through his binoculars, then whispered in Bomber's ear that he thought the sentry was asleep by the door of the outbuilding. No one else could have been seen outside. Creeping forward behind Perfection, Bomber's throat was so dry that he could not swallow and what was worse – he had a genuine desire to piss.

Stopping short of the building, Perfection signaled for them to stay and without a pause he walked casually to the sentry. Standing above him, he raised his SLR and drove the bayonet down and through his skull.

He must have died instantly as all he did was fall sideways when the bayonet was pulled out. Perfection waved for everyone to come forward. Bomber and Patrick took post by the door while Sean and Jos followed Perfection to the house.

Just as they reached the door, it opened and there stood one of the dissidents but before he could move, Sean hit hard with the butt of his rifle and he dropped like a stone. Perfection raced in followed by Jos and two shots rang out, and after a few minutes they both appeared dragging a dead dissident by the ankles. Bomber found himself staring and fascinated by the way the corpse's head bounced as it was dragged over the open ground.

Sean had rolled the unconscious one over and tied his hands behind his back. When Perfection saw him, he raised his SLR ready to slam his bayonet into him. Sean caught his arm and pulled him away. "I promised I would kill the scum," snarled Perfection at Sean like a dog ready to contest for a prize bone.

"You never promised murder," Sean said, still holding his arm in a vice-like grip.

Perfection nodded and seemed to sag. His whole body looked limp and he walked away, so close to the line of what is acceptable in war and what is not. Sean told Bomber later that Perfection had explained that he had, had the urge to kill but knew it was wrong and thanked him for stopping him.

Bomber meanwhile had used his torch to signal the PO that all was well and he could come in. This was important as they needed an Arabic speaker to reassure the wife and children that they were safe.

The PO spoke in a gentle voice through the door. Then Bomber lifted the bar and opened the door. Shining his torch on to the wife who had the children shielded behind her, an arm held out straight in front with a knife clutched in her hand. She must have smuggled it in after preparing the food as it looked like a knife for cutting vegetables.

The PO continued to speak softly and then pointed to the dead dissident clearly visible with Bomber shining his torch on the body.

After some more coaxing, she moved outside with the children following. Stopping, she fired a string of questions at the PO who answered in the same calm tone as he had used to coax her from the building. Whatever he said seemed to do the trick and she spoke to the children who stayed by the doorway. Taking Bomber's torch from his hand, she strode off and into the house.

One of the tribesmen flashed his torch in the direction of the mounds and after about five minutes, the two jeeps arrived. Sitting in the lead jeep was Blaze, him, and one section had traveled by truck to a point about a mile away, stopping there so the noise of the vehicle would not be heard. Then they had marched in the dark to the mounds where he guessed they would be.

Just then, they could see the lights of the truck and in five more minutes, it had arrived and the remains of the platoon dismounted and spread out in all round defense.

The woman had reappeared from the house carrying several bundles and pushing an old wooden box with her foot. Two of the tribesmen went and assisted her, putting the box and bundles into one of the jeeps.

The woman now called the children to her and they all went to the corral in which were a mixed bunch of six goats and sheep. Bomber found it difficult to decide which were which. The women and the children set about putting a rope about each one's neck and leading them out. The tribesmen starting laughing and Bomber realized that these would be coming with them as well.

These animals and the old man's camels were the total sum of their wealth along with whatever was in the box and bundles.

The animals and the children were loaded into the truck with the guys having a good laugh as, when passing them up, one of the goats sprayed two of them with urine. The children joined in the laughter and were rewarded with sweets from the guys.

The two bodies and the prisoner were also added to the load. A crowded truck set off back to base following the two jeeps. Bomber wedged himself in and, despite the lurching, bumping, and stink of the dead and animals, fell asleep only awaking a short distance from camp. He realized he had slept for almost five hours.

At the camp, Bomber watched the old man and his son have a tearful reunion with his family. Tears flowed. He hugged Perfection, praising him to God on their safe return and the death of the dissidents.

They heard later from the PO that they had moved into a family house near the west village. The tribesmen who had staked out the house where the mines had been delivered had successfully ambushed four dissidents there, alive or dead it was not said. Bomber suspected the latter.

A quiet period of three weeks followed with little to disturb the normal routine of guard duties and patrols. With nothing to break, the monotony Bomber began to get restless. *Perhaps*, thought Bomber, *the dissidents had decided to wait for the regiment to finish its tour up country and then try its luck with the new guys taking over to see how they reacted to a spot of bother or perhaps they had simply moved their operations to easier targets.*

Chapter 9
Spit, Polish, and Clueless

The day had arrived when they were to be relieved. Most of the Company, apart from a small rear party whose job it was to hand over all the tactical know how to the new unit, stood with their kit at the edge of the runway watching the two Beverlys coming into land. The Raider Platoon had been deployed to the north of the runway to prevent the dissidents getting into a position where they could shoot the planes down.

The Beverlys taxied in creating a mini sandstorm in their wake and finally stopped a hundred yards from the waiting Company. What happened next stayed with Bomber for years to come. The rear doors of the plane opened and after a fifteen-minute pause came the sound of regimental music and out marched a guards' band in full ceremonial uniform playing fit to bust. They were followed by guardsmen formed up in three ranks weapons at the shoulder. The guardsmen wore khakis but peaked parade caps, white belts, and with everything metal-polished so that the sun reflected and dazzled all for miles around.

"Holy mother of God, where do they think they are?" exclaimed Sean.

"Not in the Radfan that's for fucking sure," Patrick snarled. "Fucking pounces will get shot to hell going around like that."

Bomber could see all the guardsmen were untanned and he could already see the sweat staining the shirts of the men marching to the music in the burning sun.

The band stopped playing and after the shock of seeing the performance, Bomber and others realized that what they had witnessed was actually a performance designed to impress. Laughter and catcalls started from the lads. The CSM barked 'quiet' and when he said 'quiet', everyone knew to be so, and the noise stopped.

The guards' company marched off to the base with the band playing. As they left, the CSM ordered everyone onto the Beverly's. Inside the planes, the guards' personnel kit was still on board. The RAF load master did not look a happy man and the first thing Bomber had learned when dealing with the RAF was never to upset the load master, if you wanted a peaceful flight.

It appeared the guards were expecting the kit to be unloaded and taken to the camp for them. After a short discussion between the load master and the CSM, they decided to oblige, forming a chain of men in two rows. The kit was passed from hand to hand and then thrown onto the ground at the back of the planes. The lads were not too particular in the handling of the kit or where it landed.

Once completed, the company quickly boarded and the plane's engines started up and moved into position for takeoff. The back wash from the planes covered the guards' kit in a mound of sand and dirt and Bomber felt a sadistic sense of satisfaction at the result. There would be some very pissed off guardsmen when they found their kit. Later it seemed a bit petty to Bomber but it was clear the guardsmen had a lot to learn about fighting and living in the Radfan.

Bomber sat in the bucket seat and forced himself to relax as the Beverly lumbered its way down the airfield getting airborne in an incredibly short run. The pilot flew the plane to the east, then banked to the south and made a low-altitude run back over the camp to cheers from the guys. Bomber was too busy to cheer as he was trying very hard not to be sick.

Chapter 10
Crater City, an Old Volcano Waiting to Blow

Bomber stood in the shade of an orange sellers stall studying the mass and mix of humanity passing by. After the open spaces and lack of people up country, the confine of the buildings, smell, and sheer volume of people was beginning to swamp his senses.

The port city of Aden was a stopping point for Dhows from Africa and the Red Sea. Rust bucket steamers from further away places with unpronounceable names all docked at the port. The city was a melting pot. Anything could be brought or sold including people and was a perfect place for the dissidents to develop their war on the establishment and the British.

The city, as its name implied, was built in the center of a long, dead volcano crater. The side to the sea had collapsed and made it a perfect harbor, leaving two thirds of the rim of the old volcano surrounding the city.

The volume of people, noise, and smells struck the sense like a hammer ringing on an anvil. Those on their first visit could easily be overwhelmed, until by constant immersion in the city life, the senses equalize.

Foot patrols in the city were half Platoon affairs which in the case of the Regiment could be as few as twelve men as with most Infantry Regiments of the time they were under strength.

Their brief had been to stay at this road junction which had a small bank on one side and market stalls backing onto the walls of other buildings on the opposite side and observe. A number of attacks had been carried out ranging from bombs placed in vacuum flasks or toys to much larger ones in boxes being left in such places as this.

Cardboard boxes on the street were not uncommon as the rubbish collection system was haphazard, if it happened at all. Cardboard was a favorite food of the large number of goats that wandered freely in the streets.

Officials, police and army posts, and just any place where people gathered could be the targets for these indiscriminate weapons of the enemy. Spreading terror was their aim regardless of who they killed to achieve this. Getting rid of the British and the current establishment was their one goal but they also needed the population cowed and pliable.

Bomber watched the shoppers at the stalls making sure that no one left a bag, box, or anything suspicious behind when they left. After two hours, he was feeling weary. His shirt was soaked with sweat. The flies seemed to target him, determined to drive him mad. He suspected his mind was wandering when he started to believe the flies had been trained by the terrorists to break his morale by their constant attention.

Patrolling two nights later, Bomber, kneeling in the doorway of a shuttered shop, looked at his watch and was relieved to find there was only another hour to go. The night was hot and lacked even a sea breeze to cool the streets. There were few people about in the small hours. A heady aroma of exotic, unknown smells from the shop filled his senses as the dullness of sleep did its best to overpower him.

Blaze was leading the patrol. Behind him was the radio operator, Jamie McElroy, then Bomber, three more of the platoon further back on the same side of the street. On the opposite side, six more of the Platoon were stretched out, each of them hugging the shadows to remain invisible to any gunman.

Suddenly Blaze shouted a warning challenge, "Halt or I fire," and almost immediately fired two shots from his pistol, one of the new 9 mm Browning semi automatic's, before setting off at a gallop down a side alley.

The rest of the patrol followed but Jamie, hampered by the A41 radio strapped to his back while at the same time trying to send a contact report, had no chance of keeping up with the athletic Blaze. As the alley was narrow and filled with mountains of rubbish, rats and the odd goat, there was little chance of getting past Jamie.

On reaching a T-junction, Bomber called a halt not knowing which way Blaze had gone. The sound of two shots made him duck. They had come from the left. Without waiting to be told, they all set off at a run in that direction.

Working their way through the piles of debris, they came to a dead end. There two men stood facing the wall with their hands up. Ten yards away stood Blaze, pistol at the ready.

"About time, seems some people need more fitness training, Cpl. Brown."

"Yes sir, what have you got?"

"They had what looked like a bomb which they have dumped, but I know the spot and the skinny one has a gun which he dropped when I put a couple of rounds by his head."

Bomber put down his SLR and, being careful not to get in the line of fire, went forward to search the two men. At the feet of the skinny one was a Webley .45 pistol. Bomber slid it with his foot towards Sean who was also covering the pair. A quick frisk search of 'Skinny' revealed some pistol ammunition but nothing else.

The other man looked at the hard case, six-foot Bomber judged with a boxer's physic, taking greater care. He made him put his finger tips against the wall, then spread his leg and pushed his feet back until he was leaning on his fingertips at an angle against the wall. He reassured that if the man gave any trouble, he could kick his feet backwards and the man would crash to the floor.

Frisking him, he discovered a heavy semiautomatic pistol stuffed into his waistband. Bomber thought it could be a Soviet Makarov but was not sure. Two spare magazines and a notebook were in a jacket pocket and he stuffed them into the back pocket of his own trousers.

Once the two had their hands secured behind their backs. Blaze retraced the route. About twenty yards in from the road, a goat was eating a cardboard box. The skinny dissident gave a yell and threw himself to the floor while the hard case let out a string of what Bomber assumed were curses in Arabic.

The goat seemed unperturbed ignoring the fuss and was about to take another bite when Sean sent it on its way with a shove from a size-nine boot.

Patrick had grabbed the skinny one and forced him to stand but he was obviously afraid and was muttering at the hard case who shouted at him and he stopped.

Blaze called Bomber over saying, "They don't know I speak Arabic. It would appear they have set the bomb. The tough-looking one I think is the boss, so I am going to get him to disarm it."

"Is that a good idea sir? He could choose to blow us all to hell."

"Exactly, so I want you and the rest to take the skinny one out on to the road where you will be sheltered. I'll stay with the other one and make him an offer he can't refuse. Before you go, get someone to untie his hands."

"Okay sir, but could I suggest you cover him from the corner where you will stand a chance if it blows."

"I'll do that. Now get everyone clear."

Once out of harm's way, Bomber could hear Blaze talking to the hard case. What he said Bomber never knew but after a few minutes, the hard case appeared carrying the box with Blaze behind him, pistol at the ready.

Locals arrested by the army in the district of Aden had to be handed over to the local police, something that the boys did not approve of, as many of them were back out on the streets in less than twenty-four hours. Whether this was due to intimidation, corruption, or just plain laziness by the police in charging the culprits, Bomber was not sure. Arriving at the police station, Blaze, Bomber, and Sean escorted the prisoners in and put the weapons and the box on the desk. The desk Sergeant called out and an inspector appeared with several others in civilian clothes.

Blaze explained in Arabic what had happened. He opened the box and the inspector looked in. The Inspector had up to this point displayed only a mild interest in Blaze's explanation but now he suddenly paled and then he quickly moved back, ordering the station to be abandoned, which they did at amazing speed, leaving the five of them standing alone.

The hard case said something in Arabic which Blaze seem to concur with. Then Blaze ordered the two to be locked in the cells, leaving the bomb on the desk for the bomb squad to deal with.

Leaving the station, Bomber could see all the police sitting behind a row of police vehicles smoking. The rest of the patrol had spread out covering the ground away from the station.

Blaze used radio HQ to update them of the situation and they were told to wait for the special investigation team to arrive. The SB boys arrived in two unmarked cars and pulled in at the same moment the bomb squad arrived at the car park. Blaze explained to the Warrant Officer from the bomb squad where the bomb was and its condition. The Warrant Officer acknowledged and collected his tool bag from the back of his vehicle. With just this in his hand, he went into the station. He appeared a few minutes later with the bomb.

He stopped by Blaze, stating it was properly disarmed but that it was a more sophisticated device than he had previously seen. With that, he left. Rumor control had it that a few weeks later he was killed trying to disarm a much larger bomb near the same police station.

Remembering the notebook, Bomber handed it to Blaze who had a quick reading. Then he gave it to one of the British members of the investigation team, who were taking the two prisoners to their vehicle. This started an argument between the police inspector and the SB officers (Special Branch Officers). The SB Officers were beginning to get pushed around by the policemen who had suddenly found their courage and Blaze had to step in with several of the lads to separate the two groups.

After a further heated discussion, it was agreed that the prisoners would go with the SB officer but that two of the local police would go with them.

Bomber later learned from Blaze that the notebook had some useful information in regarding potential targets. The hard case turned out to be an Egyptian probably sent in to strengthen the dissidents' will to fight and to persuade them to take more direct action. He was probably responsible for the more sophisticated bomb as he seemed very competent when it came to disarming it.

It must have been considered an important result by the powers to be because Blaze was awarded the Military Cross (MC), for his action of chasing down two armed men and preventing a bomb attack.

Bomber also learnt that Perfection had been mentioned in dispatches for the hostage rescue, which meant he would wear an oak leaf on the ribbon of his campaign medal.

It was two days later that the Regiment had to deal with its first riot in Crater and the ready Platoon was sent to deal with it. The riot which was taking place in the central district or old part of the city was a clearly orchestrated event with the rioters leaving local houses and shops alone and only attacking establishment buildings.

Since the time of the army wearing red coats, there had been a standard riot drill practiced by the army. Everyone knew it was as obsolete as a wooden warship except, it would appear, the higher echelons of the army and government who always wanted to appear fair to the natives but not too worried about Tommy Atkins.

The standard drill would be to form a square of men in front of the rioters, blow a bugle, and unfurl a banner saying, "This is an unlawful assembly disburse." In the meantime, rocks, bottles, and fire bombs would be sailing through the air at the soldiers. As the soldiers had only their steel helmets, a flimsy tin riot shield barely big enough to cover the chest, and a wooden stick like baton, casualties would piled up. Of course the Commander after due consultation could order a couple of the likely looking agitators to be shot and that would disperse the crowd. However, things move much faster now than in the year of the red coats as the ready platoon were about to find out.

Later, members of the ready Platoon recounted to Bomber how they had quickly deployed from the trucks and formed a square, immediately being pelted by rocks and petrol bombs. Four or five men went down and before they could deploy the banner, the rioters vanished leaving two gunmen who opened fire with AK 47s. Fortunately, the gunmen were either inexperienced at firing the AKs on automatic or too scared to take aim and put most of their bursts wide or high but four men went down wounded. Without waiting for permission, several of the guys returned fire. One of the gunmen was killed. The other got away.

The four platoon casualties all survived, thanks to fast treatment but that was four less good men the Regiment could deploy.

Less than twenty-four hours later, Bomber and the rest of his Platoon were deployed to the same area for another riot. Before they left, Blaze gave out his orders. It was radical and unapproved but all the boys liked it.

As they arrived in the area, Bomber noticed all the shops had their shutters closed and none of the normal traffic was about. Several old cars were burning and the rioter seemed to be waiting for the army to arrive.

Stopping a long way short of the rioters, the Platoon jumped out of the vehicles. One man stayed in the cab with the driver but stood up with his head and shoulders sticking out of the hatch with a fully loaded and cocked LMG facing the rioters. The three trucks had heavy steel mesh protecting the windshields which would stop most non-explosive missiles such as rocks. Lined up abreast the trucks blocked the whole street including the pavements. Behind the trucks was one section and the depleted HQ section. While the rioters were watching this and not being sure how to react, two and three section had each taken the parallel streets either side of the main street, quickly making their way up to get level with the rioters blocking the side streets which the rioters could use to escape.

As soon as Blaze knew they were in positions, he ordered the trucks to advance at a steady pace with the boys jogging along behind them. A few hardy souls stood and threw some petrol bombs but the rest ran leaving a lone gunman standing looking bewildered. Remembering he was supposed to fire his gun, he raised it to fire only to be cut down by a burst from the LMGs.

The rioters broke and ran towards Bomber and his section blocking the side street. With rifles leveled and bayonets fixed, they stood firm shoulder to shoulder watching the rioters run towards them. The first saw the way blocked and stopped but were knocked flat and trampled by the panicked rioters behind them. They too stopped once they realized that there was no escape.

As the momentum was lost, so Bomber advanced the section pushing the panicky rioters back at the point of the bayonet. Some tried banging on the doors and shutters of the buildings either side of the narrow street but no one was opening their doors today. Soon they were back at the main road where Blaze had sealed the last escape route. Bomber estimated that they had over a hundred rioters and one dead gunman.

Blaze had called for support and told the Section Commanders that the civil and military police were on the way.

In the meantime, Blaze ordered all the prisoners to sit on the ground and put their hands on their heads, which most did with just a few needing encouragement from Perfection and a couple of the guys from HQ section. Bomber was amazed how intimidating the wickedly pointed bayonet could be when you were on the wrong end of it.

The police arrived, photographed each prisoner, and then with a lot of shouting, pushing and a few well-aimed kicks, started loading them into the police vehicles. Meanwhile the Platoon kept a tight cordon facing outwards in case any gunman tried to disrupt the proceedings.

Finally the last ones were taken away and the Platoon returned to barracks ready for a good meal and a rest. Despite the fact Blaze's tactics had not been approved by anyone, the system was quickly taken up by the other Platoons in the Regiment and no one ever deployed for a riot in square formation again.

Chapter 11
Hell and the Spider

Bomber felt his eyes, ears, and nose were full of dust, dust that clung to his body, dust that he inhaled with every hot intake of breath, dust that he felt would smother the life out of him.

Intelligence had been offered that up on the crater rim above the city was a large weapons' dump hidden in one of the many old mine workings. What they could have been mining, there no one seemed to know. The whole company was deployed to search the area. The trucks dropped them off at a rough donkey track and Bomber and the rest of the platoon started the climb up. It was hot, 110 degrees hot. Bomber could feel the heat through the soles of his boots but worse was to come. The area at the top of the rim was a warren of tunnels and holes in the ground and the heat seemed to be amplified tenfold in side of these.

If there is a hell, thought Bomber, *then this must be what it is like*. They each had two water bottles and a chuggle and Bomber, like everyone else, had soon emptied the bottles. Bomber slumped to the ground and dragged his chuggle from his back, greedily gulping the warm water, swilling his mouth and throat of the cloying dust.

"God save us," Sean croaked as they slid into yet another hell hole of a tunnel which suddenly expanded into a small cavern.

Bomber casted his mind back to his time in the Infantry Junior Leaders when they had gone caving in Yorkshire. There it had been cool under ground a bit muddy in places and sometimes a wonderful cold waterfall. God, how they could do with that now!

"You would think it would be cooler in here but it seems even hotter," Patrick muttered and made a show of searching one side of the cavern, disturbing more of the fine dust that clung to them and mixed with their sweat where it formed into a sticky paste. As their ability to sweat disappeared, the dust set like a plaster on the skin until every exposed area was set hard. When they moved, the skin looked like cracked glaze on an old earthenware pot.

Several hours later, Bomber felt himself slowing up and it seemed to him that the others were moving in slow motion. He also thought that he was slurring his words and was not sure if he was actually talking or if it was all in his head. Leaving the last tunnel they had been given to search, Bomber was confronted by an apparition. Close up it turned out to be Perfection, his normal immaculate mustache was drooping. It was caked in dust and when he spoke, little puffs of it erupted from it.

"We are leaving, form up over there in the shade." Perfection's voice, normally crisp and sharp, came out as a hoarse whisper.

The shade was an illusion as there was no relief from the heat and Bomber noticed that all were struggling to cope and looked as if they had been painted a dun color and Bomber found himself starting to giggle with the thought they had adopted the perfect camouflage.

"No bloody locals up here digging or hiding," said Jos. "What the hell were they digging for anyway?"

"Someone said it was sulfur," Muttered Patrick. "But as you say no one here now."

"Not while there are nice comfy air-conditioned buildings down there," indicated Donnie in the direction of Crater city, who for once had not produced a brew the whole day.

At a wave from Blaze, the Platoon stumbled off back down the goat track to the trucks. Gathered round the trucks were all the street urchins, some with just a ragged T-shirt and flip flops, but each with a basket containing a large block of ice and dozens of *Stim's*, the local brand soft drink, which looked tantalizingly delicious.

Each section homed in on one or other of the urchin and Bomber found himself standing the cost of two bottles each for his section as he appeared to be the only one with any money.

"You want cold drink, soldier?" yelled the urchins as they pushed each other out of the way. There was not any shortage of takers and the urchins sold everything they had in ten minutes at ten times the normal price.

"Bloody little robbers," muttered Donnie to no one in particular. "Must have made more money today than they would have in a year."

"Never saw you parting with any money," said Sean.

"No, but I will pay you back on pay day, Bomber. Have no fear."

"Some fucking chance. You still owe me a fiver from last month when I paid your Char Wallah bill," fired back Sean.

"Did I forget to give you that?" Donnie said in a feigned shock voice. "Well, pay day, the debt will be settled."

Sean grunted having run out of energy to keep the banter going.

Back in barracks with weapons cleaned and stowed, they stood under the cool running water in the shower block fully clothed and watched as the dust turned to liquid mud and slithered down the drain like a gray snake. Stripping off the sodden clothing, the same thing happened as the dust left their bodies, creating an endless line of gray escaping into the depths of the sewers.

Not to be out done by the street urchins of Crater, the camp Char Wallah appeared with his basket of cold drinks and his giant kettle of tea. Bomber wondered how he carried all the stuff plus another basket full of freshly made cheese and tomato rolls. After three-pint mugs of tea, Bomber started to feel that he had replaced some of the lost fluid but it took several more mugs of water before he felt the need to pee and he realized that they had all come very close to being completely dehydrated.

That evening, the Dammed all collected in the NAAFI bar and decided that they should pool their money and see how many beers they could afford.

Bomber went first seventeen dinar. Sean managed nine Dinar. Donnie was forced to part with his lucky coin, a dented half a crown, worth two and a half Dinar and mumbled that if he got shot now, it was their fault for forcing him to part with it.

Once the others had dug deep into their pockets, they had a grand total of thirty-four Dinars and five old East African

93

shillings. The currency in Aden had recently changed from shillings to Dinar but most establishments would still take the East African currency.

Sean took the lot to the bar and, after some haggling with the bar manager, arranged for cans of ice-cold beer to be supplied until the funds ran out.

An hour later, they were sharing the last three cans between them and discussing Blaze's award of the MC and Perfection's MiD.

"How come," slurred John, "that a Sgt. who cool as a cucumber takes out an enemy sentry with just a bayonet, then another inside a building with one shot, rescues the hostages and gets this done without any of his team getting killed, just gets a bloody MiD and an officer who chases down two men gets a fucking MC!"

Bomber was taken aback by this, not just for the content. Blaze was held in high regard by the guys in the platoon, but that he had never heard John speak more than a few words before and certainly never a full sentence.

"Just the way of the world mate," replied Jos. "But you have to admit that Blaze did a good job chasing them down and it took guts to make that hard-looking bastard disarm the bomb. He deserves a medal just for changing our riot drill which must have saved a lot of casualties. All the Platoons are using our drill now and the locals seem to have given up on riots." The last words spoken would come back to haunt them all later.

Jos had wasted his breath as John, who chin on chest was snoring gently. Sean carefully removed the can from his hand as there was at least two swallows left in it which he quickly polished off.

The duty Corporal was now coming round telling everyone to drink up and leave so the Dammed arm-in-arm weaved its way back to barracks to sleep and to hell with tomorrow.

Next morning, the platoon paraded early as first order of the day was pay parade. The senior NCOs and the rank and file were all paid in cash over the table once a week. Only officers had bank accounts.

The soldier drew as much of his pay in cash as he wished. This was paid over the table by the pay staff, with the residue being paid into his POSB (Post Office Saving Account). The wise drew just enough cash to meet their needs each week, building up a nest egg for when they would go on leave.

Bomber was careful with his money, not drinking every night when they were in barracks and always making sure he had a little spare in his pocket on the last day before payday.

Some of the boys would gamble at cards. This was strictly against QRs (Queen's Regulations) and could be punished severely. Bomber knew that despite this, there were card schools going on. Often he would be approached by those who had lost their money, asking for a payday loan with doubles back on payday. Bomber never obliged, knowing it would put them even further in debt.

Bomber mentioned it to Perfection one day and he commented that throughout history, soldiers had gambled but the stupidity of some still amazed him. However, he would raise the matter with his pal, the Regimental Provo Sgt., (police). The evening of the next payday, a card school was busted by the Provo Sgt. and his team. The school was in the tent store run by the Quarter Master's Cpl. store man, a rather fat, nasty-looking cretin by the name of Stokes.

Punishment was swift and sure. All the NCOs involved were busted to private soldiers and fined. The private soldiers were given fourteen days' restriction of privileges and a fine. Those married men amongst the group would also be getting a tough time from their wives for the loss of income.

Normally jail time should have been mandatory for this offense but the regiment was so short of manpower that it could not really afford to have anyone not ready for duty.

The Platoon had moved onto mobile patrol duties operating out of HMS Sabre, the Royal Navy's shore base in Aden. All enjoyed being at Sabre, the food was wonderful and the accommodation ten times better than in barracks.

The patrols were conducted by pairs of especially adapted Land Rovers. Each vehicle was covered in steel mesh with a hatch that could be open or closed in the roof. On the front was a steel angled bar that went straight up from the bumper above the height of the Land Rover's roof the last foot of the bar being angle forward. This was designed to snap or cut through any wire cable stretch across the road put there to decapitate the men standing up on watch in the hatch.

Each vehicle was also fitted with a C42 radio to ensure contact with the HQ at all times.

Patrol times were four hours which could consist of cruising a set route, road blocks or fast raids on isolated locations where there would not be too much local interference.

About this time, the dissidents started using a 3.5 rocket launcher to fire into either residential areas, police, or army post. So far, no one had been killed or seriously hurt but it was only a matter of time. The dissident was given the code name Spider. Bomber was not sure if this was just the name the lads had given him or it was official but the name had been adopted by all.

Needless to say he was on the priority list to stop, kill, or capture!

Bomber was beginning to feel drowsy. It was two o'clock in the morning but still the heat of the previous day lingered. They were at a road junction just outside an area of well-to-do detached houses where there had been a number of grenade attacks. The radio call came through informing them of two suspicious men seen at the back of a house occupied by a local official. Bomber was in the second vehicle and Perfection was commanding the first. They drove to the street with the house in; all seemed quiet. Perfection had his vehicle drive down the street which was a narrow one way paved road. Bomber noticed they were going the wrong way but no one expected to meet anything coming the other way.

Bomber stopped his vehicle at the corner and watched. All the houses had high walls around them with large, solid-looking double wooden gates to let a car in or out.

Just as Perfection passed a pair of these gates, Bomber saw an object come over the wall. He heard one of the escorts yell 'grenade' and the driver went straight into the IA (Immediate Action) drill which was to put his foot down and drive at high speed away from the grenade. The grenade exploded and Bomber heard several clangs against the other vehicles' steel mess. Then he ordered to drive. The driver drove full pelt for the double gates. Bomber yelled for the escorts to get down and hold on.

The Land Rover hit the gates, smashing them apart. As the vehicle stopped in an ornate courtyard, complete with a fountain, shots rang out and both escorts returned fire and a gunman toppled from the side of an ornate fountain, a pistol falling from his hand into the water.

Bomber yelled, "Stay in cover. They said there are two of them."

"You don't have to worry about him," Patrick said in a matter-of-fact manner. "The Land Rover got him."

When Bomber looked, he could see a body partly under the vehicle and it was not moving.

Just then, Perfection returned to take control. One of the escorts, Jos, had been hit in the calf by a piece of the grenade shrapnel and was being bandaged by Donnie who was also telling him to shut up moaning, saying it was only a scratch.

By now, Perfection had called the HQ who were sending the police and back up to assist.

"Better check the house. Take Sean with you," Perfection ordered Bomber.

Bomber and Sean moved to an open doorway and moved in one left, the other right. The room was dark and sparsely furnished. Bomber pointed to a door at the far end of the room where a faint light could be seen coming from under the door.

Standing either side, they could see a key in the lock, carefully trying the handle. Sean indicated it was locked from their side, which meant anyone in there had been locked in probably by the two dissidents.

Sean slowly and quietly turned the key, a large iron one in an old lock but the lock was well oiled and turned with just a couple of clicks disturbing the silence.

Bomber felt his heart beating fast and so loud that he was sure Sean could hear it. His mouth was so dry that he could not swallow. *What is on the other side of the door?* the little voice in his head kept saying over and over again.

Dead bodies, a gunman, what? Shut up, Bomber thought and nodded to Sean to open the door and for what must have been a dozen times in as many seconds' check, the safety catch was off on his rifle.

Sean gentle turned the handle and then pushed hard, as the door swung back with a crash. Bomber dashed through the opening ready to fire at anything that looked remotely hostile.

The room was a store of some kind, with old bits of furniture, a bike without a front wheel and some clothes hanging from a line in one corner. Beneath this huddled together was a woman cradling a middle-aged man. His face was covered in blood and he appeared to be unconscious, two small children clung to the woman clothes and cried softly. Bomber lowered his rifle putting the safety catch back to safe, kneeling down. Bomber could see the man had been beaten around the head, probably with a pistol butt.

Bomber told Sean to get Donnie in to see to the injured man, Donnie being their nearest to a field medic having done the field first aid course.

Leaving them to Donnie's care, Bomber went outside and reported to Perfection.

Perfection said an ambulance was on its way as the man the Land Rover flattened was still alive.

After about twenty minutes, an army ambulance arrived with a military police escort and the medics took over.

"Fucking brilliant," said Sean. "Ambulance arrives well before the police and any backup, perhaps they should give the backup job to the medics."

The MP escort was commanded by a Warrant Officer class two; unusual but everyone had to take a turn at just about everything when it was busy.

"As the police team isn't here, I'll take charge. So give me your report, Sgt.," the warrant officer said in a calm voice.

Perfection quickly briefed him and notes were taken. His Cpl. and driver checked the weapons and bagged them.

The Cpl. medic asked for a hand with the stretcher with the middle-aged man on it. Bomber asked after his condition.

"Not good. He has been badly beaten about the head and there could be some brain damage. Won't know for sure until the docs have checked him." With that, the stretcher was put in the ambulance followed by the woman and the two children.

The dissident that the Land Rover had run down was also strapped onto a stretcher and placed in the ambulance. It was then the woman went crazy and started beating him with her fists and screaming. The children started wailing and the medics had to quickly get between them. After a minute or two, the woman calmed down and went back to attending her husband. As the doors closed, Bomber was left with the vision of two young frightened children clinging to their mother's robes. The ambulance drove off at high speed followed by the MP's Land Rover with the bullet-riddled body wrapped in a body bag. For what seemed like several minutes, they all stood and stared at the departing vehicles even when they had completely disappeared from view. Perfection broke the silence by making them shore up the gates as best as could be done without tools.

After two more calls on the radio and another hour waiting, the police finally turned up. A smart, high-powered air-conditioned car stopped by the gate. A Staff Sgt. and Cpl. MP got out. They were dressed in immaculate KDs (Khaki Drills) and looked like men who did not get their hands too dirty. With them were two civilian police officers, one of which was an Inspector the other must have been the driver. The staff Sgt. strode into the courtyard like a man who expected people to jump when he appeared.

"Right. Who's in charge here and where are the gunmen?"

Perfection stepped forward and explained the situation. The staff Sgt. started berating Perfection for allowing the bodies and witnesses removed and for contaminating a crime scene.

Perfection remained calm and explained that it was not a crime scene but a combat zone and that the other MPs had done the removing and that it was not his decision.

The Staff Sgt. MP had worked himself up into a state of righteous indignation, ordering the Cpl. to arrest Perfection for what he did not say.

The lads were having none of it so a man went and stood between the MPs and Perfection. Sean spoke out in a loud, steady voice, "Fuck off, you stupid bastard. Put one hand on our Sgt. and we will top the lot of you and dump your useless bodies out there for the locals to piss on."

Bomber was not surprised at the lad's loyalty and had no doubt that his crazy Irish boys would do it.

The MP Staff Sgt. was looking bewildered and the civilian police had both taken a few steps back edging behind the fountain. The Cpl. MP seemed unperturbed and even had a slight smile on his face but then he was standing behind his boss who could not see his expression.

Bomber knew he had to step in and keep the initiative.

"I think if you radio in Staff Sgt., you will find the Warrant Officer MP in the other group took command and gave the orders, so anything you think you could charge our Sgt. with will be thrown out. I think we have made it clear that we are not going to let you deprive our patrol of its Commander, so perhaps we should leave and get on with our patrol."

The staff Sgt. didn't reply. He just stood there, his mouth open but nothing coming out.

Perfection now took control, "Mount up and let's go."

The two civilian police officers were now smiling and nodding their heads but still kept the fountain between the lads and themselves.

Backing the Land Rover out, Bomber could see that the Cpl. was talking to the staff Sgt. who seemed to have his head down, listening intently. The two civilian police officers were also gesticulating and talking. *Give it to him lads*, thought Bomber. *The toe rag needs taking down a peg or two.*

Bomber's Land Rover was somewhat the worse for wear after crashing through the gates. A bent bumper which almost touched the wheel on the driver's side and both wings a little crushed. The sidelights and indicators were smashed but the headlights still worked. One of the bullets fired at them had gouged its way through the steel mesh and starred the windshield high on the passenger side, but apart from that the old bus was fully operational.

After about a mile distance from the house, they pulled up and Perfection had a group huddle and thanked everyone for the backup. However, he thought that when they got back, the shit would hit the fan big time but they had to stick together and tell the truth.

With that thought in their head, they routinely carried out the rest of the patrol. An hour later, without any further incidents, they returned to HMS Sabre.

There was not any reception committee of armed Military Police or even their own Provo Sgt., just the Duty Operations Officer to do the patrol debrief.

They all sat in the debrief room, a cool air-condition box with a large map of Aden and beyond fixed to one wall, a bank of radio's on a bench against another. Jos was not present as he was being fussed over by the duty doctor and nurse in the medical center. With mugs of tea and thick bacon sandwiches made fresh by the on-duty navy chef, they listened as Perfection gave a straightforward and to the point account of the action.

When he got to the bit where the police arrived and what happened, the operations officer stared in disbelieve. His mouth dropped open and he stopped, Perfection asking him to repeat things several times. The duty clerk was openly smiling and scribbling furiously until the operations officer switched on and told him to stop and hand over the log and then to leave the room. The Op's Officer tore the pages from the log and stuffed them in his pocket.

He then picked up the phone and made a call to the Commanding Officer, Lt. Col. Dee. After listening for a moment, he said, "Yes sir," and put down the phone.

"You are all to wait here." Then he left the room. The duty clerk came in and sat facing the radio sets, humming 'she loves you' without any regard for the correct order of notes.

Bomber felt himself getting irritated by the clerk's humming and prayed for the radios to come alive with a report of some kind to shut him up.

A short while later, Jos hobbled into the room, mug of tea in one hand and a sandwich in the other, looking very pleased with himself.

"Got me a date with the nurse," said Jos with a smug look.

No one answered.

"What's up then, why the long faces?"

"I'd cancel the date if I were you unless you think she will visit you in nick," retorted Patrick who was raiding the clerk's table for biscuits, ignoring the feeble protests of the clerk.

Jos sat down and rested his injured leg on a chair opposite.

"How's the leg?" Bomber asked.

"Nice that someone cares, about fifty stitches and three pound of shrapnel dug out, but I will survive to nurse maid you lot some more."

"That means a splinter and two stitches by my reckoning," said Donnie who had originally bandaged his leg.

Just then, the door opened and Perfection called them all to attention. The CO entered perched himself on the OP's Officers desk and told them to sit. Looking at Perfection, he asked him to repeat the incident word for word. When Perfection had finished, he asked Bomber if he agreed to the facts. Bomber agreed. The CO asked all the others if they agreed and they did.

The CO stood and so did they. "Fine, you all did a first-class job with the dissidents but not so smart threatening the MPs but I cannot fault your loyalty even though you should have called HQ first. Go and get some sleep and we will speak later."

With that, the CO left the room.

"Well, what do you make of that?" Patrick asked.

"I think the CO is going to bat for us with the Brigade Commander," Perfection said with slow deliberation while staring at the closed door.

"What do you think, Bomber?" Sean sounded worried, as being the only married man in the section, he had more to lose.

"I think the MP Cpl. will confirm our action in a favorable way. I got the impression he was not the best of pals with the Staff Sgt. and maybe his loyalty is to his Corp and not the individual."

"You are joking," said Donnie. "They stick like shit to a blanket that lot. Mark my words."

"Well, thank you for cheering us all up, Donnie you prat," snapped back Sean.

Perfection opened the door and spoke, "Well, no good worrying about it now. Get some sleep. It will be sun up in a couple of hours."

Sleep alluded Bomber as he lay on his bed and mulled things over. He decided he was proud of the way the lads had responded to the situation but it had not been the smartest way to deal with the stroppy MP Staff Sgt. and who knows how the Brigade Commander would act when it came to discipline.

As the sun rose, he fell into a troubled sleep and had a nightmare about a demented MP Staff Sgt. laughing as he locked him into a cell.

After brunch, the Platoon Commander informed them that they were to smarten themselves up and be at the debriefing room in twenty minutes.

Outside of the briefing room, the RSM (Regimental Sergeant Major) was waiting. He formed them up in two ranks, his face and demeanor giving nothing away on what was to come. There was no sign of Perfection or the Platoon Commander and Bomber had a sinking feeling they were in for the chop big time.

The door opened and the RSM marched them in halting in the middle of the room and then ordering right turn. Standing in front of them was the Brigadier and the CO. The Platoon Commander and Perfection stood to one side also at attention.

"Stand at ease please, RSM," the Brigadier said in a calm but firm voice.

Here it comes, thought Bomber, Colchester nick and a dishonorable discharge.

"Firstly," said the Brigadier, "I wish to congratulate you all on getting the grenade men. Intelligence informs me that they are the ones who have been orchestrating most of the attacks in that area." The Brigadier spoke in a calm, measured voice.

He paused and then said, "A report from the Military Police indicts that they made some errors in their follow-up procedures to the incident and have apologized. So I do not expect anything like it will occur again!" The Brigadier emphasized the last sentence and gave a look of 'better bloody not lads'. The Brigadier then seemed to relax and half sat on the edge of the Ops Officer's desk.

"Now your CO tells me you are one of his best at improvisation and getting jobs done, so any ideas of dealing with the 'Spider', eh?"

So it's official, Bomber thought. *Everyone calls him the Spider*. The others looked at Bomber. They had discussed this endlessly over mugs of tea and cold beers. Now they were willing him to speak up.

"Well," said the Brigadier impatiently.

Bomber took a deep breath and spoke up, "We have discussed this a lot, sir, and we think the best tactic would be covert OPs with a sniper included. Stake out all his favorite target areas and be patient, sir."

"Excellent, Christopher sound like a job for those rogues you call the Raider Platoon, eh!" The Brigadier said, smiling to the CO.

"Right chaps. Keep up the good work and get me some more dissident, eh!"

With that, the RSM called them all to attention and the Brigadier strode from the room giving a casual salute as he did followed by the CO and the RSM.

"Fuck me with a revolving fir tree," exclaimed Patrick.

"All right," snapped Perfection. "Pay attention to the Platoon Commander."

Blaze had a smile on his face a mile wide, "You are the luckiest bastards alive, escape a grenade attack, get the ones who did it, threaten to shoot dead four policemen and get away with a mild ticking off from the Brigade Commander, incredible."

"The suggestion for the Spider was good but the CO has already decided to deploy the Recce boys on the OPs, but it shows you are all on the case, well done. I suggest you all get some food and some more sleep as you are on the late patrol tonight. Carry on, Sgt."

The talk later was endless about what had happened at the upper echelon of power for them to have got off so lightly, in fact scot free. After the Brigadier's little talk, he was referred to by the lads as 'Eh'.

The CO must be counting the favors we now owe him, thought Bomber.

"You're quiet, Bomber," said Sean.

"Well, I don't think we have got off with it. I think we will be in line for whatever shit job comes up next and we will be watched like hawks for anything we get wrong. The MPs or at least one S/Sgt. will be gunning for us, so my advice is watch your backs."

"That's a bit fucking bent thinking. What's the matter with you?" Patrick snapped. "Next, you will be saying the Regiment had got it in for us as well."

"The CO has had to eat humble pie with the Brigadier, thanks to us. So when something nasty comes up, he is going to think, I know just the rabble to sacrifice on that job."

Patrol that night was a subdued affair and despite the busy time of car checks and searches, the time seemed to have slowed down and by the end of the four hours, it felt like they had been on the go for twelve hours and Bomber was physically and mentally drained.

The week at Sabre came to a close without any further incidents and a two-day break in barracks was followed by the platoon taking its turn at Flag Staff house.

Bomber studied the houses and building on the walk around with the Platoon Commander. There was a variety of buildings which housed guards, housed staff, vehicles, and all the other personnel and equipment required to look after the needs of the Commanders of the three services and their families. Three very smart colonial type houses stood at the top of a high point overlooking Aden; the view was stunning.

The Platoon's role in the security of Flag Staff had three parts at which everyone took a turn. Leading up to Flag Staff was a steep road which was the only road in or out.

Near the top of the road by the final hair pin turn into the complex was a checkpoint with a large pivotal steel barrier. This was manned by an unarmed sentry. It was his job to check the identity of those entering and to call the guardroom should a search be required.

Providing armed protection fifteen yards further up the slope was a sentry manning a GPMG in a sandbag Sanger. Both sentries could alert the guardroom, which was situated directly above the barrier sentry on the next level of road, by pressing a bell push, which set of an alarm at the Guard Commanders post, an armed response would immediately go to the sentry location.

The second job was part ceremonial and part tactical. On the opposite side of the complex was a steep drop which protected the rear of the houses. Here on a flat point stood a sentry box, the sort depicted on picture postcards. This could be seen from below by any of the local populace.

The sentry here was in smart khakis and beret armed with a rifle. The sentry was allowed to march around the area but was also expected to stand in full view for part of the time. Bomber thought this a little bizarre in a combat zone as the sentry was a perfect target for any sniper who was a half-decent shot. With this in mind, when he was there he made sure he kept on the move to ensure he was a difficult target to hit.

The final task was a foot patrol conducted at irregular intervals by a pair of sentries around the complex with certain areas near the houses out of bounds except in an emergency.

Like HMS Sabre, the deployment lasted for one week but the accommodation and food was not of the same high standard as the RN provided.

On the third day, Bomber was standing outside the guardroom with Blaze and Perfection looking down on the barrier sentry when the roar of a high-powered engine could be heard coming up the hill. Screeching around the last hair pin bend before the barrier sentry came, the latest Volvo sports car, the type that 'Simon Templer', the 'Saint' had made famous in the TV series, except this was not driven by the 'Saint' but the army commanders latest ADC (Aide de Camp), a rather pompous Captain from some Donkcy Walloper Regiment, (cavalry). With a screeching of rubber on tar mac, he pulled up in front of the barrier.

The sentry a Norfolk lad called Pent, peered at the driver and recognizing him pushed down on the barrier which was very heavy and needed two hands to raise it. As the barrier was raised, the car pulled forward so it was part under the barrier. The ADC put his head out of the window and shouted at the sentry, "Don't you know who I am?"

The sentry replied, "Yes sir, you are the ADC."

"Well bloody well, salute me you lazy devil."

"Are you sure sir? I will have to take my hands off the barrier."

Now the ADC was red in the face with indignation, to be asked if he was sure by a country bumpkin of a sentry. "Of course I'm sure, you moron."

With that, the sentry took his hands off the barrier and threw up an immaculate salute and, as expected, the barrier came down at high speed. The heavy steel bar designed to stop a speeding vehicle landed directly on the bonnet of the car with an almighty crash.

The force generated by a solid steel nine-inch barrier bar sprung the bonnet up in two halves. The bar finished its journey down tearing through hoses and the top of the engine block. The windshield popped out and a cloud of steam rose from the ruptured hoses.

Blaze and Perfection were almost doubled over with laughter and Bomber found himself struggling to keep himself in check. As the ADC climbed out with a look of utter disbelief on his face, Bomber heard the sentry say, "Who's the fucking moron now, sir?"

Blaze and Perfection fortunately missed the comment as they were on their way down to the scene of the devastation. By now, the noise of the crash had reached all those that were not on duty. Now they were crowding to look over the wall down at the ADC who was walking around his car, swearing all sorts of revenge on the sentry. Pent was now stood to attention with a complete look of innocence and Bomber knew he couldn't give a damn.

The ADC turned his anger on to Blaze as he approached the barrier. Blaze saluted the ADC and then ordered Perfection to get the car towed away as it was now blocking the road. He then asked the ADC to walk with him to the guardroom. As they did, Bomber could hear the ADC insisting that the sentry be charged. With what he was not sure, as he had only done as he was ordered. He knew Pent would not have to buy any beers for a while and would be forced to tell the story many times.

Bomber hustled every one back to the restroom before Blaze and the ADC arrived and stood by the guardroom door and saluted as they arrived, opened the door, and closed it once they went in.

Despite trying, Bomber could not hear what was said but the ADC left after a few minutes with a face like a wet weekend. Blaze asked Bomber to get Perfection and relieve the sentry and send him in.

What Blaze did or said to calm the situation, Bomber did not know but a tow truck came and took the ADC car away that afternoon and the ADC never insisted on being saluted by the barrier sentry again.

The rest of the week passed without further incident and the platoon was rotated to one of the least liked duties, the security detail for Sheikh Othman police station.

Sheikh Othman was a mix of decent houses and shanties with the police station roughly in the center. A small square two-story building surrounded by an eight-foot high stonewall topped with barbwire.

The ground floor contained cells, reception area, interview rooms, two of which now became restrooms for the half platoon, a small kitchen, and toilets. The top floor had several rooms, one of which was the platoon HQ in which the Platoon Sgt. or Commander plus the radio operator monitored what was going on. At night, a sentry would be placed on the roof above to watch the streets around the station.

Patrols would go out with the local police to give them a beefed up level of protection while they went about their normal duties, duties that seemed to diminish with each passing day.

Bombers section and two section plus a couple from the HQ section commanded by Blaze were on their way there in a truck when a radio call came through to proceed to the causeway road leading to Little Aden where the oil terminal was situated.

Once there, they had to set up a road block and lookout for a pickup truck with two armed men in it. Perfection and the other half of the Platoon would proceed to and take over the police station at Sheikh Othman.

On arrival at the causeway, Blaze deployed two cut-off teams about hundred and fifty yards either side of the road block with Bomber commanding the mainland side cut-off. With him was Sean manning the GPMG, Patrick, and Jos.

After about twenty minutes, Bomber and Patrick spotted what look like the pickup truck described in the radio message and radioed Blaze to warn him.

The occupants of the vehicle spotted the slowing down of the traffic and then must have seen the road block and abruptly stopped, then started to try and turn around in the traffic which caused cars to swerve and honk their horns.

Blaze must have spotted what was happening and he and three others started to run towards the pickup. Suddenly a figure stood up in the back of the truck and opened fire with an AK47 at the advancing four who dived for cover. The vehicle driver had managed to force a way through the traffic shunting several cars out of the way. As it drove back towards Bomber, he could see that if they fired the GPMG to stop it, they could hit other vehicles and innocent civilians, so ordered rifle fire only. They were all in good cover on the right side of the road behind a low stonewall.

When the pickup was about thirty yards away, the gunman, standing in the back looking over the cab, must have seen them and started firing wildly in their direction and Bomber ordered them to open fire. Jos had been told to shoot at the engine area while Bomber and Patrick took the cab and gunman.

The pickup seemed to shudder and then swerved violently to the right leaving the road and crashing on its side. Bomber and Patrick covered by the other two raced over to the wrecked pickup. The gunman had been thrown clear and lay face-down on the rocky ground, the AK47 some ten feet off to his left. Carefully they approached the cab. The front screen had been pushed out by the force of one of the men going through it and who now lay on his side partly over the bonnet and held in place by his legs being trapped in the cab. His neck looked broken and he had clearly been hit in the chest by one of the shots, judging by the amount of blood leaking out.

The other man was still in the cab lying against the driver's door as still as a man would be with most of his head shot away. Bomber studied the bodies and suddenly realized he was not affected by their deaths or the brutality of it, just another day at the office and felt a coldness that made him shiver.

A panting Blaze and the other three gathered around the cab and checked the bodies and found an AK47 on the seat. Patrick who had pulled a tarpaulin from the back of the pickup called out, "I think we should walk away quickly before we get blown to hell." To emphasize this, he was walking backwards away from the vehicle.

Bomber and Blaze took a quick look. The back of the vehicle was packed with large gas cylinders laid flat and tightly strapped down. In between were bundles of what looked like commercial explosives attached to a long length of safety fuse.

"Well, I don't think it will blow but we had better clear the area and call the bomb squad," Blaze remarked in a matter-of-fact manner.

Having cleared the area, they waited for the bomb squad and the police to arrive and for once, Donnie did not produce any tea.

"Hope we don't have the same tosser as last time; can't go through that again," Sean spoke quietly to Bomber referring to the MPs.

"Not likely and even if it is, I don't think we will have a problem with Blaze being here."

Just then, a lot of radio traffic came through. Something had happened at the Sheikh Othman police station and there were casualties. A voice cut through the radio traffic ordering the Sheikh Othman operator to switch frequencies in a standard operating procedure so as not to block the normal working channel.

"Shit," Jos exclaimed, "I hope it's not any of ours that have been clobbered."

Later once the bomb squad had made the bomb safe and the police had taken over the scene, they were ordered to go to the

Sheikh Othman police station. A feeling of pending doom took over and the chatter dried up, no one wishing to speculate on who had been injured or killed.

As the truck drew into the area near the police station, they passed through a cordon of soldiers from *B* Company who seemed to be working their way out from the station.

Jumping from the truck in the compound, they could all detect the distinct odor of an explosion lingering in the air.

"We are taking over the station," Blaze announced. "It appears the 'Spider' hit the room at the top with a rocket and the radio operator Jensen and the Pl. Sgt. have been injured. They have been taken off to hospital. Apparently Jensen saved the Pl. Sgt.'s life in there before the medics arrived."

"Cpl. Brown, take your section to the top floor. I want a man at every window covering all the streets and buildings. Anything that looks a threat, shoot it." The tone in which he spoke left Bomber in no doubt that Blaze was as mad as hell and would not tolerate any threat to the station or them.

"Yes sir," said Bomber, his mind running through various scenarios. Would the Spider try again with so many troops around? Is he getting cocky and thinks he is unstoppable? Well, as Sgt. Cocker said, complacency will get you killed.

Entering the radio room, Bomber could see what had happened. A rocket had hit the window sill and ricocheted up into the ceiling, exploding and sending shrapnel everywhere. Dark patches of drying blood covered the desk and floor.

Turning to Sean, Bomber said, "Let's get all the spare sandbags from downstairs and block every window except for a shooting hole."

An hour later, all the windows were sandbagged and manned.

The evening and night passed quietly and while Bomber and the rest were enjoying a cup of tea. News came through that Perfection was badly hurt but stable. Jensen had numerous shrapnel wounds to the back of his legs and body but none life-threatening.

Bomber wondered if Jensen would be able to sprint again. He was in the Regiment's athletics team and was their best four-hundred-and-forty-yard man. If they had not been called to do the road block at Little Aden, it could have been Blaze and Jonah

Jones being taken to hospital. Two nights later, the Spider struck again in the Ma-ala area, except that this time one of the covert OP's snipers got a shot off at him and the follow-up team found blood on the roof of the building but not a body or launcher. He must have had some help with him or it wasn't him that had been hit. Five nights later, the Spider struck again, firing a rocket at a block of flats that had service families and other civilians living in it. The damage was not severe and there were not any casualties but it was the signal to consider sending families and nonessential civilians home to the UK. It amazed Bomber how outside of his world others seemed to carry on an almost normal life. Bomber could not imagine what a 'normal life' would feel like anymore.

Chapter 12
Going Native

Bomber and the lads had just finished cleaning their weapons and were handing them into the armory when Doyle, now their platoon Sgt., in place of the wounded Perfection, came to them and said, "Right new job, you are all to draw out pistols and report to the thirty-yard range and look lively."

At the range was the Recce Platoon Sgt., a tall Norfolk man called Ward. Rumor had it he was a successful poacher before joining the army. During the EOKA campaign in Cyprus, he had been awarded the MM (Military Medal) and was a highly regarded specialist in close quarter combat and shooting.

For three hours, he took them through center point shooting, snap shooting, and close kill shooting.

Bomber found himself enjoying working with the 9 mm pistol taking on three targets in snap shooting and found that he always put the first round into the chest area of the target and the second into the head. Ward explained this was due to the semiautomatic pistols recoil system raising the barrel placing the second shot higher. Bomber worked hard at hitting the targets in a different order on each exposure. Encouraged by Ward, he eventually could hit all three targets in quick succession while on the move. Ward called a halt and announced the end of the session, declaring, "You are just okay but better keep practicing every chance you get." Then he marched off looking a little put out.

"Take no notice," said Doyle, "the job you are going to do he thinks the Recce lads should have it, but they are fully employed on OPs and anti-Spider duties."

Next, they were taken to the QM store and handed a bag of smelly local civilian clothing of dubious origin. From there, they were quick march to the barbers.

"Well! Come on, Sgt.," said Sean, "what's going on?"

Bomber knew better than to ask. If Doyle wasn't telling them of his own free will, they weren't supposed to know. However, he had a horrible suspicion that this might be the first of the CO's favors being called in.

Doyle did not answer and just pointed to the barber's chairs and said, "Sit and relax. You don't even have to pay for any of this," and laughed.

In turn, those who had light or brown hair had it dyed black and then a stain was applied to their faces, necks, arms, and lower legs until they were all nut-brown. With a lot of grumbling and coarse bantering, they left the barber chair looking a lot different to when they went in.

After this, they were taken to the training wing building where they found all their belongings had been dumped next to camp beds.

"Okay," said Doyle, "into the lecture room."

In the lecture room was the Pl. Commander and the Regiment's Operations Officer a Captain by the name of Wallis-Brown, who was tall and gaunt-looking and reminded Bomber of an eagle waiting to swoop on its unsuspecting prey.

Blaze started by saying, "The Commanding Officer has asked for volunteers for this assignment and I take it that as you have all been to the range and I can see you have all been to the barbers, that you have volunteered, which makes me very proud of you."

Heads turned to Doyle who gave a look of 'face front, you suckers'.

The Ops Officer took over, "As you are well aware, the number of grenade attacks especially on uniformed patrols has increased quite dramatically."

Bomber thought his voice matched that of an eagle giving a screech that sounded the death knell for some poor creature and thought it could be us.

"It has been decided in the strictest secrecy that we will deploy soldiers disguised as locals at night to hunt down these grenadiers." Bomber inwardly smiled at the old-fashioned term for those that throw grenades.

He paused for effect. "And you volunteers are going to do this. Now no one, not even the police or any other military unit knows you are out there, so you are on your own for good reason. We know the FRA and the local police are riddled with informers, so they will not be told or you may become the hunted instead of the hunters. Lt. Blaze is going to fill in the details which just leaves me to wish you good hunting and to take care."

The look he gave actually convinced Bomber he really meant the last sentence, which instead of heartening him made him feel even more in doubt of the sanity or chances of surviving the assignment.

For the next hour, Blaze pointed out locations of frequent grenade attacks. The operation procedures they were to stick to and emergency drills. At the end of it, Bomber thought, *Shit. We really are on our own out there. If the enemy don't get us, our own side could well shoot us.*

"Finally," continued Blaze, "you will stay in here during daylight, blinds drawn. There is a kitchen at the end of the hall and showers but you will not wash or shave until told to do so. Meals will be put into the kitchen at night when you are not here and you can reheat them on your return. No one is to see you or talk to you except me or the Ops Officer. Any questions?" No one spoke. "Good luck, you will deploy at twenty-one hundred tonight as briefed."

With that, both he and Doyle left.

"Fuck me," Sean said with some venom. "That bastard Doyle suckered us and has now cleared off to the Sgt.'s mess for an ice-cold beer, the Londonderry bastard."

"Can someone tell me when we were asked to volunteer and when I said yes?" asked Jos, hands held wide and a look of bewilderment on his face.

"It don't matter now. There is no way we could back down and Doyle knew that, but I have to say the job sounds like it could be worth doing." Bomber spoke and he hoped with conviction even though his stomach was churning and told him this could be more dangerous than playing with sweaty plastic explosives.

"Anyway, I think it was all set up as payback for the MP incident. I can just see the CO and Ops Officer saying we know just the reprobates for this sort of thing, 'The Dammed'."

It took about an hour to sort out the camp beds and hang up the kit and clothing amidst a constant series of volunteering stories. Then they heard a voice outside and then a key in the lock. The door swung open and there in the doorway stood an Arab, off the street in ragged clothes, holding a large box in his arms and two other boxes at his feet.

"Who the fuck are you?" Patrick demanded being nearer to the door than anyone else.

The Arab kept his head down, pushing one of the boxes further into the room with his foot. Mumbling, he then turned and dragged the other box in, then pushed the door closed.

Now Patrick was angry at being ignored and stepped forward to grab him when Bomber clicked.

"Hold it, Patrick. I think it's someone we all know."

The Arab put the boxes down and said "Got ya" in his unmistakable Londonderry accent.

"You didn't think I would have volunteered the Dammed without coming myself to have some fun, do ya?"

"Well, I will be Dammed," said Sean. "I thought you was a bloody local, but then they do mostly look like that in Londonderry."

"Careful, you Ballymena Mick, or I might not let you have one of the pressy I have in this box."

After some more lighthearted insults, Doyle unpacked the boxes. In one was the nine-millimeter pistols each with three magazines and boxes of ammunition. Unwrapping a cloth, Doyle had everyone gather around and said, "These are not official but the QM has given me them on the quiet and they may come in handy if it gets desperate."

Out of the clothes he produced eight daggers of the type used by Second World War Commandos. Sliding one out of its sheaf, Bomber studied the narrow blade shaped to easily slide between the ribs to the heart and hoped he would never have to use one. Jos made everyone jump when he spun round and threw the knife with force and accuracy at the door where it stuck in the center of the cross piece of the door.

"Lucky," said Donnie. "Bet you a pound you can't do it again?"

"Save your money," Sean said, smiling. "He can do that with his eyes closed."

After some prodding, it appeared Jos had been taught to throw a knife by his grandfather who had been in a circus act known as 'Marvelous Martin' and that his grandmother had the scars to prove she was his assistant.

After some sleep and hot food from the kitchen, they dressed in the Arab clothing. It was unwashed and smelly. Every one chose the darkest clothes as they would be lurking in the shadows and needed to blend in and be unseen.

At twenty, thirty hours, three battered cars pulled up and were left outside the training wing with the keys in the ignition. The drivers walked away and did not look back. Bomber and Jos had been teamed together. Everyone would work in teams of two, within a two-street distance of each other. This way they could cover a fairly large area but if needed to, they could go to the assistance of each other.

The area chosen for the first night was Al Qahira off the main thorough fare, which had a large number of dirty sewage riddled alleyways and streets not used by the patrols or most other people.

The alleyways were ideal for the grenadiers to throw a grenade and disappear quickly, a strategy that they would adopt if they had a contact.

Squatting in the shadow of a locked doorway, Bomber was invisible to anyone walking by even as close as a few steps away. Jos was almost opposite in a similar doorway; both had their pistols in hand cocked and ready for action.

Like many hot countries, the evenings and late into the night was when most people did a lot of shopping, business, and generally going about their lives. So between evening and two in the morning was a favorite time for the grenadiers.

Struggling to cope with the smell, Bomber tried to breathe gently through his nose. The ally was full of human and animal shit and a slow trickle of smelly water passed within a few inches of his feet. The whine of mosquitoes was constant and after almost three hours, the only thing in the alley other than themselves was a goat that seemed to take a liking to Jos but eventually got bored and wandered off. Bomber was just about to ease his cramped legs when he heard footsteps coming down the alley towards the main thoroughfare.

Easing his grip then re-gripping the nine-millimeter pistol, he felt his mouth go dry and his heart began to race. *Is this it?* he thought. *Has Jos heard it too?*

Two shadows pasted Bomber, one tall, the other short, both trying to keep their feet clear of the sewage. As they passed, Bomber he eased himself up, ready to deal with whatever was about to happen. The shadows did not stop as they reached the end of the alley. They moved into the light of the main road. Bomber could see it was a man and a boy of about twelve. The man paused for a moment and then turned left and went on the boy by his side. The man had his hand protectively on the boy's shoulder.

Bomber felt his legs trembling and he realized he had been holding his breath. He saw a slight movement in the shadow where Jos was slowly re-squatting down and Bomber did the same.

The whine of the mosquitoes and the smell was beginning to get to Bomber and he wondered if he could stay in the alley much longer. His wondering was interrupted by the sound of more footsteps coming along the alleyway. He quickly focused his mind and again, rechecked his grip on the pistol, not too tight, safety catch off, and slowed the breathing down.

A lone shadow went past and stopped about ten feet in from the end of the alley where the shadow was not washed away by the ambient light from the street.

The figure crouched and waited, so did Bomber. When the figure stood up, so did bomber and he sensed rather than saw that Jos had done the same.

The figure got tensed and suddenly bowled under arm and released a grenade into the street. At almost the same time, both Bomber and Jos opened fire and the figure collapsed. The grenade exploded in the street and Bomber glimpsed a police Land Rover racing away. Bomber thought he had heard other shots and had definitely heard a second grenade explode further away.

Joss was already searching the body and pulled out a second grenade and a six-shot Webley .45 pistol.

In a pocket, he discovered a notebook and some money. They took the notebook. The money was scattered over the body, with the pistol and grenade left for the police or army patrol to find.

Hearing the shouts of a military patrol coming up the street and a police siren, they bugged out the opposite way back to where they had left the car. Getting in the car, Bomber felt himself shaking and sweating more than usual and was glad that Jos was doing the driving. Jos looked grim and stared straight ahead over the steering wheel and drove at a steady speed through the traffic to barracks.

The barrack guard had been briefed on the cars and the number plates and after a quick glance at the occupants, they were waved through. Bomber thought that this was wrong but could not come up with an alternative but would talk to Doyle about it.

Parking the car at the training center, they went into the room unloading the nine-millimeter pistols just inside the door. Bomber went straight into the kitchen, put the kettle on, and then drank two large mugs of water. 'God, what's that smell?' Looking down, Bomber could see his feet were covered in shit. Carefully pulling off his shoes, he washed them thoroughly in the sink, thinking, *We have to have a better way than this to clean the shit off.*

The kettle boiled and Bomber made eight mugs of tea as he could hear the other two cars pulling up. Going through, he saw Jos coming out of the toilets, looking sheepish.

"Just thrown up, felt really sick, not sure if it was the shooting and searching the body or the sitting in all that shit for hours."

Bomber nodded and pushed a mug of tea into his hands.

The door opened and in came Doyle and the rest of the section. Doyle was swearing and muttering dire threats against the world.

Sitting at the table that served as a dining area, briefing table, map board, and any other thing they needed to do on it, the story came out. Doyle and Jamie McElroy had the same situation as they had. So as Doyle explained it, the bombers had intended to get both police Land Rovers at the same time. After they had shot their grenade man, they started searching him when shots were fired at them from an army patrol.

"We were okay," explained Jamie. "It was those wankers from *C* Company and they couldn't hit fuck all if it was stood next to them."

"Yes, but we had to leg it really fast and we could have easily been either shot by our own side or caught and exposed," snapped Doyle.

Just then, the door opened and in came Blaze and the Ops Officer. The Ops Officer was all smiles and congratulations. A debrief followed and the Ops Officer was keen to keep up the initiative and wanted them out again tonight. It was already four in the morning.

After they left, Donnie took on the role as chef reheating the food that had been left on the stove. Doyle went to the fridge and pulled out some cans of beer he had hidden at the back.

"Come on. Let's celebrate a job well done." He raised a can and made a toast to the Dammed.

"To the Dammed, Dammed in name, dammed in life, and I'm dammed if anyone will get to know what we have damn well done." With that, he tossed back his head and gulped down the beer.

"What do you think he means by that, Bomber," Jos asked quietly.

"No one will acknowledge that we are out there in civvies knocking off local dissidents and not calling in the police after. We are unofficial, not recognized. If we get caught, they will probably say we were doing it on our own initiative."

"But if we get caught, they wouldn't just abandon us, would they?"

"They could and we would all be in deep shit, me old mate that's what."

Bomber sipped his beer, wanting it to last as the cool liquid washed away the foul taste in his mouth that the last words he had spoken had created.

After eating and having another beer, they settled down and slept. Bomber kept seeing a gun firing and a figure falling to the ground over and over again. *It's so easy*, a small voice kept repeating in his head. Bomber wondered later if he had been dreaming or had been awake and was just thinking it.

Bomber woke to a mug of tea being plunked down beside him by Donnie. Bomber realized he had a headache and searched his wash bag for some aspirin. Failing to find any, he swore out loud. Next second, a packet landed on his chest tossed over by Jos.

"Headache?" Joss asked. Bomber nodded.

"I had this bloody dream last night of the shooting and me standing over the body. Feel like I haven't slept a wink, fuck it." Jos put his head down on the table and pretended to snore.

Breakfast instead of supper was a subdued affair. They had just cleaned up and dressed in their new civvies when Blaze and the Ops Officer arrived for the briefing.

They were to move several blocks over and repeat the previous night stake out. This they did and repeated it for a further three nights without any success, which was not entirely true as there were no grenade attacks either. The word was obviously out that the culprits were being hunted.

The next night, they moved to the Sheikh Othman area into a location that was a lot cleaner than the filth-laden alleyways they had endured night after night.

In their four pairs, they were spread over three blocks and adopted the same routine as before. Unlike the previous nights, the roads seemed empty of traffic and people, making Bomber uneasy for no other reason than the fact that it was so different from all the other nights.

It was one o'clock in the morning and Bomber was struggling to stay alert and had to keep pinching himself to stay awake. Suddenly the sound of gunfire erupted to the right of their position where Sean and Donnie were located. The light crack, crack of the nine-millimeter pistols was echoed by heavier automatic fire.

Bomber thought hell this is trouble and called Jos. They set out at a run through the empty street towards the sound of the increasing gunfire. Rounding a corner, Bomber saw three men behind a pickup truck armed with AK47s. They were firing towards the alley that Sean and Donnie were in. One of the men had already been hit and was lying on the floor but was still firing his weapon from under the pickup. One other dressed in some sort of military uniform was firing over the top of the bonnet of the truck while the other seemed to be struggling to reload his AK47.

The men had no idea that they had Bomber and Jos less than twenty yards behind them, crouching next to a car on the other side of the road. With a nod to Jos, they opened fire. The fire was doubled when from the left Doyle and Jamie joined in.

In less time than it took Bomber to empty the pistols magazine and reload, the three men lay bleeding and dying in the road. A call to Sean was acknowledged that they were okay.

Doyle and Jamie had sprinted to the vehicle and quickly kicked the weapons away from the dying men. Jos looked in the back of the pickup truck and let out a whistle that drew Bomber's attention to the back of the vehicle. Inside was an assembled three-inch mortar ready to fire with six mortar bombs laid out on the sandbags used to line the bottom of the truck to absorb the impact.

Before they could search further, they could hear the distinctive whirr of a Military Land Rover tires on tarmac and the faint wailing of a police vehicle's siren.

"Let's go," Doyle barked and led the way down Sean's alley. Five minutes later, they split up and went to their cars and drove back towards the barracks. As Bomber's car rounded a bend just five hundred yards from camp, they could see Doyle's car ahead stopped by a road block.

Bomber and Jos were sharing a car with John and Patrick. Patrick was driving and pulled up.

"Fuck it. What now?" muttered Patrick, turning off the car headlights.

It was dark and there were no streetlights to illuminate them on the empty road.

"Back up slowly, Patrick, and reverse down that side road behind us and we can wait it out," instructed Bomber.

As they did so, a dark shape the size of a truck drove straight into the back of the car and before they could recover, they were being dragged out of the car by strong hands. Bomber opened his mouth to speak but instead dropped to his knees as a rifle butt struck him firmly in the stomach.

As he lay on the road struggling to breathe and feeling he wanted to vomit, he noticed the vehicle that had rammed them was a Saracen armored personnel carrier.

"So what have we got here then? Four fucking rag heads trying to avoid our nice little road block eh?"

A familiar voice, thought Bomber. *Must be someone from our Regiment.*

"And tooled up Cpl., look at this four lovely new nine-millimeter pistols," said a voice.

Bomber had not felt his pistol being removed from his waist holster but it had gone.

"Good enough reason to top them, Cpl.," said the second voice which Bomber now recognized.

Regaining his breath, Bomber spoke loudly, "Fuck off, Ridley. Even at this range you would miss, you fat knacker."

Chuckles and laughter came from Bomber's left where the others were face-down on the road.

"The only thing that Ridley's ever shot is his big toe to get out of Op Nutcracker," Patrick spoke loudly for all to hear. "That's why he has been shunted over to *C* Company. His section could not stand the shame of him."

This brought more laughter. *So that's the story*, thought Bomber.

"Okay, on your feet," said the first voice and Bomber struggled to stand and looked at Cpl. Mortimer who was studying them with a puzzled expression on his face.

"So who are you and what are you doing?" demanded Mortimer.

"Sorry, can't tell you, Cpl., but I'm sure the others have guessed who we are and if you radio in the car registration number to HQ, they will tell you to let us pass." Bomber looked at the rear of the car as he finished speaking.

Patrick stood by him and said, "Not sure the MTO (Motor Transport Officer) going to be happy about the state of the car."

Bomber could see that the back end had been smashed completely in forcing the boot lid open and one of the tires had been punctured by the impact.

Cpl. Mortimer had gone into the Saracen and Bomber could hear him on the radio. Ridley stood a short distance away with his SLR pointing at them. The look on his face was one of pure hate.

"Alright, you are clear to go. The main road block has been informed, so you can get through without being stopped," Mortimer spoke with his head sticking out of the hatch of the Saracen.

Retrieving the pistols, they gathered at the car. "Well, we are not going anywhere in this." Jos kicked the flat tire as he spoke, "We will have to walk back and get the MT to recover the car."

The walk back to camp was a subdued affair. Bomber's stomach hurt, making him walk slightly hunched over.

Patrick talked quietly to Bomber about Ridley, "Time's coming for a reckoning with that bastard. Should have fixed him a long time ago."

Bomber shuddered to think what retribution Patrick would inflict on Ridley.

Back in the training wing, the Ops Officer and Blaze were already debriefing the others.

"Well, a real coup," said the OP's Officer. "They were obviously planning something big with the set up they had. The mortar had been stolen from the FRAs a week ago. One of the men you shot was a turncoat from the FRA the other two have already been identified as on the wanted list by the Int. (Intelligence) boys. Now what happened to you four?"

The Op's officer listened to Bomber relate the road block incident.

"Well, not to worry. You are all being pulled off this duty, too many questions now being asked by the police and the civvies above us."

"But we are getting good results," objected Doyle.

"I know but it all being made official now and its being taken over by specialists, so you will be going back to normal duties. The CO is very pleased with you all. Well done. Oh! We have put a few beers in the fridge for you. Stay in and have a good sleep. Lt. Blaze will see you later."

When they had left, Patrick threw his jacket against the wall and exploded with a series of swear words that seemed to impress even Doyle.

"Oh, being made official now, fancy that," Patrick kicked a chair clear across the room in his anger. "Fucking specialists taking over. Well, what the fuck are we shagging amateurs? We had better result than the whole bloody police force and SB combined. Shit, I feel like I've been shagged by a grizzly and not even kissed goodbye." With that, he slumped onto his camp bed still cursing.

Bomber sat at the table feeling empty. He knew that there would be no official recognition for what they had achieved and that those taking over the mantle would collect the rewards for the hours spent sitting in sewage-ridden alleys and preventing the deaths of police, soldiers, and perhaps civilians as well.

The others were chipping in with comments but mostly they were so deflated that they made no effort to outdo Patrick's tirade.

"Oh, stop your fucking bleating. You lot sound like a bunch of Taigs on an orange day parade," Doyle growled. "Donnie, get those beers out of the fridge and let's wind down and decide what we tell everyone we have been up to when we rejoin the platoon tomorrow."

The OP's officer had left two slabs of beer in the fridge. That's forty-eight cans, a total of six each. *Clever*, thought Bomber. *Just enough to let of steam but not enough to get pissed and cause trouble.*

"There's steak here as well," shouted Donnie from the kitchen. "I'll get them on the stove."

"He will make someone a lovely wife one day," Sean said, laughing through gulps of beer.

"I heard that, you Ballymena Mick."

The mood lightened and the banter and beer flowed, the steaks tasted good and by the time they had finished, all they could do was collapse on their beds, where the events of the night, food, beer, and exhaustion overwhelmed them.

Bomber slept for almost ten hours but was having the same recurring dream. In it, he saw the first dissident with the grenade they shot. He kept shooting him but every time he walked to him, he wasn't dead, just looking up and mouthing words that he couldn't hear.

When Bomber awoke, the others were still asleep, except for Doyle. He was in the kitchen drinking tea and indicated a mug for Bomber already loaded. Sipping his tea, he looked at Doyle and said, "I noticed you only had a couple of beers last night and you look great. Still off the rum?"

Doyle nodded. "No rum and I have a strict rule: no more than two cans of beer and you're right. I look better and feel great. Well, I did until we got pulled off this job. I thought we were making a real difference. Now the others will take over and every dissident will know where, when, and who before they even deploy. Fucking waste. That's what it is."

"Well, it could not have lasted. Someone was bound to work it out sooner or later. That's provided we didn't get shot first."

They were interrupted by the others getting up and coming in for tea and toast.

An hour later, they had cleaned the pistols and magazines, replaced the spare ammunition in the other box and packed their kit.

At noon, Lt. Blaze arrived and told them the story was they had been working with the FRA helping out the training team and they had dyed their skin and hair to blend in and not make it obvious that they were not official training team. "Now remember you are bound by the official secrets act and cannot talk to anyone about what you have been up to."

"Anyway," went on Blaze, "it won't be a problem. We are deploying up country again tomorrow to Thumair."

"Tomorrow! That's a bit short notice, isn't it sir?" exclaimed Patrick, which earned him a hard look from Doyle.

"Yes, it is. We were expecting at least another month on the coast, but I think the dissidents are trying to regain control of the Sacred Road again, so we are going there to beef up the locals and Brit unit that are already there."

"So you need to get back to the platoon lines and see that everything is ready for a Company Commander's inspection at eighteen hundred hours."

"Right sir. Okay, you lot, let's go. Oh, and I'm two daggers missing, so make sure they are in the box before you leave."

Patrick and Jos looked a bit sheepish and slid the daggers out of the inside of their shirts and dropped them in the box. Doyle pretended not to notice, but Bomber saw him smiling.

Chapter 13
RAD Force

As they approached the mountains, the pilot was having a hard time keeping the aircraft on an even keel. Rising thermals caused by the heat of the day made the plane buck and rise alarmingly. Bomber even had a glimpse of two eagles soaring on these thermals level with the plane when they had crossed the last mountain peaks before the descent to Thumair.

The landing was a stomach-churning steep descent; the dirt airstrip was small and surrounded by rugged mountains. Bomber tried to appear unconcerned but looking at the faces of those next to him, they too thought it a little scary. Gripping his knees hard, he prayed that the RAF pilot was not having an off day. He didn't need to worry as the blue job set the Beverly down like a mother laying a baby in its crib.

The RAD FORCE HQ was a heavily fortified camp next to the air strip. Fortified pickets on the mountain ridges protected the camp from attack. Thumair was at the meeting point of some important *wadis*, acting as routes through the mountains. Whoever dominated this junction was in control of who moved in or out of the mountains.

No sooner were they off the plane than they were assembled in the dining tent and a briefing was given by the PO and the Company Commander.

The PO droned on about the political situation and how important it was that everyone remained alert to the ever-changing situation.

"What the hell is he talking about?" Patrick hissed.

"No idea," Sean whispered back.

However, everyone sat up and took notice when he started saying the NLF was uniting more and more of the tribes and therefore were able to put greater numbers on the ground than ever before.

The PO talked stats and figures for another ten minutes, eventually getting to the part that would directly affect them.

"Now," he intoned like a bored padre giving a sermon to men he knew had little faith in his words. "As for our area in and around Thumair, there has been an increase in activity especially at night. Heavy machinegun attacks, some mortar fire and mines being placed on the roads. As of today, there have been no direct attempts to take any of the pickets or an attack on the main camp but it cannot be ruled out." He finished by looking at the faces staring back at him and then, with a shrug of his shoulders, handed over the rest of the briefing to the Company Commander.

The Company Commander stood and hit the table in front of him which made everyone sit up. "We," he barked, "are going to take an aggressive approach and we will not be just sitting on our backsides in the pickets or the camp. We will be doing sweeps of the area and more ambush patrols at night." He left little doubt that he was not in any mood to accept anything less than complete domination of the area, so there was little hope of a cushy time at Thumair.

The briefing broke up with platoons being given their jobs for the next ten days. Bomber felt relieved that they would be upon one of the high points first. The Dammed had Charlie picket, a key location which covered the main *wadi* running north to south through the area.

After forty-eight hours of studying maps of the surrounding terrain, sorting equipment and going over contact drills, they were ready to move out to their respective locations. An hour before dawn, Bomber and his section found themselves setting off behind six camels loaded with food, ammunition, and water. The camels were in the charge of a local who had sworn loyalty to the government. He was assisted by two others. All were armed with .303 Lee Enfield bolt action rifles and had two bandoliers of ammunition slung across their chests.

As they left the camp to cross the airfield, Bomber split the section and flanked either side of the camels. The locals looked surprised at this, talking and laughing as if they knew something he did not. *What do they know?* mused Bomber. *When the next attack is coming or am I just getting over cautious?* Then

Cocker's words came back to him: "Complacency has killed many a men."

It took two hours to reach the top of the ridge and Charlie picket was a mere pimple on it. The forward slope looked into the interior and the reverse back to the airfield and camp. The place was occupied by a section of Royal Marines who were packed up and more than ready to leave.

The Cpl. introduced himself and took Bomber to the main Sanger, quickly pointing out the relevant trouble spots and the main *wadi* they were to watch from dawn to dusk after which a patrol would take over the task laying up in an ambush.

Within minutes, they had left following the camels down the hillside. Bomber looked around and was not impressed. The ammunition and stores carried up by the camels had been left where the handlers had pulled them from their backs. The Sangers were little more than a pile of rocks and a hundred and sixty pounder tent on the reverse slope sagged sadly; several of the camp beds had one or two legs missing.

"What a shithole," Sean said with disgust. "No one has put themselves out to make this place defensible or worth living in."

"You're right there, and if the PO is right, we better do something about it. Jos, get the radio working and contact Pl HQ (Platoon Headquarters). John, man the GPMG and watch that *wadi*. The rest of us will get the stores sorted."

Going around with Sean, they made notes of what needed to be done. The two Sangers were flimsy with only a double thickness of rocks and no sandbags to reinforce the rocks. Both lacked overhead cover and the barbwire was limited to one strand wrapped around a few stakes.

On the reverse side of the ridge, the single eight-man tent needed sandbags to provide protection against small arms fire or shrapnel from mortar rounds. An ammunition bunker had been part dug into the side of the slope. It was too shallow and too far from the action to allow easy access to the reserve ammunition.

Donnie was busy organizing rations and producing a brew. "I'll build a lightproof oven later so we can have a hot brew at night. Lazy bastards have not even made a proper latrine, not that we can dig a pit here. What we need is an empty forty-gallon oil drum and a couple of planks to sit on."

Once they had completed the list of what they needed, Bomber got onto the radio and spoke to Blaze. He was not surprised to hear Bomber's request for stores. Two other pickets had made similar requests for assistance.

Most of the units who had been there before them had been on short rotation tours unlike the regiment which was on a two-year tour. All they wanted was an easy life and back home as soon as possible. It was obvious that no one of senior rank had been to visit recently which was probably why so little had been done to improve the Sangers and living area. Bomber was determined to get the position in order. The priority would be the main Sanger. They started by reinforcing the front wall with a third layer of rocks. It was backbreaking work in the unrelenting heat dragging rocks up from the lower slope.

Jos suddenly called Bomber to the radio. It was Blaze informing him that a Bristol Belvedere was going to lift some of the heavy stuff up to them shortly and that a camel train would bring the rest.

The Belvedere was the only twin rotary helicopter the RAF had. It was powerful enough to lift heavy loads in the hot, thin air at Thumair. Bomber and Sean watched as the helicopter lifted off from the runway with a cargo net slung underneath. The helicopter worked its way up in spirals until it was level with the ridge. The downwash from the rotors hurled around small rocks and any debris that was in its way.

Donnie and Patrick had collapsed the tent and were laying on it to stop the down wash blowing it away, as the helicopter edged in to their position.

Hovering with the net about five feet from the ground, the load master released it. Then the chopper was gone. The net was full of filled sandbags, three sheets of corrugated iron and six lengths of wood, twelve foot long, of nine by nine inches.

The chopper returned twenty minutes later with more stores including a forty-gallon empty, oil drum. *Now we can get cracking*, thought Bomber. To his surprise, the chopper returned once more but after it had dropped the cargo net, it hovered with its wheels touching the ridge and six men jumped out. The Belvedere had a very high-set landing gear. The drop from the doorway was considerable and Bomber was amazed that no one broke a leg.

As the chopper wheeled away, Bomber found himself looking into the bearded face of the Regiment's Pioneer Platoon Sgt. He by tradition always sported a beard.

"Some jump, Sgt.," said Bomber with admiration.

"Getting better at it but the first time was a ball breaker. Well, Cpl. Brown, we are here to set up some barbwire entanglements but we have not got long."

Sgt. Thomas was a stout man tremendously strong and good at his job which could be just about anything the Commanding Officer wished. It said something about the importance of Charlie picket that he had been spared to help strengthen the defenses.

Showing Thomas the site, they mapped out an area for the barbwire entanglement to protect the position. Thomas set two of his team to sort out a toilet while he and the rest got on with fixing the barbwire to the steel stakes hammered into the iron hard ground.

Bomber and the rest set about sandbagging the main Sanger and rigging the overhead cover. There was not enough to equipment the second Sanger as he would like to, so priority was given to the main one.

With just an hour to go to dusk, the Pioneers had finished and made their way down towards the main camp. Bomber had Sean and Patrick provide cover for them with the LMG until they reached the runway.

Eating a meal of curried everything, which was Donnie's specialty, Bomber discussed the sentry roster and sleeping arrangements. The tent was not safe from mortar fire but as it was on the reverse slope, it should be safe from any direct fire but not mortar rounds which could easily be lobbed over the ridge. However, as the PO had indicated that attacks were likely, they all elected to sleep at night in the main Sanger. As from midnight to an hour before dawn, they would be half on sentry and half resting, so there would just be enough room for the seven of them. The other Sanger would remain unmanned until they could make it bullet and mortar-proof.

Studying the ground to their front, they looked at the range and DF card the marines had left. From this, they worked out ranges for the GPMG and the LMG. The two-inch mortar with two dozen para illuminating rounds and the same number of high explosive rounds was stored in the other Sanger, as it could not be fired inside the main one due to the overhead cover. The mortar and the flare pistol, which fire an illuminating cartridge, were their main nighttime defensive lighting system. Without it, they would be blind to any one approaching the ridge. After some discussion, it was decided to place trip flares further down the slope so they would be set off by anyone approaching from that direction.

The night passed without incident. The next day was spent increasing the thickness and height of the second Sanger walls. Bomber's request for more sandbags, wood, and corrugated iron was met with a wait out. So he knew that there would be no support for a while and they would just have to make the best they could with the rocks lying around on the ground.

Apart from their machineguns and the mortar, the picket was also equipped with a 3.5 rocket launcher which could be used to cover the *wadi* road. Not that the road or roads through the *wadis* looked like roads. They were just flattened out due to centuries of camel trains and in later year's trucks driving through.

Every morning, the length of *wadi* under the watch of Charlie picket was swept for mines by two sappers or two of the pioneers with handheld mine sweepers. Following behind them was a ferret armored car with a Browning .303 machinegun to give them protection. On the third morning, Jos called Bomber to the Sanger. He and John had the dawn to eight watch each morning.

"Bomber," Jos said staring down into the *wadi*, "watch this. Every morning they sweep the road and when they get to that rock island with the bushes on it, they go to the left. Now in a few minutes, they will come back getting a lift on the Ferret sitting on the front. Watch what happens."

Bomber waited patiently wondering what he would see. After about fifteen minutes, the Ferret came in sight with the two pioneers/sappers sitting on the front.

On reaching the rock island, the driver drove around it to the left, in other words, to the side that had not been cleared of any mines.

"Shit, the bloody idiots," Bomber exclaimed.

"Yes, and they have done this every morning so far and if we have noticed, you can bet your boots that there are other eyes watching who will also have notice. So it's just a matter of time before boom."

Bomber agreed and got on the radio, calling Pl HQ with the information. A short while later, Blaze called back and asked for more details and Bomber explained what had been observed.

On day-four, a large camel train arrived at the picket carrying sandbags and the other items needed to strengthen the second Sanger. The camels did not look to happy about the heavy loads and while kneeling down to be unloaded, they had a habit of turning their heads towards whoever was doing the unloading and trying to take a bite out of an arm or leg. This seemed to amuse the camel handlers and produced great peals of laughter from them.

Donnie lost his cool after one near miss to many. Fetching his rifle, he cocked it, putting a round in the chamber and threatened to shoot the camel that was giving him grief. After this, the handlers held the head of any camel being unloaded which made Donnie happy but rather spoiled their fun.

The afternoon work progressed well, but there were only enough sandbags to reinforce the front wall of the second Sanger and to make the pillars for the roof beams. The corrugated iron roof had only one layer of bags, not ideal but it would have to do.

It was just about four in the afternoon and Donnie was shouting char time when everyone hit the deck as a vicious crack, crack, passed overhead. Scrambling for cover and weapons, they all made for the main Sanger. Patrick was on duty and had already sent a contact report to HQ over the radio.

Jamming on his steel helmet, Bomber scanned the foreground, then the middle ground, and finally the distance but saw nothing to indicate where the attack came from.

"Did you see anything, Patrick?" Bomber asked, not really expecting an exact location.

"Not a thing, but I think it came from somewhere to our north between pointed peak and the gap."

Both were marked on the range card and had several red dots against them, showing they had been used in the past to attack the picket. The range was too great for their weapons to be really effective.

The radio squawked and it was Blaze asking for more details. Bomber gave the reference that Patrick had suggested.

Next minute, a sustained burst of fire erupted around the second position, some of it hitting the new sandbagged wall at the front.

"Someone doesn't like our work," Sean shouted and they both ducked as the next burst hit around them.

"I think it's coming from just left of the Gap," said Patrick calmly. Bomber noticed he had not even ducked but was observing through the binoculars.

Okay, Bomber thought, *at that range, they must be using one of the heavy 12.6 mm machineguns mounted on a tripod and we cannot effectively counter that without a tripod for the GPMG.*

Bomber grabbed the radio mike and gave the details to Blaze asking for some defensive fire from the 81 mm mortars at base camp.

Blaze said a Wilco and every one waited.

"There," said Patrick with the binoculars still clamped to his eyes. "Tell them add one hundred and fire for effect."

The first mortar round fired was normally a ranging shot and the drop shorts as the mortar lads were often called and were dead on target.

They all watched as a dozen explosions covered the area by the Gap, the sound only reaching them several seconds later.

After the smoke and dust cleared, Bomber told Patrick to keep watching and to scan the area for any movement.

For about fifteen minutes or so, nothing happened. Then all hell was let loose with a sustained burst hitting the second Sanger and then the fire switched to them. *Thank God we did the work or this place would have disintegrated by now*, Bomber thought as he called the details over the radio to Blaze. Suddenly the firing stopped and they nearly jumped out of their skins as two Hunter jet fighters roared over the ridge. Lining up, they poured high explosive rockets towards the Gap. The Hawker Hunter jetfighter was equipped with two pods of eighteen 2.68 inch rockets and the pilots took turns circling and firing at the gap area. Once the rockets had been exhausted, they dived in blasting the ridge with their four 30 mm Aden cannons.

"Glad I am not on the end of that lot," Patrick stated, still with the binoculars glued to his eyes.

After two runs each with the cannons, the Hunters continued to circle for about ten more minutes before returning in the direction they came from as they flew over Bomber's position they waggled there wings.

"I take back all I have ever said about the blue jobs," Sean said with some sincerity, "and the next ones I meet I'll buy them a beer."

"Amen to that," echoed the others.

Bomber took the binoculars from Patrick and spent a long time studying the gap area but could not see any sign of movement.

After another half hour, they cautiously left the safety of the Sanger to examine the damage. The second one with only one layer of sandbags at the front had partially collapsed. The heavy caliber rounds had torn through the bags and shattered the rock wall behind it. Bomber set Sean, Jos, and John to repairing the wall. No one needed encouragement to work hard as they knew without the Sangers, they would be sitting ducks on the ridge for any dissident who wanted to take a pot shot at them.

The main position had fared better; the double thickness of bags had absorbed the force of the round and those that had penetrated to the rock wall beneath had been stopped, proving to Bomber that the rock wall had to be at least three feet thick with a double layer of bags to provide adequate protection against heavy machinegun fire at long range but he was not convinced it was enough if it came down to a range of two hundred yards.

As darkness descended, it remained quiet and Donnie produced a hot curried 'everything' which they ate huddled together in the main Sanger and it seemed to put new life into them. Gulping mugs of tea, the banter started up.

"Seems we have really pissed off the dissidents by fortifying the ridge. I wonder what we can do to upset the fuckers some more?" Patrick seemed keen to bring on the agro.

"You do what you want. I'm more for a quiet life," muttered John who was scraping the large compo biscuit tin Donnie used as a cooking pot, vainly trying to get more curry out of it in the dark.

Speaking quietly while the others listened, Bomber said, "We really need to think what this attack is about?"

"Was it just a token gesture to show they could do it, a matter of pride, or is it something more?"

"Like what?" asked Donnie.

"Well, we know Charlie picket is the key to holding the *wadi*, by day and at night the company patrol it and set up ambushes. So if they want to control the area and have a strong point to shoot up the main camp and airfield, then taking over Charlie picket or making it untenable would be a priority for their freedom of movement, yes?"

Leaving the question hanging, Bomber waited to see who would speak first.

Sean started, "Well, I guess that they would have to kill the people manning the picket and then take the position under cover of darkness."

"Let's look at it from their point. They have rattled our cage with heavy MG fire and if they are watching, they will have seen us moving around after it, so they know we are still in one piece. They couldn't risk another go and get mortared and strafed by the RAF again in daylight. So if you have everything still in place and you have ranged in during daylight, why not have another go when it's dark and the mortars will not be as effective and the RAF will not do any night attacks in the mountains?"

"Fuck me. I hate the way you think. Will they come at us tonight?" Jos asked.

"I've no idea, but I don't think that show was for fun, so we best be prepared. The other Sanger won't take much punishment until we can repair it properly. So, we will move the mortar and ammo to here and we can fire it from the doorway. Sean, can you place a couple of your pull grenades in there in case someone reaches it? Jos, break open more GPMG belts and bandoliers for the rifles. Sean, while you are at the grenades, I think we will have some extras in here. Anyone think of anything else?"

"More para illuminating," said John. "There is never enough when it's a long night."

Once the work was completed, they settled down, half of them on watch, the others resting and trying to sleep.

Bomber found he could not rest. His mind kept going over every scenario. Had he covered all eventualities?

At some stage, he must have dozed off as the next thing he knew, Patrick was shaking him and saying, "Come on, our turn to take watch."

Standing beside Sean, Bomber asked if they had heard any noise from the *wadi*.

"No," said Sean and moved to the back to rest.

It was close to one o'clock in the morning when Patrick nudged Bomber and mouthed in his ear with a cupped hand, "I'm not sure but I think I heard some loose rocks being knocked together lower down. It could be in the *wadi* or on the slope below us."

Donnie who was on the left of Bomber gave him a nudged, pointing down the slope. Bomber cupped his ear to help catch any sound. On a still night in the mountains, sound could travel a long way.

Suddenly Donnie grab Bomber's arm, pulling him down and shouting 'incoming', but before the words were out of his mouth, Bomber heard the sound of bullets passing over head and the thud as others hit the sandbags.

Patrick was already on the radio giving out the contact report and the others were scrambling to their stand to positions.

Bomber told John to fire the para illuminating round from the mortar as soon as he fired the Flare pistol. The Flare cartridge cast a silver light to their front and was just dying out when the para illuminating round blazed out dazzling all around for hundreds of yards.

Bomber remembered his training, keeping his left eye closed so when they went into darkness, he would still have some night vision in one eye.

Everyone was scanning their arc of fire but there was nothing to be seen. Then from down in the *wadi*, a furious fire fight erupted. Bomber ordered John to fire more illuminating rounds in that direction and Patrick yelled and pointed to figures in the *wadi* and Bomber guessed there were thirty or more tribesmen and directed the GPMG onto them, keeping the fire firmly directed to those figures in the open area as they all knew one of their own ambush patrols was down there and they probably started the firefight and would be tucked down tight to one side of the *wadi*.

According to the range card, it was six hundred yards to the ambush zone with a drop of some eight hundred feet, meaning that without a tripod, they were at the limit for accurate fire. Bomber made a mental note to request a tripod for the GPMG.

Bomber told Sean to keep the LMG covering the front just in case they too came under attack. A few seconds later, they were sprayed by fire from the heavy MG again, but this time it did some damage. The LMG flew from Sean's grasp and hit John who was crouched in the doorway on his head. John slumped to the floor with a groan. Donnie was on to him immediately and grabbing the mortar, Bomber put up another round.

The radio was squawking and Bomber grabbed the mike. It was Blaze telling him that a mortar DF was being fired at the same spot as early that day to shut the heavy MG up, and they were to keep firing into the *wadi* until told to stop.

They could all see the explosions of the mortar bombs and hear the sound a second or two later after about thirty explosions, the mortar fire stopped and the heavy MG remained silent.

They took turns using the GPMG, firing short bursts of three to five rounds at any spot that might conceal dissident but away from where there the ambush patrol fire was coming from. The ambush position was marked by the white-hot streak of tracer rounds that crossed the ground immediately in front of the ambush position. Despite being an arid landscape, the *wadi* contained many bushes and trees, probably getting water from deep down that had been trapped there after some long past rains. The combination of boulders trees and bushes that littered the sides of the *wadi* made it easy for anyone to hide and remain safe until daylight. Then it would be the job of a fighting patrol to winkle them out.

The para-illuminating fired from the two-inch mortar kept the landscape cast in a silvery light as the flare drifted down on its parachute. It also emphasized the shadows cast by the tree, bushes, and boulders, and it was at these shadows they directed the fire from the GPMG.

Finally they received orders to stop firing and it was a chance to take stock. John was okay, his steel helmet taking most of the force of the LMG hitting him. Sean had a sprained wrist and a bruised shoulder. The LMG barrel had a large gouge in it where a round had struck it. Sean was lucky to be alive.

At dawn, they could hear helicopters on the airfield and at first, light three Whirlwinds lifted off and headed towards Charlie picket. As they gained altitude, two Hunters jet fighters screeched overhead and went streaking towards the Gap but did not fire.

The helicopters labored in the hot, thin air, clawing their way slowly over Charlie picket. As they flew steadily towards the Gap, the tail end chopper suddenly lost altitude and then it clipped the hillside. The rotating blades hit the slope and then the helicopter was rolling and bouncing down the hillside. Bomber thought he could see bodies coming out of the door. Finally the chopper came to a halt and Sean was on the radio reporting the incident. The wreck was too far away for them to be of assistance other than reporting the incident.

Meanwhile, the other two had reached the Gap and deposited the troops who would conduct a search for any dissidents dead or alive.

"Jesus Christ!" shouted Patrick, pointing at the downed helicopter. Figures could be seen crawling out of the wreckage. Some were standing up. Others lay where they had crawled too. Suddenly the air was filled with a roar as a Belvedere flew low over them and headed towards the wreck. It hovered close to the wreckage and figures jumped down. Then it went lower, down the hillside to a point where it could land.

The two helicopters from the gap were now returning and flew back over Charlie picket. Faces could be seen peering down at them.

Watching in stunned silence, they could see casualties being lifted into the Belvedere which eventually took off and roared over them. This time, the downwash blew the hundred and sixty pounder tent down, cursing Patrick and Sean who were nearest threw themselves onto it, so it did not take off and disappear. The Belvedere did not stop at the airfield and Bomber guessed it was going on to Aden and the hospital.

Meanwhile in the *wadi* where the firefight took place last night, a fighting patrol was sweeping through the ambush site and beyond. A Ferret armored car followed behind with two trucks and occasionally the patrol would stop and something, maybe a body, was loaded onto one of the trucks.

Bomber had the damage repaired the best they could and had asked for a replacement barrel for the LMG, a tripod for the GPMG, and more sandbags to be included in the next camel train to them.

As news filtered through on the night's activities, the number of dead in the ambush varied from five to twelve depending on who was telling the story and a patrol was following a number of blood trials guided by some of the friendly locals.

The check at the Gap found empty cases from a 12.6 mm MG but no body parts. The downed helicopter cost two dead and four with various injuries. One of the injured was a friend of Bomber's who had trained at the IJLB with him and was an outstanding footballer tipped to make the army team. *What now for him?* thought Bomber. *How badly hurt is he?*

The next two days and nights past quietly and they all stood too on their last day at Charlie picket. Donnie was just brewing up the first cup of tea of the day, and Bomber and Patrick were at the GPMG watching the two Pioneers followed by the Ferret sweep the road for mines. Finally, the Ferret came back with the two Pioneers sitting on the front as usual. After their report to Pl HQ regarding the correct side to pass the rock island on, the drivers had followed instructions.

Patrick suddenly gripped Bomber's arm and said, "He's going to go the wrong way round the rock island, the stupid bastard."

Bomber watched as one of the Pioneers waved their arms at the driver's hatch but the Ferret driver either did not see or was too late to change direction. Just as Bomber and Patrick thought they were clear, an explosion lifted the front of the Ferret in to the air. Both passengers were thrown from the vehicle and crashed to the ground yards away from the Ferret that was now on its side.

Bomber snatched the radio mike and reported to Platoon HQ. Within minutes, three vehicles raced from the main camp, one of which being an ambulance. Everyone at Charlie picket watched as the medics took charge while a section stood guard. Two others worked their way around the Ferret with mine sweepers before a recovery vehicle hooked up the Ferret and towed it away.

"Bloody hell! We shouldn't be losing people to stuff like this," Sean said with passion. "Either the driver ignored orders or if the driver is new, someone didn't brief him."

Bomber thought it was more likely the driver just forgot which way to go. Looking down, Bomber saw he had let his tea grow cold and felt slightly embarrassed by it. 'Why?' he asked himself. 'Should I be embarrassed or is it guilt?'

'Guilt that we were up here safe, drinking tea, and could see what was going to happen but were helpless to stop it.'

Bomber gulped down the cold tea and with it, he hoped the guilt and shame of being so helpless.

Being in the action and taking casualties was one thing; being a helpless spectator was hard to deal with.

Due to this incident, the handover of Charlie picket was late. By midafternoon, a section from one Platoon had arrived to take over. They had been in the ambush last night and spent most of the handover telling and re-telling the story of the contact to whoever was nearest.

They also heard that the Pioneer Cpl., on the Ferret, had lost a leg and had serious head injuries but was still alive. The other one had concussion and a broken arm. Both the driver and commander had concussion but were going to be okay. It seemed the driver just plain forgot which side to go and got it wrong.

"Stupid bastard," one of the incoming sections said.

"Or just unlucky," said Patrick. "Just don't be too quick to judge. It could be you that makes the next mistake."

Mistakes cost lives. Complacency costs lives, and what else? Too many variables, thought Bomber. *All we can do is cover as many bases as we can think of and physically cover. So don't get sloppy or think it won't happen to you, because it can*, the little voice in his head whispered.

With this going round and round in his head, Bomber and his section made their way back to base camp following the camels. One of which was letting off very loud, smelly farts. Perhaps it had eaten some of Donnie's curried everything.

Back at base, their Platoon took on the patrol tasks. The company commander was keen to keep the dissidents on the back foot after the recent success of the ambush and decided that they were to push up the *wadi* and winkle out any suspects lurking in buildings or caves.

To do this, the platoon would have the support of a dozen local friendlies, who would be more able to identify dissidents. Two Saladin armored cars, these six wheeled eleven, and half ton beasts had a 76 mm gun and two machineguns which was a lot of firepower. It could also stand a mine blast and could still operate with two of its wheels blown off.

A beefed up Company HQ would back up the Platoon in case of heavy opposition, consisting of the Company Commander with three radio operators, the CSM commanding an ad hoc group of store men, drivers, four pioneers, and several odd and sods from the mortar and anti-tank platoon who normally never left camp. Giving a total of sixteen reinforcements should they be required.

Bomber had a notion the Pioneers were itching for some action to redress the injuries to their two colleagues.

Entering the point where the ambush took place, they were soon out of sight of Charlie picket. The Dammed were on point operating up to four hundred yards ahead of the rest of the platoon. Behind the platoon two of the Pioneers swept the dirt road for mines with the two Saladin following close behind.

Jos and Patrick were in the lead while Bomber and the rest of the section stayed close behind in a loose diamond formation. They had one local friendly with them carrying the mandatory .303 rifle over his shoulder and all the time he would be saying in his camp-learnt English, "No fucking ragheads here, Cpl."

Bomber, using a combination of English and mime, managed to convince him only to tell him when the ragheads were actually there.

Taking turns at point, Bomber found himself with John carefully moving forward while all the time scanning for anything that would indicate an ambush. At the same time thinking that they were out front with no one sweeping for anti-personnel mines when the best protected items, the Saladins got the road swept for them.

The terrain rose very gently upwards and was typical of most of the country, stony with hardy bushes and trees on either side, good ambush country. John signaled for Bomber to come to him and indicated a side trail that was obviously used as there were goat and sheep droppings.

The trail was not wide and Bomber told John to wait there for the rest of the section. He moved forward slowly and carefully. After fifty feet, he saw a cord stretched tight across the track. Scanning the area, he could not see any sign of a trap, so he bent down and followed the cord to one side, finding it hooked over a forked stick, attached to several old tin cans, inside of which were some stones.

So it's an alarm, not a booby trap, thought bomber, making his way back to John and the rest of the section. They waited for the Platoon to catch up. When Blaze arrived, Bomber briefed him and he radio back to the Company HQ.

After a short conversation, they were told to follow up and investigate and Bomber led the way, marking the alarm cord so everyone could step over it without setting it off.

The smell was the first thing he noticed. *Animals?* he wondered. Then he noticed bees buzzing around. Bomber recalled that bees were never too far from a water source of some sort. Suddenly they were in a small clearing; a corral made of cut bushes and branches was empty. To the right of the corral by a rock face was a log with the middle cut out to make a trough. By the trough, Bomber could see a small bubbling of water coming from the bottom of the rock face. Several bees could be seen dipping down to drink from it. Behind the corral was a small cave and Bomber could hear the sound of a woman talking in low tones and the occasional reply from a child. He signaled the section to split and circle the corral and come up to the cave from each side. There, they discovered two small children and a woman. The woman grabbed the children and pulled them to her and stared defiantly at Bomber, who gently put his rifle down and held his hands out to the side to show he meant no harm.

Blaze and a friendly spoke to the woman. It transpired that she and her husband, who was further up the side *wadi* grazing the animals, had left their village some months ago. The village, which was further up the main valley, was being occupied by dissidents who took whatever they wanted especially livestock for food.

She told them that there was originally up to twenty dissidents and some others who were not locals or Yemenis but the numbers changed, sometimes more, sometimes less.

After a chat between the Company Commander and Blaze, it was decided to push hard for the village. Once they were closer, they would send two of the friendlies to recce the place.

Being released from point, Bomber and the section rejoined the Platoon. The pace became much faster now and the Saladins had been dropped further back so that the engine noise would not betray the presents of the troops.

Four hours later, they halted. Hot and thirsty, they had a chance to gulp down some tepid water and then they waited. Movement and voices informed them that the friendlies were back. After twenty minutes, everyone was on the move again.

Doyle led Bomber and his section, circling out left until they had got behind the village. Then he radioed that they were in position. Their job was to act as cut-offs and stop anyone escaping further up the valley.

Bomber could just make out the village, not that it would qualify as a village anywhere else. It consisted of a collection of perhaps a dozen mud-built houses with flat roofs. A larger house had two men on the roof who Bomber guessed were sentries. They were slouched against the parapet smoking. They had clearly not seen or heard anything as yet. Bomber kept his binoculars on the two men. Suddenly one of them appeared to stand up straight. Then he collapsed. The second one did the same a split second later. Bomber heard the two shots that had killed them. Both shots sounded like .303 Lee Enfield's rifles.

Now there was the distinctive sound of AK47 chattering away and then answered by the clearer crack of the SLR and continuous chatter of a GPMG. The silence that followed lasted a few moments. Then they could hear the engine rumble of a Saladin's. Heavy fire came from the AK47s and then a *boom* as one of the Saladins' 76 mm gun fired.

No more shots were fired. Half an hour later, they received a radio call to go to the village. As they entered the village, they could see the locals were gathered in one corner of a rough square. They were angry and some were throwing stones and shouting but not at the soldiers but at five figures squatting on the ground and guarded by one section, lying near the open door of the larger building were four bodies. The two from the roof and the others must have been in the house when the Saladin put a 76 mm shell through the wall. A group of women and children spat on the bodies and were shouting insults and pointing at them.

After a while, the Company Commander sat down with the village elders. Tea was offered with some figs.

It appeared the dissidents had arrived some six months before, demanding that they joined the fight against the government and the British. When the village headman refused, they shot him and his two young sons who tried to stop them. The dissidents took over the dead man's house which was the one the Saladin had fired into. As the dissidents' numbers were greater than the village men, they had to agree to shelter and feed them.

Several days ago, the dissidents, except other than the ones that were sitting or lying there, went away. When they came back, there was not so many and some were wounded. The next day, they left heading north towards the border taking the village donkeys and camels to carry the wounded. This gave them a two-day head start on the Platoon. It was a little over two and a half days to the border for men on foot.

The Company Commander ordered a section to be loaded onto the back of each Saladin, and with Blaze they set out in hot pursuit. To Bomber's disappointment, they were not included. Instead, they were ordered to go onto the roof of the large building and keep watch.

Aware of how easily the dissident sentries had been shot on the roof, Bomber ordered that no one was to stand up but to make gaps in the mud parapets and watch through the holes.

Using their bayonets, they dug at the mud.

"Bloody hell! It's only mud but it's harder than rock," Jos complained.

"Just keep digging and hope there is not a dissident out there lining up on your fat head, mate," Patrick replied with a laugh but the possibility was not lost on any of them.

After an hour of hard work, they had made good observation holes. Bomber sent Donnie down to the floor below to rustle up some food and tea. Then they could go down in twos to eat.

Later, Bomber was joined on the roof by two of their friendly locals, one of whom was the 'no fucking ragheads here, Cpl.' who the boys had taken a shine to calling him 'No Fuck'.

Despite Bomber telling them to keep down, neither seemed to worry about standing with their heads above the parapet while smoking their foul-smelling cigarettes. An hour before last light, everyone stood too.

All was quiet. The sun was casting long shadows. Birds were flitting in and out of the trees before settling down.

The shot, when it came, made Bomber jump and he scanned through one of the observation holes easing the safety catch off his SLR. Shouts came from the local who had been standing next to 'No Fuck' and he was crawling away from 'No Fuck' who had collapsed. The shot had hit him squarely in the center of his head and blood was spreading like a cloak around him.

As they had heard the bang at the same time as 'No Fuck had collapsed, they knew the shooter was close. Patrick was already firing back and shouting directions. The shooter was less than fifty yards away on the top of an adjacent but lower building and now everyone was pouring fire at the rooftop and the one lone gunman.

Bomber had to shout 'cease fire' three times before they all stopped. The CSM was up at the doorway shouting for a report and Bomber briefed him and he set off back down the stairs.

A few minutes later, the CSM and four others appeared on the shooters roof and inspected a bundle that was lying there. Turning his attention to Donnie who had crawled over to 'No Fuck', when Donnie looked at Bomber, he knew the round had killed him instantly. *Stupid! Stupid! Stupid!* the voice in Bomber's head screamed. *You should have forced them to stay down on the roof. It's your fault!*

Bomber knew even if he had forced them to sit or lie down as soon as his back was turned, they would have been standing and smoking. But the guilt was there.

The company clerks head appeared in the doorway informing them that a house to house search was to be carried out and a torch signal plus the radio would be used to warn them when any of the searchers were going onto the roof of any house.

Later, Bomber learnt from the CSM that the owner of the house, which the shooter had used, had been stabbed to death inside the house. As they were talking, a shout went up. Then a real hue and cry started. The locals had found another dissident hiding. They had dragged him into the open by the well. The attack on him was a frenzy; men, women, and even children joined in. Knifes, clubs, and rocks rained down on him until all that was left was an unrecognizable mess of torn flesh and bloody clothing. The villagers, their anger spent, walked away from the body. It was left to the CSM and three luckless lads to bury the remains.

"Well, it's all happening here. Just needs some beers and dancing girls and we will be complete," muttered Sean in an attempt to lighten the mood.

"Don't think we will get the last two, but we could do with the two-inch mortar and a load of para-illuminating rounds up here. John, go see the CSM and get the mortar and rounds." Thinking he had been very slack in staying ahead of the game, Bomber discussed what else they should do with Sean.

"Not much else we can do. The CSM has the perimeter covered. We just need to stay alert during the night. So I think I'll get some kip now. Wake me when you want." With that, he turned on his side and within seconds was asleep.

John came back with two of the Pioneers' lugging boxes of mortar rounds. Plunking the two-inch mortar next to Bomber, he indicated the two Pioneers, reinforcements.

Sedgwick, the taller of the two, spoke, "I cleared it with the CSM and he said if you are happy, we can stay up here and do sentry with your guys."

Bomber teamed them up with Sean and Patrick with strict instructions that they were to do exactly what Sean and Patrick told them.

Bomber, lying on his back, looked up at the uncountable host of stars and mulled over why they had not made a thorough house to house search when they arrived. Perhaps they had put too much reliance on the locals to check their own houses. After all, they all had weapons and could have asked for backup from us.

I should have asked the CSM what weapon they found, he thought to himself. *Could the shooter have been a villager, not a dissident after all?*

They had only heard one shot so if it was an AK47, the shooter would have set it to automatic and fired a burst. A .303 Lee Enfield would have only been able to fire one shot at a time. What did he hope to gain with so many of them on the roof? Perhaps he had not known that a section of troops were there.

146

After all, he would not have been able to see any of them from below; the roof he had been on was a lot lower, so all he could have seen was the two friendlies' heads and shoulders. He couldn't have known that there was manned gun slits pointing in his direction.

Bomber rolled over and informed Sean he was going down to find the CSM. He found the CSM talking to the Company Commander. Seeing him, they stopped and asked what he wanted.

Bomber told them his thoughts and the Company Commander told him that they were looking into just that.

The weapon was a .303 but it belonged to the stabbed homeowner verified by his wife who had been locked in another room with her children. The dissident, for that what he was, was not a local or a Yemeni but probably an Egyptian. "Trouble was your lads put so much lead into him that he was torn apart so it was a little difficult to be sure."

The next morning, Blaze and the Saladins returned less a section and two of the friendlies. After about what Blaze estimated as a day's march they found the animals abandoned. Blaze assumed that the dissidents had then changed to trucks or other vehicles. They had pushed on to the border but they didn't see any of them.

The missing section and friendlies had been bringing the animals back. As soon as the villagers heard this, they set out to reclaim their animals.

After further discussion with the village elders who swore loyalty to the government, it was agreed that the building the soldiers occupied at present would be fortified and that two LMGs and a two-inch mortar with plenty of ammunition for both would be given as a present to the village to deter any more occupation by other dissidents.

The next two days were spent mixing mud and straw, some for bricks and some were used to thicken the parapet on the roof until it was at least two feet thick. Firing slits were improved and the hole made by the Saladin's 76 mm gun was repaired. Bomber was impressed by how effective the mud was at absorbing high velocity rounds and that it required a heavy weapon like the 76 mm to knock a hole in the thick walls.

After the bricks and mud had been applied a smooth mixture of camel dung and mud was applied which apparently made the wall more weatherproof.

Passing by Patrick, as he mixed the mess up, one of one section made the mistake of saying, "You Micks have found your right place, I see." Before Bomber could intervene, Patrick had hit him hard in the midriff and then shoved his head deep into the mixture.

The locals stopped working and looked on in amazement when Patrick pulled the unfortunate out of the evil-smelling concoction. He dumped him hard onto the ground and said in a low warning voice, "Say anything else shithead and I will make you part of this house."

Some of the other members of one section decided to intervene but Sean stepped in front of them, saying, "Pick him up and go away unless of course you want to play with me fuck nuts?"

Even with odds of four to one, such was Sean's reputation as a fighter. They hesitated and Bomber stepped in. "Leave it lads. We don't need to fight amongst ourselves. He asked for it, so just take him for a wash-down."

The tension eased and they all moved away. A short while later as Bomber was cleaning himself up, one section's commander, a tall, red-faced Cpl. by the name of Moore, approached him. Moore shoved his face close to Bomber and snarled, "This is not finished. I'll have that fucking Mick's hide when we get back to base you, fucker."

Bomber didn't even think; he just reacted, grasping Moore's shirt in both hands. He used Moore's weight against him by leaning back and pivoting fast to the left, spinning Moore round, then he let go of the shirt.

Moore went backwards, caught his heels on some drying bricks and went down. Bomber was on him like a cat and stamped down hard on Moore's left knee. A cry of pain was stopped by two quick hard punches to Moore's face. Bomber could feel the nose flatten under the force of the punches which gave him a feeling of sadistic satisfaction.

Bomber was just about to deliver a further blow when strong arms encircled him from behind and lifted him completely off the ground and away into the building.

Sean's voice spoke in to his ear, "If I let you go, will you stay calm?"

He felt the anger drain away as quickly as it had risen and nodded an agreement. Sean released him, laughing and saying, "That clown didn't know what was going on, because he was bigger than you by a mile. He thought he could walk all over you."

Jos and John were also there, now large grins on their faces, looking very pleased and Jos said, "Don't worry about him whining to the Platoon Commander. We already told him if he does, we will give him a battering he'll never recover from. Mind you he'll take a while to heal from the way he is hobbling right now."

By now, the whole section was gathered around Bomber who felt a sense of bewilderment, both from their mindset that he had done a good job and his own sense of shame for losing it and risking the hard-won tape on his arm.

"Well, I think he is good enough to be made an honorary Ulster man. What do you think boys?" Patrick looked at the others and Jos spoke up, "I guess it depends on what foot he kicks with?"

Bomber later learnt this meant if he was a Catholic or Protestant.

"He stamps more than kicks," laughed Patrick, "so I don't think it matters, all in favor?" A raise of hands brought a chorus of 'he's one of us'.

Bomber had a feeling this would be costly club to be in, if today was any measure of the future.

Later that evening, the CSM had a word with Bomber. Bomber liked the CSM. He was a big man, who had seen some action in the past, but carried himself quietly and had the respect of everyone.

"I hear that lanky toe rag Moore was trying it on with you today and came off worse. Now this is nothing official. The Company Commander is happy to turn a blind eye and I'm happy that you have put Moore in his place. However, don't make a habit of it. There's a system. Use it. Go to your Platoon Sgt. First, then to me. Doing too much with your fists can backfire on you. Got it?"

"Yes sir," and after a pause, "Thanks sir!"

"It's okay. Remember you have had good training at IJLB and it shows. Keep your nose clean and you could rise up the ranks quicker than the best of them." With that, he walked away quietly circling the village houses followed at a distance by two of the HQ team with rifles at the ready.

Chapter 14
Curly and Camels

It took all morning to weave a way to the pass at the top of the ridge following a narrow but well used path. The route over the ridge was not suitable for the Saladins, so they, the CSM and some of the Company HQ group, would go back the way that we had approached the village.

The Company Commander believing they had achieved all that they could in the village decided to return to Thumair but by a different route. The route was by a *wadi* which flowed in the general direction to Thumair, meeting at a junction close to the camp. This *wadi* was divided from the village by a high, steep rocky ridge.

A guide was provided by the village elders and it turned out to be the son of the man stabbed to death by the dissident. Bomber thought that the boy could not be more than twelve but he carried his father's rifle as if he was born to it, which he probably was.

It had been a punishing climb from the village. Bomber felt his leg muscles cramping and greedily gulped water to rehydrate his body. He could see an easy and more direct way down which led to a narrow defile with thorny bushes growing on its sides. Blaze ordered Bomber's section to take point and gave him instructions to proceed with caution as it was an ideal place for an ambush.

Bomber didn't need any encouragement to be cautious as he already had a bad feeling about this. Taking the lead, he stopped and studied the ground for signs of fresh footprints and continually sniffed the air for smoke, either from a fire or cigarettes. In the bottom of the defile, he could see where it opened into the *wadi*. The heat was stifling. It felt as if he had been covered in a hot blanket. *Well*, he thought, *if we run out of water here, we will be well and truly screwed.* The path they followed was obviously well used by animals as dried droppings were plentiful. Tough bushes and stunted trees lined either side of the path. The bushes had nasty thorns that ripped through clothing and skin with ease. Every now and again he would hear a soft curse as someone got to close to a bush. As they progressed along the path, the *wadi* was getting wider until it was not possible to see both sides without doing a one-eighty.

The guide, who the boys had named Curly, was with them. His real name was 'Mo' but his mass of curly black locks ensured that he would forever be Curly to the boys. After an hour, Curly tugged on Bomber's arm, pointing to a small side trail. He smiled and mimicked the action of drinking. Ten yards down the trail, they were amazed to see a small spring with flowering bushes and tiny flowers growing close by. Bomber had all the water bottles refilled and stared in wonder at this little oasis of a few square yards in such an arid place. He waited for Blaze to arrive, showing him the spring which flowed for less than ten feet before the water disappeared below the stones.

After another hour, they came to another side trail. This one was wider and it looked well used with footprints and fresh camel dung on the ground.

Curly looked apprehensive and made a shooting sign with his hand. Waiting for Blaze to reach him, he relayed what Curly had indicated.

After briefing the Company Commander using the radio, they moved cautiously forward. Sean and Bomber were leading with Blaze and the rest of the section was close behind. Doyle and the rest of the platoon followed leaving a gap of a hundred yards. The pace was slow; neither of them wished to be careless and walk into a booby trap or ambush.

Thirty minutes later, they were crouched behind bushes looking at six tribesmen stretched out on blankets. They could not see if they were armed, so they had no way of knowing if they were dissidents or not. Four camels with packs on their backs were hobbled and resting to one side of the men.

Word was sent back to Doyle to quietly bring the Platoon forward as they did so, the camels appeared to get nervous and one of the men stood up and looked around but not seeing any thing, he sat down again.

Blaze sent Bomber and his section to try and get to the rear of the group but despite going slowly and carefully, he was worried that one of the men would hear the stones that they dislodged as they circled them.

Once more, Bomber could hear the camels getting restless. Again, one of the men stood up but this time he just turned and emptied his bladder onto the ground. It was then that Bomber noticed that all the men were chewing slowly and methodically and one word sprang to mind, *Qut*. The local leaf that was a mood enhancing drug that gave the user a feeling of wellbeing but was not recommended if you wished to remain alert.

Crouching low, they waited for Blaze to make his move. When he did, it was almost funny to witness. He just marched the whole platoon straight at the group who stopped chewing in amazement before fumbling for their weapons that had been out of sight on the blankets. The lads were on them fast wrenching their weapons away then pinning the men to the ground. One less stupefied than the others decided to run. He was stopped short as Sean stepped out from behind a bush, dropping him with a stroke from his rifle butt.

The mix of weapons wasn't convincing enough on its own that they were dissidents despite Curly insisting they were Qotaibi. A search of the eight camel loads revealed that each bundle contained *Qut. Enough to keep the whole of the Middle East chewing for months*, guessed Bomber. Blaze was watching the men as the bundles were searched and when nothing was found, Blaze ordered another search, this time taking off the saddle packs, a carved wooden and cloth padded arrangement. They felt heavy, too heavy. Turning them over, they found a gap between the wood and the padding containing a nice fat British made anti-tank mine. Now the tribesmen were very agitated, two of them talking fit to bust.

The older of the men insisted they were being forced to carry the mines but Blaze and Curly were not to be persuaded and the men were secured with cord taken from the camel packs. Carefully checking each camel saddle, they found four mines and some plastic explosives, about twenty pounds in weight with some detonators and detonator cord.

No one likes the look of the plastic explosives. It was old and sweaty a sign. It was past its best and unstable. Blaze agreed and ordered it to be wrapped in a blanket and given to one of the men to carry. The unlucky one had his hands freed and then had the blanket with the explosives dumped in his arms. He gave the impression he was not too happy about the honor. Bomber hoped that when they moved off, he would be put a couple of hundred yards or so away from him.

Radioing in the find, Blaze was ordered to return to the Company Commander on the main *wadi* path. From there, they continued their patrol to Thumair. The camels with the *Qut* and mines trailed behind with the luckless dissidents walking in the middle, everyone trying to keep a good distance away from the one carrying the plastic explosives.

Arriving at camp as the last of the daylight faded, Bomber could feel his body wanting to give up. They all needed rehydration and some hot food but that would have to wait while they handed the dissidents over to the base camp interrogation team and the OP's officer for questioning.

The Platoon headed straight for the dining tent for a large dinner and endless mugs of tea. While eating, he listened to the boys telling anyone in earshot how they had captured a vicious gang of dissidents. Each time the story was told, it became stretched until it had built into a battle of World War Two proportions.

After an exciting start to their time at Rad Force HQ, the remainder of the stay was something of an anticlimax. Long, hot, and dusty foot patrols, ambushes, and another spell on picket duty ended without further incident. Blaze and Doyle put this down to the dissidents having plenty of space to avoid any unit giving them too much trouble knowing they could not be everywhere. They could simply operate somewhere else or wait for them to leave and then see if the next unit was as proactive in chasing them down.

They watched as the plane started its steep descent to the Thumair airstrip, the pilot pulling the aircraft up at the last minute to bump along the dirt strip in a cloud of dust. Taxiing to the edge of the runway, Bomber could see faces at the windows. When the doors opened, a company of wild-looking Jocks (Scottish Regiment) disembarked. They looked a tough bunch and Bomber had to escort them to the camp accommodation. On the way, one of the Sgts. fired a string of questions at Bomber who could not understand one word. Fortunately, a Cpl. next to him translated the questions into English and Bomber was able to give answers. The Sgt. didn't seem impressed. The Cpl. explained that the Sgt. was from the old dock area of Glasgow and they practically had their own language which even he found hard to understand at times. He, the Cpl., was from the East Coast of Scotland but, as a young boy, had lived in Chester for a few years.

Having arrived at the accommodation, Bomber shook the Cpl. by the hand and wished him good luck, turned, and set off back to the plane which would take him back to the coast. After a long, hot shower, some of char wallahs cheese and tomato rolls washed down with a mug of tea, life felt remarkably pleasant. *The simple things can make all the difference*, thought Bomber.

Chapter 15
A Sad Christmas and
Rowdy New Year!

It was Christmas day. Bomber and his section along with two section were on main gate guard duty at the entrance to Waterloo lines. It was hot, dusty, and the flies seemed to take delight in tormenting them as they sweated in the heat of the afternoon. No matter how many times he swatted the flies away or moved to another position, the flies regrouped and came back. The introduction of a new vehicle pass scheme was causing long delays. People were getting frustrated at the delays. It was just as annoying for the guards who had to do the checking and searching. All the commercial vehicles had to be searched then provided with a guard while they were in the camp. This took time, care, and a lot of manpower.

When a group of FRA soldiers, who did not have passes for their cars, were told to park in the outside car park, tempers flared. One of the FRA soldiers flagged down a car leaving the camp. It stopped. Out of the car stepped a tall, middle-aged man in civilian clothing. Bomber watched him approach, thinking he looked familiar.

As he approached the gate, something clicked in Bomber's mind. He had been a Company Commander at IJLB when Bomber was training there and was originally from one of the Scottish Regiments. Bomber racked his brains to remember his name. Then it came to him, Major Black.

Bomber took the initiative as soon as Black stopped in front of him and before he could opened his mouth, Bomber said, "Good afternoon, Major Black sir. I'm sorry I cannot let these soldiers bring their cars in. It's the new orders and they lack the necessary passes."

He looked a little taken aback that this young-looking Cpl. should know his name.

Looking intently at Bomber, he spoke loudly and said, "Now look here. I'm the second in command of the FRA unit. I can vouch for all these men and you can let them take their cars in."

Bomber had already pressed the bell push by the side of the gate to summon the guard commander knowing Black was not going to back off.

"Sorry sir. I cannot do that. The new orders are very strict."

Black's face went red and he was speaking with a growl in his voice, "You will do as I say or…"

Before he could finish, the Guard Commander arrived and butted in, "What seems to be the trouble here, sir?"

Wood, the Guard Commander, was a large bear-like man, who was an army heavyweight boxer. He had been an ex IJLB boy but a few years ahead of Bomber. Now a Sgt., he was not the sort of person who could be easily intimidated.

Black looked at Wood and went through the explanation again, emphasizing the point that he had ordered Bomber to let the cars in.

"I see," Wood said. "These new passes and the orders seem to be causing all sorts of problems, sir. But the Cpl. is quite right. They cannot bring their cars in. The Duty Field Officer was very firm on this when he briefed us this morning. I can ask him to come to the guardroom to speak to you if you like."

Black was ready to blow a gasket. His face was now bright red and spittle was appearing on his lips as he worked himself up, but before he had a chance to speak, the sound of a grenade exploding in the camp made everyone turn. The explosion came from the direction of the officer married quarters. A stunned silence was broken by John.

"That's a grenade," then realizing that no one needed telling, John went to the Sanger and took up a fire position covering the road.

"Lock the gate, no one in or out," ordered Wood, who was already running back to the guardroom.

Bomber and Jos slammed and locked the gates shut, then went into the Sanger with the sentry and John manning the LMG.

Black was last seen talking to the now locked out FRA soldiers who got into their cars and drove away.

"Guess everyone thinks this lockdown will last a while," John spoke in a resigned voice knowing that they would not get relieved while the lockdown was in place.

At that moment, the camp siren went off and the rest of the guard deployed and the reserve platoon turned up in a Land Rover and two trucks ready to go wherever they were ordered.

Everything went quiet. The noise of people waiting to enter the camp had died away. Those stranded outside the gate had stopped talking. They were now staring at the thin plume of smoke rising above the buildings into the still air.

Twenty minutes later, an RMP vehicle pulled up at the guardroom. Dragging a sorry-looking local from the back of the vehicle, they frog-marched him into the guardroom.

Bomber discovered later that a grenade had been thrown into a children's party at an RAF officer's house. Apparently there was a fatality. A young girl, and some of her friends, had been wounded. The local with the RMPs were believed to be the culprit.

Lockdown remained in place for another hour while searches were carried out on all locals within the camp to ensure that they had not got any weapons on them.

Bomber got the order to re-open the gate having been told only British and FRA personnel could be allowed back in. Civilian workers and others had to be turned away. Arab workers and civilians were being removed from the lines checked and searched again at the gate before being released.

"Thank God our char wallah was at the guardroom and Wood said to keep him there," Jos chirped. "At least we can still get a brew and a cheese and tom roll whenever we want."

Char whallah was a thin six-foot-six Somali who was always happy serving tea from his giant kettle. He always turned up at first light, midmorning, the afternoon, and in the evening. He even gave tick for those who did not have any money until payday.

Bomber never heard of anyone one not paying what they owed. On reflection, Bomber wondered why he and the others had never asked him his real name.

It was New Year's Eve, Bomber plus about every off-duty squaddie and a large number of American sailors were celebrating at the NAAFI Lido Club. Several US Navy ships were docked at HMS Sabre for Christmas and the New Year. The club was a large single-story building with the longest bar that Bomber had ever seen. An army of barmen was keeping the drinks flowing nonstop.

The back of the building opened out onto a wide, pleasant veranda, beach, and safe swimming area. The swimming area was protected by a strong shark fence built of wood and steel mesh.

There were no women present in the bar. Single young ladies were in very short supply in Aden. Bomber and the lads were sharing a table with four US Navy sailors and were keeping each other amused by taking turns singing songs and telling stories.

A little after midnight and the singing of 'Auld Lang Syne', the noise started to die down and then the Lido became almost completely silent. One of the US Navy boys at their table was telling a story about getting locked in the paint store on his ship because he forgot to put a clip on the door in place. Along with the rest of the table, he had not noticed the descending silence. When Bomber looked up, he saw about thirty US Navy men in helmets with shore patrol written on them; all were carrying long clubs.

Two of them now stood directly behind our sailor and without warning or any provocation, one of them smashed his club down on to the back of his head. Blood cascaded down over the table as he went face down completely out. Patrick, who was sitting next to him, let out a wild and furious Irish roar before hitting the shore patrol culprit in the midriff and then pummeled him to the floor. The second shore patrol man tried to use his club on Patrick, but he was grabbed and beaten with his own club.

All hell was now let loose as the angry squaddies and sailors fuelled by large quantity of alcohol launched themselves at the shore patrol. Hopelessly outnumbered, the shore patrol didn't stand a chance and were beaten mercilessly in a way they could never have thought possible a few minutes previously.

Each one of the patrol was stripped naked and thrown into the sea and kept there, unable to escape either back up, the beach, or out to sea due to the shark fence.

Our unlucky navy boy was being patched up by the NAAFI manager who had called for an ambulance and the RMPs. Our navy boy was not looking too good. He kept drifting in and out of consciousness, and despite the manager's attempts with bar towels, he could not stem the bleeding.

The MPs arrived but stayed in the car park except for the MP Warrant Officer, who Bomber recognized as the one who had been at the grenade attack when they crashed the gates.

He calmly walked to the sea's edge and held up his hands for silence. After a few cat calls, every one became quiet. Then he spoke in a firm but friendly voice, "Okay lads, I think this lot have learnt their lesson. I'm going to take them out now and send them back to their ships."

With that, he waved for them to come out. A narrow lane opened up through the crowd and they walked stark naked in single file through the jeers of all and out of the Lido.

As the last of them left, the Warrant Officer said, "The bar is still open lads for another half hour and the buses are here to take you back to barracks when you have finished."

Cheering broke out and then someone decided to start a conga line and take it through the Lido the sea and back through the bar. As they passed the bar, more bottles of beer were handed over. Bomber thought this would be a good time to leave and with the rest of the section, they climbed aboard an empty bus and slept all the way back to the barracks.

Bomber woke early the next morning feeling as if his mouth had been sandblasted and a band was playing in his head. After a shaved, shower, and getting dressed in fresh KDs, he found char wallah doing the rounds with his giant kettle. Bomber took his tea and stood on the veranda, watching the waves break on the shore through the chain link security fence and tasting the salty tang on the morning breeze as it washed over him. As the tea cleansed his mouth, he began to feel more human.

Out on the beach, he could see a horse and rider galloping along the shoreline. The horse was gray and moved with powerful strides which created small plumes of spray as its hooves struck the wet sand. The rider moved easily with the rhythm of the horse. As they drew closer, he recognized the rider as his Platoon Commander Richard Blaze.

Finishing his tea, he then went into the rooms occupied by his section and ensured everyone was up, before walking to the dining hall and helping himself to breakfast – eggs, bacon, beans, toast, and of course another mug of tea.

As he was eating, Sean and Patrick joined him. Patrick had the biggest pile of food that anyone could have crammed onto the plate and Bomber wondered how he managed to eat so much but still stay slim? Sean, on the other hand, had a modest portion but seemed to increase in girth after each meal.

Sean said it was a family trait. He took after his Dad and Patrick, the Mother in physique, but both took after the mother facially. Patrick qualified that by saying Dad was not pretty to look at having been a bare knuckle fighter doing the rounds of pubs. The pubs would hold, illegal, but very lucrative fight nights either in the cellar or in the pub backyard.

Apparently, he was very successful and made a reputation for himself. He also made a lot of money. His career ended when he took a beating that left him somewhat punch drunk and unable to work for a long time.

He now worked as the pot man at his local pub which had lots of black and white photographs of him as a fighter and customers would often ask to be photographed with him.

The day was spent carrying out routine stuff, in the morning a session on the thirty-yard range, weapon cleaning then a double period of physical training in the gym run by a huge instructor who later became a Commonwealth champion and Olympian at field events.

After lunch, they rested through the heat of the afternoon, and later the Company had a swimming competition between the Platoons. It was a hilarious event. Everyone had to take part in each race and try each stroke, breast, crawl, and backstroke. How none of them drowned, Bomber could only wonder. He had no idea how the scoring worked but watching those who had never tried backstroke before had everyone in stitches. Some seemed to do more under the water than on top of it.

Bomber was surprised that evening by the lads coming in to his room and then insisting on taking him to the NAAFI for a beer. As he entered, a loud cheer broke out and the singing of happy birthday. Bomber wondered how they had known. Then he realized as Blaze and Doyle stepped forward and Blaze pushed a beer into Bomber's hand, saying, "Happy birthday. I wondered sometimes if you would make eighteen." He laughed and then slapped him on the back.

They had even organized a curry supper but before they could start eating, someone shouted speech and others took up the chant.

What the hell do I say? thought Bomber.

"Come on, get on with it the beer getting warm," cried a voice.

"Okay," said Bomber, "I would just like to say thank you for the party and beer. Thanks for everything we have shared together and for looking out for each other and here's a toast to the best Platoon in the Regiment." Bomber raised his glass amid loud cheers and a chorus of 'the best Platoon'.

The evening past in a haze of corny jokes about 'letting kids into a man's army', and 'I joined when they needed men not just feeding them'.

'Cesar was in charge when I joined' and so on.

As the evening went on, Bomber was glad that the next day would be a day off as he was sure he would have a hell of a hangover in the morning.

"Well, you survived some action and have made acting corporal," said Doyle, slapping Bomber on the back with such force that he thought his spine would be permanently damaged. "They did a good job on you at that… what's it called again?"

"Infantry Junior Leaders' Regiment," he replied proudly.

"That's it. Tell me how it worked?"

"If you pass the exam at the recruiting office at fifteen, you go to Oswestry, Park Hall Camp. There you spend two years doing all the stuff to turn you into, as they call it, a junior leader."

"So what's the difference to recruit training?"

They go into things in more depths than they do at recruit training. Lots of drill, weapon training, range work, tactics, survival stuff, and so-called character and leadership development. The courses include education in English, military accounting and more."

By now, a small group had gathered and Bomber had an audience including Blaze who interjected, "Who were the instructors for this unit?"

"It's mostly senior NCOs and officers from the different Infantry Regiments. I was in a Company that covered six different Regiments. We had instructors from each including our own." Bomber rattled off a couple of names that both Blaze and Doyle recognized them.

"Well, I had no idea that the army had such a place. Let's hope they keep up the good work."

As the party broke up, Bomber wandered back to his room wondering how so much had happened to him in such short a time. How had he survived some of the things that had come his way? But mostly, how lucky he was to be in such a good platoon that had now become his family!

Chapter 16
Justice, Torture, and Death

Two days later, Bomber and the Dammed were back on foot patrols out of the Police barracks in Crater city. The barracks was a grim place comprising of several large stone-built two-story blocks surrounded by a high solid-looking wall. The main entrance was covered by a sentry box manned by a lone policeman armed with an LMG.

Bomber and the rest of the Platoon were not happy about the policeman and the LMG pointing at them when they came in the gates. If he decides to become a turncoat, he could cut down a patrol in a very short time particularly if they were in a vehicle.

Blaze must have felt the same as he ordered that when approaching and leaving the police station by vehicle that they would dismount from the vehicles and split to both sides of the road and wave the vehicles in or out. This would result in them being multiple targets with a chance of returning fire on anyone foolish enough to fire at them.

The daytime patrols were accompanied by at least one police officer who dealt with the routine law and order, the patrol protecting him from being killed while carrying out his duties. On the whole, the policemen were friendly with the soldiers but occasionally a surly one who clearly resented the soldiers would be allocated to the patrol.

This never worked well and some even tried to start trouble by stirring up the locals as they went round with the patrol. On one such day, Blaze took the offending policeman into a side alley and gave him a real dressing down in his own language which seemed to shock and frighten the man. He was never allocated to any of our patrols again.

It was on one of these patrols that Bomber saw mob justice handed out for the first time. They were standing in a small

164

market areas when a shout went up and suddenly a small mob had a boy of about thirteen pinned down on the ground and were beating him. Bomber later described it as being like a pack of hyenas on a downed antelope. By the time the patrol had forced its way through and pushed back the mob, the boy was dead.

Bomber looked at the body of the boy. He looked starved. His ragged clothes had been ripped away revealing the wounds on his body, one of which looked like a stab wound. His face had been hit so many times that it was a pulp. Feeling sad and drained, Bomber felt unable to comprehend what had happened and why.

The police officer was talking to those that had not dispersed. He said they had told him that the boy was a thief who had been caught taking food from one of the stalls. *It appeared*, he thought, *it was acceptable for the mob to dish out their type of justice even on a child.*

The policeman made no attempt to arrest anyone or take down any notes. He merely asked Blaze to radio in for a vehicle to take the body away.

The patrol kept the area clear of curious onlookers until the police Land Rover arrived. The driver and passenger took some cloth from the vehicle and wrapped the body in it. Then without any care, they threw the body into the back of the Land Rover. The way they lifted the body and tossed it so easily into the back of the vehicle told Bomber that it could not have weighed more than about four or five stone.

Bomber reflected on how desperate the boy must have been to try and steal food in broad daylight in a crowded market place, crowded with people who he knew would show him little mercy if caught. He was beginning to think clearly again and he saw that there were beggars on almost every corner of the market. Some were blind. Others had limbs missing.

One in particular, who was never too far away from the patrol, was a legless man, squatting on a board with small wheels fitted to it. The man held a wooden block in each hand and used these to propel himself along by pushing on the ground.

Bomber or one of the lads often gave him a few Dinars or buy him an ice cold drink when they happened to be by a Stim seller.

He would always smile and pour out words praising us to Allah. The lads began thinking of him as a sort of lucky mascot becoming known as 'Speedy' because he could scoot along at quite a pace on his board.

Bomber wondered if he was friendly or someone paid by the NLF to keep tags on the patrols' movements.

Night patrols were different in that a policeman was rarely allocated to accompany them. This was explained as a shortage of funds to pay officer's overtime or they were on sick leave.

Bomber and the others put it down to the fact that they were more likely to be attacked at night and the police did not want to be around.

The heat of the day seemed to be trapped between the buildings and even at two in the morning, it was hot enough to sap the energy from the body and make the mind drowsy. Bomber looked back along the street scanning alleyways and shuttered windows but saw nothing to alarm him. Ten yards ahead of him he saw Blaze stop at an alleyway and bent down before moving on. As Bomber drew level with the same alleyway, he saw Speedy looking up at him. Speedy smiled and for the first time he noticed that Speedy had beautiful even white teeth, his only good feature in a scarred and broken body.

At a junction where the patrol should have gone straight ahead, Blaze stopped telling Bomber and his section to take cover and watch while he and the rest went left and circled round to come back one block on when they would be facing back towards them.

"Is this a tip off from Speedy?" Bomber asked.

"Yes," replied Blaze, "there may be some gunmen in the alleyway half way down the street. Once I am in position, we will move down to flush them out and you can take out anyone trying to escape your way."

Bomber and the other members of the section took cover using doorways and vehicles and then waited. Looking down the street, Bomber could see an alleyway on both sides of the street. He wondered if there was a gunman or was it a set up?

Twenty minutes or so later, Bomber could see the rest of the patrol leap frogging down the street towards the alleyway. Suddenly from the right-hand side, a burst of automatic fire was sprayed into the street. The gunman had fired without aiming his

166

weapon, just poking it round the corner and pulling the trigger emptying the magazine. The patrol immediately returned fire but Bomber and his section could not fire for fear of hitting their own men.

After a few moments, Bomber watched the patrol approach the alleyway but apart from a few empty cases, the alley was empty. The dissidents could have escaped through any of a dozen doorways leading into the buildings in the alley or through the warren of side alleys.

It was clear that without the warning the patrol would have been hit hard from close range. Bomber wondered if Speedy was an informant in the pay of the sneaky beakies or had he just warned us because he did not believe in the violence of the dissidents.

After picking up the empty cases and pushing through the alley for a few blocks, the Platoon gave up and headed back towards the police station. Just as they were arriving at the police station, they heard the distinctive crack of pistol fire a few blocks away and Blaze led the patrol in that direction but was stopped by the radio operator telling him HQ had said to ignore it.

It later filtered down that it was two undercover patrols from different units mistaking each other for dissident and having a shootout. Luckily, they realized the error and stopped shooting at each other before there were any casualties.

"Crappy shooting if you ask me," said Sean when we heard and laughed. Speaking to Bomber in a hushed voice, he said, "Could've been us if we had stayed on that job."

Bomber agreed. With so many groups operating in the city and not knowing who was who, it could easily end up with a friendly on friendly shoot out.

It was three days later that Doyle and his patrol found the body on a small patch of waste ground. Speedy had been brutally tortured. His bright white teeth had been smashed. His tongue had been cut out and both hands crudely hacked off. It appeared he had been allowed to bleed to death.

"Jesus Christ!" exclaimed Jos, "the poor bastard suffered enough in life without any legs, reduced to begging living on scraps sleeping in doorway. What sort of sick bastard would do that to him?"

Bomber felt that the world was full of pain and death but the wrong people were on the receiving end of it. Speedy had chosen for whatever reason to help them and Speedy's choice cost him a painful death that he did not deserve.

Bomber felt deflated and wondered if his death had been the result of them showing some kindness to Speedy in public and the dissidents had decided to make an example of him or had he been spotted tipping them off.

Bomber could see that the torture and death of Speedy had affected the lads a lot and they swore revenge. As they did not know who his killers were, their anger would be vented on anyone who crossed them in the next few days. They could all be seen as Speedy killers.

On reflection, Bomber noticed a hardening and less tolerant attitude in the Platoon and especially in his, as he now thought of them, Irish lads. He wondered if he himself had changed and if anyone had noticed. He had found himself becoming less affected by the squalor, pain, and death that were the daily diet in this Godforsaken place. He knew that in the future he would shoot to kill at the slightest hint of a threat to himself or the Platoon.

The Crater patrols drew to an end and everyone was happy to leave the City. The Platoon was moved to standby duty based in the barracks. This consisted of being dressed, armed and ready to go at thirty minutes' notice. That meant that they could relax, read, or play cards, or just catch up on sleep. The notice could change to fifteen minutes indicating that a deployment was about to happen but the lads still treated it as thirty minutes' standby but knowing that they had to be faster out of the blocks if called.

'Immediate' meant just that sitting in the vehicles engines running. Unlike the units that were now being brought in on six-month tours and being equipped with the Saracen armored personnel carrier (APC), the regiment was still using trucks which were vulnerable to small arms fire and grenade attacks. So the drill was to sit in the back with two looking over the cab, ready to fire and the rest facing outwards in the back plus two facing rearwards.

Some of the drivers with the help of the various platoons had placed sandbags inside the floor of the truck and against the sides to give some protection. Other than that, it was a tin hat and army issue shirt for protection.

It was at this time, about February 1965, that some bright sparks in the higher echelons of power decided that everyone needed to know when to fire their weapons. Every soldier was issued with a card telling them when they could open fire. As it was printed on yellow paper, it became known as the 'Yellow Card'. None of the lads were impressed by this and Blaze had to remind them that it was a directive that they could not ignore.

At about the same time, rewards were being offered to the locals for information leading to finds of weapons and explosives or the handing in of, without any questions being asked.

Sean had one of the leaflets that were in Arabic and English and he read out the price list. "This is great. We can make some money out of this," he exclaimed. "For a grenade you get twenty-five Dinars, a machine-gun, four hundred Dinars, and a Bazooka six hundred, and the list goes on."

Bomber was amused by the idea and smiling, pointed out, "Only one problem with that Sean. They will not give money to us for anything we find."

"Aye, but I have a plan for that. We find the stuff grab a local we know and then split it forty, sixty, then that way we will have plenty of beer coupons." Sean said it with such conviction that he began to think he was actually serious, was he?

"Trouble is the Rag Head you pick will take it into the police station and claim the reward the police will throw him in the cells and take the money for themselves. So you are pissing in the wind me old mate." John's utterance was a bit of a surprise. Not normally given to speaking long sentences, he sat down as if worn out by the effort and closed his eyes ending Sean's moneymaking scheme there and then.

The 'Yellow Card' became a topic for endless discussion. Finally, it stopped when Doyle told them to shut up and follow orders. Bomber pointed out that the politicians who a year ago had little interest in the events in Aden, now were suddenly worried about world opinion, with big bad British soldiers Willy Nilly shooting poor Arab tribesmen whenever they felt like it.

It seemed that Egyptian President Nasser pot stirring and propaganda was paying off and many politicians were asking the question: why are we here in Aden? It had little importance to

British trade routes anymore? Perhaps they didn't think the peaceful people of Aden had a right to live their lives without fear of being killed just because they were of a different tribe or religion.

Bomber thought the reward scheme had some merits but the rational that the local population would risk their lives or that of their families for such paltry amounts he considered laughable.

Too little too late was also the sections' considered opinion. Nasser had been running his propaganda campaign against the British in the Middle East since the Suez debacle. With every Arab now able to obtain a cheap transistor radio, he could broadcast his anti-British tirade twenty-four hours a day every day of the year, reaching even the remotest villages.

There was also the appearance of the NLF's own leaflets instructing the locals on how to sabotage the police, army, and government such as, pouring sugar into petrol tanks of vehicles, setting fire to cars, and destroying air conditioners at offices or houses.

As far as Bomber could tell, this was about as effective as the British reward scheme leaflets.

The day had past peacefully and Bomber felt refreshed but for some reason restless. Then at four in the morning, the Platoon was put on immediate and almost without pause or briefing, they roared out of camp heading towards Sheikh Othman. Just on the fringe of the Soukh (market), they set up two road blocks. A few minutes later, more vehicles arrived, setting up more road blocks, until no one could enter or leave the area without going through an army checkpoint.

The orders were clear no one in or out.

As the dawn brightened the sky, more troops and police arrived. It was clear to Bomber that this was going to be a large-scale cordon and search operation that could well take all day. Bomber had seen several different cap badges including the Royal Marines in the troops that were deployed.

Slowly the Soukh came to life and as people emerged and started opening up their stalls and roadside shops. Bomber was amazed at how little interest was shown in the presents of so many soldiers and police.

When he mentioned it to Sean, he replied, "You can bet your boots that someone in the police has already tipped them off."

"Could well be right, but let's hope we get some result for the effort."

The heat of the day was beginning to increase and so was the temperature of some of the locals that wanted to leave. Soon an unruly crowd had gathered at their roadblock. Bomber could see several men on the fringe of the crowd stirring it up. Pointing these out to Doyle, he replied, "I see the wee bastards and I want you to get three of your guys to target them from the back of the vehicle where they can keep a close eye on them."

Now the crowd was beginning to pull at the coil of barbed wire and Doyle ordered fix bayonets which were present over the wire. The people at the front touching the wire tried to pull back but were forced forward by the surge of people at the back and the troublemakers continued to urge them on.

Doyle realized that the people at the front would be pushed down onto the wire and crushed by the people behind unless fast action was taken. He ordered two of the guys to each fire a warning shot into the air.

The shots rang out and the crowd, with the exception of those caught in the wire, scattered, most running back into the stalls. Using the radio, Doyle explained the situation while the unfortunates were worked free from the wire and released.

Checking with John and Jos, who were on the truck watching the agitators who could be seen standing together by one of the stalls talking and looking at the road block, the tallest one of the three seemed to be in charge and Doyle, already one step ahead of more trouble, ordered a snatch party to go after them to stop them geeing up another crowd.

Bomber and his lads were given the job. Doyle would stand on the vehicle and pass direction over the radio if the trio moved.

Working away from the agitators stall so that they could approach unseen from the left, Bomber was glad he had the backing of his guys who he knew he could rely on in a close quarter skirmish.

When they were two stalls away, Bomber knew that they would soon be seen and bunched everyone up, then charged catching the agitators by surprise. This amazed Bomber as he had expected the locals to have passed the word.

Seeing the soldiers coming at them, the three turned to run. Two of them crashed into the stall in a panic. The third jumped over them and fled into the Soukh. They were on the other two in a flash pinning them to the floor and secured their hands behind their back. There was little point on trying to chase down the third man. He would have disappeared into the maze of stalls and buildings.

The stall holder started shouting and waving his hands at the devastation of his stall and vegetable. A small crowd had gathered and presented a danger to Bomber and his small group especially if they turned nasty. Roughly pushing their way through the crowd, they frog-marched the two men back to the road block. The Company Commander and CSM were already there with his Company HQ team. The CSM took charge of the agitators and searched them. The Company Commander surprised everyone by marching over to the stallholder with three of his team members. He spoke to the stallholder and then helped to put the stall back together. He then paid over a fist full of Dinars as compensation to the stallholder and then shook hands with him and it was clear that the locals witnessing this act were impressed and thought that the stallholder had been fairly treated.

Bomber was not surprised that they never had any more trouble at the road block for the rest of the day.

The CSM had found dozens of leaflets in Arabic on the two men probably anti-British stuff and two wicked-looking flick knifes, which could be openly purchased in the market.

A police Land Rover had arrived and the two agitators were handed over and with a few punches, curses, and kicks, from the police. They were persuaded to get into the vehicle. It was obvious these police officers were not sympathetic to their cause.

At about midday, they were ordered to open the road block but to stay in position as the searchers and others withdrew. As they drove away, Bomber felt his empty stomach growl for the want of food. It had been sixteen hours since they had had supper the evening before, more than food he could have murder one of char wallahs pint mugs of tea.

Back in barracks, they enjoyed a late lunch or early supper. As they were on thirty minutes' standby, they all crashed out on top of their beds to get some much-needed sleep. Bomber felt himself sink into a bottomless pit of darkness and even the monotonous clanking of the wobbly ceiling fan could not disturb him.

The next day started like any other with a cheery shout of "Char boss?" from char wallah. He sipped his tea and watched the sea break on the shore – breakfast, weapon cleaning, and just waiting. The British Forces Broadcasting Service (BFBS) never went off the air and was a favorite with all the guys. So when the music stopped and a voice a little shaken but defiant announced that the station was under attack, everyone sat up and took notice. The station was at Steamer Point and housed in a strong-looking stone building but had little in the way of security.

On hearing the announcement, the Platoon got ready and loaded up on to the vehicles and by the time Blaze and Doyle arrived a few minutes later, the engines were running.

On arrival at the station, they put a cordon two hundred yards out and Blaze went to inspect the damage and check for casualties. Bomber watch as a vehicle patrol from HMS Sabre circled the building in a clockwise direction and wondered what they hope to achieve.

It had been a rocket attack. It had struck the building causing very little damage to the station ability to broadcast and there weren't any casualties.

So the Spider strikes again. *Time he was taken out before he really gets lucky*, thought Bomber.

He didn't need to brief his section to pay particular attention to rooftops and the back of pickup trucks. He knew they would be doing that. However, he went round and instead spoke to each, discussing the likely sites from their positions.

Suddenly the radios were full of reports of another explosion at Steamer Point. They did not need to be told; they could hear it and see the smoke.

While Doyle stayed at the station with half the platoon, Blaze led Bomber and one section at the run towards the explosion which they now could see was at a restaurant that was a favorite of many of the British civilians' workers. There would not be any soldiers in there as they had been banned from going out of barracks earlier in the year.

Blaze halted the men about hundred and fifty yards away in case anyone was waiting to have a go at the security forces, ambulances, or police as they arrived.

Bomber could see people helping others out of the restaurant. Some just staggered around or slumped down on the ground once clear of the smoking building.

Blaze sent Bomber and his section to the left of the building to clear that side and the back while he and one section worked the front and the right-hand side.

As of Donnie, his medic side coming out wanted to go and help the people but that was left to the paramedics and ambulance service. Their job was to make sure no further attacks happen and if possible trap the original culprits. Meeting up with Blaze, Bomber told him as far as could be determined no one was lurking in wait to attack the security forces arriving but not to rule out the Spider.

Deploying so that they could cover all sides of the building and protecting the ambulances and medic who were now on the scene patching people up and taking them away to hospital, Bomber wondered how many other vulnerable buildings like this would be hit in the coming days. There was no way the army could cover every location.

The fire service arrived and damped down the building which for some reason had not caught fire but had large amounts of black smoke billowing from it.

They returned to barracks feeling a little deflated at not catching anyone for the two attacks but if they thought they were going to get a rest, they were mistaking. The Company Commander had called a briefing which took place in the dining room and the Company Commander had the look of a man who meant business. The Company was to deploy to a village called Danaba or Dana on some maps and cordon it ready for a search. Two soldiers had been killed there today but two had escaped and had reported that the place was full of dissidents.

Chapter 17
Their Finest Hour!

Leaving at last light, they bumped and rumbled along with a large escort of Saladins. They took turns at trying to sleep but just when Bomber started to nod off, the truck would hit another set of deep pot holes, jolting him so hard that his teeth felt that they would come loose.

Eventually they came to a halt and completed the rest of the journey on foot. Circling the village was not too difficult but it was clear they had not gone undetected as the village dogs started snarling and barking fit to wake the dead.

As dawn broke, the Saladins rumbled up and took station their powerful guns trained on the village. Bomber felt himself shudder at his thoughts that if the dissidents were there and decided to fight, a lot of innocent people would be killed.

As the sky brightened, Bomber had his first good look at the village. It was larger than he had thought it would be. On one side, he could see was a cluster of mud houses the color of dung. Some were hovels, others larger and more cared for. To one side stood a larger, more impressive building that had once had a covering of paint over the mud dung rendering but now it had faded and in places disappeared completely giving an overall impression of neglected dominance over the rest of the village.

Twelve policemen had accompanied the Company Commander. The senior of them had a megaphone which he now raised to his mouth and spoke rapidly into it. Whatever he said had doors opening and people stared sullenly at the police and soldiers. Next, the search teams moved in and began a systematic search of the houses while the police and some British guys in civvies questioned the inhabitants.

Bomber later discovered that the civvies were Special Branch (SB) who would be trying to identify any wanted dissidents on their list.

Bomber found himself getting bored after three hours of standing in the cordon and as the next of his section to his left and right were too far away to speak to, there was little to help the time slip by.

Just as Bomber was thinking about opening fire on the plague of flies that were driving him mad, the CSM came along and told him to pull his section out and report to the Platoon Commander. Their position was being taken by one of the search teams that were being relieved for a rest. "Please to be out of the cordon." Bomber hurried the section to Blaze who stood in the shadow of one of the Saladins.

At Blaze's feet was an assortment of shovels, picks, and long steel probes that could be pushed into the earth for about six feet or into mud walls to locate any buried object, crude but effective.

Armed now with the search kit, they slung their rifles on their right shoulders with a slack sling. Should anything occur, the rifle could be swiveled forward underhand and into the firing position in a second.

Blaze led them to a small cluster of huts at the back of the grand house and instructed three of them to search the huts and Bomber, Jos, and John to scour the ground outside to see if they could detect any recently disturbed ground.

In the grounds surrounding the buildings were some sad-looking trees, the largest being a fig and some stunted date palms and what might be an apricot tree but Bomber was not sure. Secured by some lengths of rope to the fig tree were two goats, one of which had somehow gained the lowest large branch which stuck out from the trunk like an accusing finger and was happily eating the leaves and any green figs it could reach.

They spread out and quartered the ground after half an hour. They had not seen any sign of recent disturbance. Bomber was about to move to another spot when John called him over and pointed to a spot clear of the trees.

"What is it?" Bomber asked.

"Well, under the trees, there's leaves and stuff. Everywhere else is just dust and stones. Over there away from the trees, we have leaves as well as stones."

"Well spotted. Let's try it." And the three of them started to probe. The probe went in fairly easily, indicating loose soil and just as Jos had pushed it in about three quarters of its length, it stopped hard.

"Could just be a rock but the soil is loose, so it could be worth a dig," Jos looked at Bomber for support. Bomber nodded and grabbed a shovel.

Attracted by the digging, Blaze came over and watched. The soil came out easily. No pick axe was required and Bomber guessed that this was done in a hurry, perhaps just yesterday and passed his thoughts to Blaze who agreed.

Just as Bomber thought it was a setup, his shovel struck something metallic and he felt a surge of excitement. Now down on all fours, he and Jos cleared the dirt away with their hands.

Finally they pulled free an LMG wrapped in a thin blanked with ten magazines fully loaded. Beneath this was another bundle and when opened, there was a gasp. None of them had seen anything like this before and Blaze had to explain it, it was a Soviet-made rocket-propelled grenade launcher or RPG and was issued in great numbers to Soviet troops.

It looked a lot less clumsy than a 3.5 rocket launcher and Blaze explained that it was capable of destroying a Saladin.

In with the launcher were three of the rocket grenades and further scrapping around, Jos found a box containing ten British 36 grenades.

Blaze had sent for the Company Commander who was extremely pleased with the find and urged them all on to see what else they could find. Before anyone could start searching, a shout went up from one of the huts and they ran toward it, weapons at the ready.

The hut had a small doorway but no windows and contained three stalls in two of which were sad-looking donkeys munching on some dry grass. In the second stall stood Sean and to the side, Patrick, who had his rifle trained onto the section of wall where Sean's probe had gone through.

"Watch and listen," Sean said in a hushed voice.

He removed the probe and then inserted it in a lower point; a muffle cry was heard.

"Break the wall down," ordered Blaze, "and get those donkeys out of here."

With the stalls cleared, Sean could swing a pick axe and quickly brought down the thin partition wall that revealed a tall thin man trying to hold his hands up.

Getting him out was easy but Blaze wanted to know how he got in there and he showed them a cleverly made piece of wall near the joint of one of the stalls that could be removed and then pulled in place once he was inside. Even with their torches it was hard to detect.

The news of the discovery had reached the SB team and two of them came hotfooting to the group. After some discussion and checking various photographs, they agreed that it was the village leader who was a known supporter of the dissidents.

Handcuffing the luckless man, they marched away extremely happy but without so much as well done, lads had the rest of the day off and some beers on us.

Hopes were high now in the team and they were sure they would dig up a lot more goodies, but after another two hours they had discovered nothing. Hot, thirsty, and hungry they were sent to the CQMS who had arrived with a truck containing large hay boxes containing tea and stew and he was ladling it out in great quantities.

Sitting handcuffed by one of the Saladins was half a dozen sorry-looking men. Bomber guessed they were fifteen to thirty years old. Now and again, another would be added until there was ten altogether.

Donnie took out his water bottle and went to the men and gave them water, holding the bottle to their lips. They all drank greedily, gulping at the water as only very thirsty men could do.

"Oi!" snapped a voice from the side of the Saladin. It was the sentry who was supposedly guarding the men. "What the fuck do you think you are doing?" The sentry was one of the Saladin drivers and not known to the Dammed. Donnie looked him slowly up and down and the contempt on his face was clear to all. Donnie took a step towards the sentry who, seeing the look on Donnie's face, back peddled a few paces, nervously pulling his Sterling sub machinegun from his side to the front.

Donnie's arm shot out and pushed the Sterling up and back so the barrel struck the sentry under the chin and at the same time put his leg behind the shocked sentry who went down on his back side with Donnie still pushing the Sterling hard into the luckless man's chest.

Donnie's face was now just inches away from sentry and he spoke slowly and with venom.

"I'm doing it, you stupid bastard, because dead men cannot tell us anything and I'm saving you from a charge of murder by letting them die of thirst, you arsehole."

"What's going on?" a calm voice demanded. It was the CQMS, a stocky ruddy-faced individual who Bomber had never heard raise his voice.

"The sentry was objecting to us, giving the prisoners some water C/Sgt." (CQMS was addressed as Color Sgt.) Bomber had put his mess tin down and had stood up to speak.

"Well, they are not in our charge but the rules state they should be treated in the correct manner and given food and water," the C/Sgt. had spoken directly to the sentry whom Donnie had released and was now sitting looking bewildered.

"I'll have a word with the Provost Sgt. in a minute and get them fed and watered. In the meantime, no more trouble," he said this while looking at Bomber. With that, he turned and went back to ladling out food.

"Didn't know Donnie cared so much," Bomber said to Sean.

"He has always had a soft spot; should have been a medic not a bloody foot slogger. He's right though. Sometimes a little humanity in these situations can win us friends."

"Do you think we will find any more likely lads in the village?" asked Jos who had got a second helping of stew.

"I think the real fighters got clear before we turned up," said Sean.

"You think the police tipped them off or they just did a runner after the two squaddies were killed?" Bomber replied.

"Probably just did a runner. They must have known we would come after them."

"What do you make of these leaflets?" Jos asked, waving a piece of paper with Arabic writing on.

Bomber looked at the paper and then called over one of the policemen who had been speaking in English to the Platoon Commander earlier. The policeman explained that it was telling the villagers to leave the village by seven tomorrow morning with their belongings and livestock. After seven, the RAF would come and destroy the village.

"Fuck me. That's a bit bloody drastic. What have the kids and women done to deserve to have their homes destroyed?" said Sean. As the only married man with kids in the section, he felt protective towards them.

"Seems to me we will just be making enemies of those that were probably neutral before," said Bomber.

"I know if someone came and destroyed my house and village, I would want revenge." Sean was now getting angry at the thought of it happening in his home in Northern Ireland.

"Maybe the idea is to deny shelter and a base to the dissidents by people who are already sympathetic to their cause." The comments came from the Platoon Commander who was standing behind them holding a mess tin full of stew.

Doyle was beside him looking a bit annoyed by the indiscretion.

"We were not questioning orders sir, but the necessity of such an action in winning this war, sir." Bomber was now standing to address Blaze.

"It's perfectly natural to discuss these things but you have to see the bigger picture and understand the complexities of not just winning the battle but the whole war."

"Yes sir," they said in unison.

Blaze nodded and then walked away. Doyle followed but paused and said quietly, "You prats, look around before you speak in future," and strode off after Blaze.

"Sounds like a lot of bollocks to me. It will still make the neutrals hate us," Sean snapped and Bomber had to agree.

Two hours later, they were pulled back about three quarters of a mile and set up an OP and as the shadows lengthened, they could see through the binoculars, a trail of people trekking away from the village with their livestock. *Heading to God-knows-where*, thought Bomber, *no shelter or fire to cook on and to see their homes destroyed in the morning.*

The night passed slowly and even with Donnie producing mugs of tea at regular intervals, it did not seem to lift the gloom that had settlcd over them.

The dawn broke and the sun climbed up into the sky, bringing with it the sound of jet engines. They came in fast and low. Venom jet fighters fitted with rocket pods blasted the village at exactly five minutes after seven by Bomber's watch.

Jet after jet swooped and released its rockets. Bomber was not sure if it was an endless line of Venoms or just a few going round in a circle taking turns to blast the village.

The rocket attack lasted for what seemed hours but eventually ceased. The whole village was obscured by dust. In fact it had been pretty much like that since the first rockets exploded. So how the pilots knew what they were firing at, Bomber could only guess.

"Somebody, tell me that was the RAF's finest hour," John said, spitting dust from his mouth that had drifted as far as their position. Finally the dust cloud dispersed on the fresh breeze that had sprung up.

"I don't think they have finished," Patrick muttered, pointing up at a line of four engine propeller-driven Shackleton bombers. The Shackleton was similar in looks to the old World War Two Lancaster bomber and the non-flyers could be forgiven for thinking that was what they were. But these were sleeker, more powerful and sophisticated. Normally used by Coastal Command, they could carry an enormous load of various types of munitions.

Four of them flying in line a stern, passed high overhead, Bomber could not guess their altitude but hoped like hell that they were far enough away from the village in case any bombs fell short.

They all could hear the fall of the bombs and suddenly the rubble of the village exploded into the sky, the shockwave reaching them a second or two later. Again, the view was obscured by the dust cloud rising, signaling the final death blow of the village.

Back in barracks, they heard about a large house just north of Aden city which had received the same treatment. Apparently, it belonged to the man responsible for the Steamer Point restaurant bombing.

He was nowhere to be found, so those in the house were given just enough time to pack up and leave before the RAF flattened it.

'Petty revenge or justice?' Bomber was not sure but things were getting a lot worse with retaliation becoming. It seemed more indiscriminate and perhaps this was the reality of this type of warfare.

Chapter 18
Ambush, Raids, and Booby Traps

The Company was once again paraded in the dining room and the Company Commander and an SB Officer gave a situation and political briefing.

At the start, the emphasis was on what was happening between FLOSY and the NFL. The current FLOSY leader one Mohammed Salem Basindwah was in exile in Cairo and considered himself a politician rather than a terrorist and was trying to run FLOSY as a political group rather than a terrorist group. The NFL lacked any conventional organization but was headed by a Qahtan Shaabi and he was gaining in popularity and had undoubtedly got the lion share of arms, ammunition, and support from Egypt, which meant the local tribes in the hinterland were beginning to flock, no matter how loosely to the NFL. On the coast, their support in Aden and the surrounding villages was also growing and was more organized.

The SB officer glibly glossed over the FRA and the National Guard as if they no longer existed and Bomber guessed that they had become so infiltrated that for practical reasons, they were out of the fight unless they decided to turn on us.

There then was a short pep talk on how well the army was doing against the dissidents and that we were winning.

Bomber heard some snorts of derision at that, indicating that not all were convinced of this.

Now came the end line, all about how we were to stabilize the situation here in Aden for a peaceful handover to an elected assembly and so on.

Jos who had lost interest some time ago muttered, "Fat chance of that happening. This lot could not agree on anyone to lead them except at the point of a gun."

After the Company was dismissed, Bomber and the section headed to the NAAFI for some ice-cold beer. Settling down, they heard talk from one of the other Company guys, a Cpl. called Mathews, of a big increase in grenade and shooting attacks.

"They have mostly been in the Shekh Othman, Crater and the Ma'alla area, almost two hundred in just three days," he said.

However, he was somewhat dismissive of the grenade attacks. "It's just throwing blind and then legging it, so sometimes they miss by miles. The shootings, now they're different. Close up, in the street walking up behind the target and pop in the back of the head then away. Professionally done, so make sure you have someone watching your back on patrol."

Mathews took a sip of his beer and carried on. "The SB guy doing the talking today. He's from the Aden Intelligence Centre (AIC), apparently undermanned as only we Brits could be. Most of them are ex-colonial police officers from defunct British colonies."

Mathews now had a captive audience and paused, looking at his empty beer glass. Sean pushed a fresh can to him. He nodded filled his glass and carried on. "They have built a new detention center at Mansura manned by RAF and Army MPs. The center is far better than our barracks. Very smart, I know I delivered a prisoner there just two days ago."

Several days later on a hot and humid evening, Bomber and Doyle were on vehicle patrol. They had driven through Crater city and came up to the top of the hill, where the road past through a col. This was the main way into the city from the inland side. They heard an explosion but did not see the explosion site. A radio call informed them that it was a rocket attack on the AIC building which was just over the col. Driving hard, they crested the rise and looked down to the building which was on their left. Leaving the vehicles, they split either side of the road leapfrogging; they made their way towards the building.

The building had suffered little damage and as the staff did not work there at night, there were no casualties but they were ordered to stay put and secure the area.

An hour later, two SB turned up in a yellow mini car. After a brief word with Doyle, they entered the building. Bomber recognized one of them as the one who gave the company briefing a few days ago. After a lengthy wait, they finally got the order to return to base.

Three days later, the vehicles were making hard work of climbing up the hill on the same road. Suddenly they heard multiple gunshots from further up the hill. They pushed the vehicle to the limit, eventually arriving at a small roundabout just before the same AIC building. On the far side of the roundabout sat a bullet-riddled yellow mini.

They spread out and took cover looking for any likely target. Donnie with the first aid bag went to the vehicle without any thought for his own safety.

Bomber cursed him and applauded him at the same time. It took guts to think of the other guy rather than a gunman waiting to take out the first to arrive at the scene.

Turning to look at Bomber, Donnie gave a thumbs-down. Doyle called it in to HQ.

Bomber with Sean approached the vehicle. Bomber saw it was their SB man who had given the talk to the Company. He had been shot numerous times at close range and Bomber guessed there were between thirty and fifty spent case on the ground.

Shaking his head, Sean said, "Must have been two or three of them, didn't stand a chance poor sod."

Now people were coming out of the AIC building several had pistols in their hands, all wanting to know if the car occupant was still alive.

Bomber and Sean shook their heads and muttered "Sorry" to each in turn.

The area was soon crowded, SB men, MPs, and an ambulance. The MPs took over and Bomber was relieved to get away and carry on with their patrol. As they did, he could not help thinking the personnel security for those guys was crap. What a stupidly exposed place to have the AIC!

Unprotected against rocket attack and car bombs, no hard protection by the army and traveling in easily identifiable civilian cars, crazy and a waste of a valuable man. *Valuable man*, thought Bomber. *We don't even know his name.*

The section heard later on the grapevine that the AIC had been moved to a safe compound in the oil refinery at little Aden, a much better protected area but as always too late for some.

Two days had passed. The platoon was at the thirty-meter range zeroing their weapons. When the operations officer turned up and took the platoon commander to one side.

"What do you think that's about?" asked Sean.

"Whatever it is, you can bet we get the shitty end of the stick," Patrick replied.

When the operations officer had left, Blaze called everyone together. "As you know, the AIC is seriously under manned for active operations. The army is to assist the SB with teams to conduct raids and the picking up of dissident. To this end, we will deploy to Little Aden for the next two weeks, so pack your kit and be ready to move in two hours."

On arrival at Little Aden Oil Refinery, the platoon was split into three groups. Two ten-man assault teams were allocated to one SB officer and the remainder of the platoon would act as personnel bodyguards for the SB officers when off duty, traveling to and from the AIC and any other time as deemed necessary. Someone had decided they could not afford to lose any more of the intelligence community.

Bomber and three section plus two of one section and Blaze made up one team and Doyle was to lead the other.

They practice over and over again blocking off a building and doing entry and house clearing drills. Soft entry's, hard entry's, man down and so on, until Blaze was satisfied that they had covered every possible scenario and could react to almost any situation that might arise.

At one o'clock in the morning, Bomber was woken from a deep sleep by Doyle shaking him and flashing a torch. "Get the lads together for a briefing in the main building in ten minutes."

Rolling off his camp bed and pulling on his boots, Bomber called to Sean and the others to shake a leg and get moving. Assembled in the building were all the teams and bodyguards, some seventy soldiers from two different regiments.

One of the SB men stood in the front and started the briefing. He was a tall, weather-beaten-looking fellow, the sort that had been around, the seen-it-done-it type.

"We are after this man," he said, passing a sheaf of photographs around. "His name is Mohammed Salam Basindwah, leader of FLOSY. We have heard that he has left Cairo. He is here to see family and do some reorganizing of

FLOSY." He paused and waited while the photographs did the rounds.

"He could be at any of five different locations and our aim is to hit them all at once. One team per location, your team leaders," he paused, and nodded towards five of the SB officers, "they will brief you. I cannot emphasize strongly enough the importance of hitting each target at the same time. We will leave at O four hundred hours."

With that, the team leaders took over. Our SB man introduced himself as simply number one and we were to be team number one. He had a street map with the house we would search. He had drawn in doorways, one front and one at the back. The front one was easy enough facing the street but the rear had a high wall forming a courtyard. The wall had a small keyhole doorway that would be strong and secured.

Two ladders would be taken to access the courtyard. Bomber, Sean, Jos, and John were allocated the task of entering the yard and securing the backdoor.

At four o'clock, they drove slowly and as quietly as possible from the AIC. Bomber's Land Rover had the two ladders secured one on each side of the vehicle. In all, there were three vehicles per team and as each team broke off to its own location. Bomber felt a thrill, as for once they had the initiative and were taking the fight to the enemy rather than just responding to an attack.

Cruising the vehicles with lights off and engines just idling enough to keep moving until they moved to within about a hundred yards of the target house, then they waited. Finally after what had seemed an eternity, number one gave the signal to go.

Jogging with the ladders between them, Bomber entered the alley behind the house, carefully placing the ladder against the wall. He climbed up to the top reaching down for the other ladder. Sitting on the wall, he felt exposed and vulnerable and quickly positioned the ladder down the other side. Almost falling down the ladder in his haste, Bomber landed awkwardly and his rifle caught him in the midriff, winding him. Luckily the others moved fast and were at the door by the time Bomber had regained his feet.

Joining the others, Bomber knew he had been lucky. If there had been an armed guard at the back, he would have been dead by now.

He had no time for reflection as they heard the crash of the front door being broken in. Without being told, Sean swung the heavy door ram at the lock. The door ram was a yard-long piece of heavy timber fitted with an iron ram at the front. Two webbing strap handles allowed the handler to get a full swing and drive the ram home. It was heavy and solid and Sean was just the man to use it.

With one swing, the door shattered around the lock and collapsed in under the weight of Sean and the ram. Then they were in and leapfrogging through. They cleared all the rooms at the back. Working their way upstairs, they could hear frightened cries of family members in the bedrooms. From the briefing, Bomber knew this was the target's family home and would be fully occupied.

At a large and grand-looking wooden door, Bomber paused, waiting for the others to get ready. Trying the handle, Bomber felt the door give and then flung it open. Sean and Jos dived into the room breaking left and right. Bomber followed. John had been left at the rear door to prevent anyone who may get past them from leaving.

In the room which was pleasantly decorated with several wall tapestry and some solid-looking carved furniture was a large bed with a terrified women in it, covering herself with a blanket pulled up to her neck.

Searching the room and checking under the bed took seconds and revealed nothing. Bomber could see that the bed had been slept in by two people from the pillows, so where was the other person?

They moved the chest of draws from the wall – nothing. Jos went to the shuttered window and pulled it open and let out a shout. Reaching down, he grabbed an arm and pulled. Bomber raced over to assist and they had an arm each at the end of which was an overweight bearded man wearing just some shorts. With some encouragement, he climbed back in through the window looking frightened and exhausted from hanging by his fingers to the windowsill.

Number one arrived and confirmed this was their man who was then allowed to get dressed. The women was shouting and wailing to such a pitch that Bomber was just about to tell Sean to take her out of the room when the man spoke to her quietly in Arabic and she subsided to a gentle sobbing.

Back at the AIC, the SB officers were over the moon. This was their biggest coup so far and was seen as a strike back for the killing of their colleague at the old center.

Two days later, Bomber saw number one who was their team leader and he looked down and angry both at the same time. Bomber asked what the problem was and he blurted out in an uncharacteristic display of anger that Mohammed Salam Basindwah had been released put on a plane and sent back to Cairo.

Realizing he might have said too much, he shut up, turned, and walked away. Entering the main build, he slammed the door so violently that the wall shook.

Bomber passed the information to Blaze who said he already knew but that I was not to discuss it with the lads or anyone else.

As if to make up for the loss of their prize, they went out on raids every night. Number one would come for them at about midnight, brief them and they would head out in the dead hours, entering a building, arresting the occupants, never women or children, search and collect anything of interest and return to the AIC before dawn.

If they were acting on solid intelligence, Soukh gossip or even a whim of the SB officer, Bomber never knew but they were busy. Each night was the same and everything was running smoothly until the tenth night of their two-week stint.

As usual, number one came in around midnight and briefed the team on a house to be hit in the Sheikh Othman area. All the team knew the area well from endless patrols and it was a bit like grenade alley. Not a night or day went by without a patrol being attacked by a grenade or occasionally a shooter.

Blazed asked how reliable the information was and number one shrugged and said, "About as good as we get off the street."

Blaze suggested we exercise extreme caution on dealing with this one as it could be a setup. Number one agreed and Blaze outlined a plan of approach.

Two blocks out from the target house, the team dismounted from the Land Rovers leaving one escort with each driver. Blaze led the remainder via alleyways and areas in shadow until they could see the building, which was now about fifty yards away.

Blaze told Bomber to stay there while he took John and Donnie to the rear of the building and then he would radio for the vehicles to move.

The plan was simple. The vehicles would drive to the corner of the street and see if any fire was directed at them. If it was, they would withdraw and we would return fire. If no enemy fire occurred, then the vehicles would do a drive past. If nothing happened, then Bomber, Patrick, and Sean would enter the house.

As the vehicles were approaching, number one touched Bomber's arm and pointed to a figure on the flat roof raising itself up as if just being disturbed by the noise of the engines.

"I've got him," whispered Sean from the shadow of a doorway.

The vehicles were now paused at the corner and Bomber detected rather than saw a slight movement at the wooden-slatted shutter of the window below the figure on the roof. At first, he could not work it out but, then he realized that one of the lower slats was missing and the first couple of inches of a rifle barrel were poking out with the moonlight glinting clearly off it.

The lead vehicle started to move slowly forward and the window gunman must have panicked, for he opened fire too early, hitting the radiator area of the vehicle. The driver did a textbook shoulder roll out of the vehicle and sprinted away. At the same time, the escort returned fire as did Bomber at the shutter which disintegrated under the impact of three SLRs 7.62 mm high velocity rounds cutting through it.

Sean had concentrated on the roof but no fire had come from there; either the figure had not been a gunman or he was caught off guard by the shutter man opening fire without any warning.

As soon as the firing stopped, Blaze ordered everyone forward. Sean lugging the battering ram never even stopped but crashed into the door as he hit it with the ram. The left side of the door caved inwards at an angle and Sean disappeared in a heap on the inside. Bomber dodged Sean and went right against the wall and there was a series of grunts and swearing from Sean as Patrick, number one, and Jamie, who had been the vehicle escort trod on him as they charged in and covered the room.

The only light in the room was from the doorway. A weak moon washed the entrance but did not penetrate any further. As

Bomber allowed himself time for his eyes to adjust to the darkness, he could just make out a stairs going up directly in front of him.

Now, thought Bomber, *torches or stay in the dark?*

"Can anyone see anything?" Bomber hissed.

"I think there's a doorway on the left of the stairs but can't see bugger all else," whispered Patrick.

Just then, two shots rang out from the rear of the house. Bomber almost dived to the floor but managed to stop himself. He was grateful for the darkness in that the others could not see how jumpy he was. The shots were unmistakable that of an SLR.

"Right," said Bomber, getting control of his vocal cords again. "Torches on. Patrick, take the door Jamie with me up the stairs."

As they moved in the torchlight, Bomber froze and screamed, "Freeze. No one move."

Glinting in the torchlight was a tripwire stretched across the stairs. Attached at both ends was a grenade. "Didn't know you could do that," mumbled Bomber to himself, "Must have taken a very steady hand to get the tension just right."

Patrick was examining the second door and fixed at the top was a grenade rigged so when the door was opened, it would pull the pin and blow the unlucky person to hell and back.

Patrick shouted through the door where he could hear Blaze and told him the door was rigged and to wait for him to fix it.

Jamie produced the wire cutters from his side pouch and on close examination, Bomber decided it was safe to cut the wires of both, which they did.

"I wonder why they didn't rig the front door," Sean said and went to examine it. Then he swore, "Look at this." Set in a small hole in the floor were two grenades with wires attached to the pins. Both wires had snapped without the pins coming out because they were still splayed instead of being straightened. One was partially out and Sean gingerly pushed it back in.

"We came very close to getting full of shrapnel," Sean said in a subdued voice.

Patrick had unbolted the door to let Blaze in and Bomber explained the situation. There had been no sound from upstairs during this time and that worried Bomber.

The two shots they had heard was Blaze shooting a man carrying an AK47 descending the back outside stairs to the yard.

Heart thumping furiously, Bomber slowly climbed the stairs, rifle held at waist-level but pointing straight at the doorway at the top.

The SLR's long barrel meant it was not the best weapon for this work and Bomber wished he had the Sterling sub machinegun in his hands which was ideal for house clearing. The one advantage of the SLR was the bullets would pass through almost any brick or wood at close range.

Stopping on the short landing and using his torch, he searched carefully for any wires or signs of tampering. The bare boards looked dusty and had footprints on them. *A good sign or not?* Bomber wondered.

Looking down, he could just make out Jamie looking up at him and he signaled him to come up.

Jamie came up like a scalded cat as if he did not want to put any weight on the steps and took up a kneeling position to one side with his SLR pointing at the door and nodded to Bomber. Jamie's face looked tense and Bomber guessed his must look the same.

Bomber felt himself sweating heavily and his stomach was in a knot. One more second and he felt he would lose control of his bowels and shit himself. Angrily wiping the sweat away from his eyes, Bomber stepped forward and tried the wooden latch of the door. It lifted easily and Bomber pushed it hard and it swung open with a thump as it connected with the wall. They both waited. Then taking his torch, he swung the beam through the doorway into the room. He could not see any wires in the entrance but what he could see was a body lying on its back as if asleep. An AK47 lay to one side and several magazines were stacked under the window. Shattered shutters let in a pattern of moonlight painting the body with a series of sig sag of light and shadows.

An open door and half a dozen steps to the left lead to the roof but Bomber felt drained and called down room clear but that the roof still needed clearing. Sean, Jos, and Blaze came up. Sean and Jos went cautiously up the steps to clear the roof and to stand sentry there in case any trouble started out on the street, but the vehicles had blocked the road and the escorts and drivers were alert and ready.

"Well done," said Blaze to Bomber and Jamie. "I've called for the meat wagon and once they arrive and number one has finished searching bodies, we are out of here."

Bomber tried not to look at the dead body. It was clear he had been shot in the face and upper chest but it must have been the wood splinters that had torn the flesh away from his face.

Bomber walked to a corner and tried to be sick but nothing came up except some bile which burned his throat. He spat it out and stepped away just as number one came into the room. He looked grim and gingerly searched the body, all the while muttering to himself that he was too fucking old for this shit over and over.

Bomber felt for him. He was probably in late forties or early fifties, a little overweight and had the face of a man who liked a few gins or whiskeys each evening. 'Probably spent most of his life working in various shit holes around the world dealing with the dross and then ended up here risking his neck and for what? Low pay, an overseas allowance and a crummy pension that would probably not keep him in food and clothes in his old age. Just another ex-colonial trying to adapt to a changing world.'

"But some sucker has to do it, eh!" Bomber was taken by surprise as number one stood up and looked at Bomber. Even in the dim light of the torches, he felt as if number one was seeing right into his mind and knew what he had been thinking.

"Guess so, but right now I think I would rather be a postman in Blighty."

Number one laughed and said, "Maybe but you would be bored out of your skull after day one. The likes of us are addicted to this stuff and the both of us will do this until we are pensioned off or killed whichever comes first, mark my words."

Bomber felt that his whole life had been mapped out for him in that one sentence. Would he soldier on until he dropped or was killed? He knew in his heart that he would never be anything other than a soldier.

"That's the meat wagon arriving. Let's get out of here before the locals get up the courage to come and have a look at us."

At the ACI, the three teams that had been deployed that night had all experienced similar incidents. The other two had both been on the end of coordinated grenade attacks with damage to vehicles but fortunately only one flesh wound to one of the escorts. However, it was clear that the dissidents had decided to take out the teams but had been unlucky to not score a kill. Bomber rationalized that was how it could go some times.

The head man said that a full review of intelligence gathering, the source and the response, would be carried out in detail the next day.

With that, they all went for some breakfast, followed by a shower and wonderful sleep. Except that Bomber kept dreaming he was climbing an endless flight of stairs and each step had a tripwire and when he looked down to his feet, he saw the shattered and torn face of the gunman.

Bomber was relieved when chatting with the others, over tea that afternoon, to hear they had similarly disturbed sleep, meaning he was not the only one.

Donnie, who had just returned from scrounging another mug of tea from the cook house, said excitedly, "Did you hear about Mac?"

Cpl. 'Mac' McBride and Bomber had worked together in Bomber's first section.

"What? Stop slurping that brew and tell us," demanded Sean.

"He escorted the head man back home last night. That's the first time he has let anyone do that, but I guess with what's happening. He thought it was a good idea."

"Will you fucking well get on with it? You're like a gibbering baboon but not as smart," snapped Sean, getting angry with Donnie's longwinded explanation.

"Alright, well, when they got to his flat, Mac went in first and waiting with a pistol in his hand was a gunman. When he saw Mac, he ran for it out through the kitchen and Mac sent him on his way with a burst from his SMG." Donnie finished with a flourish and took a large gulp of tea looking quite smug at being first with the story.

Later, Blaze and Doyle gathered everyone together including those on escort to the SB men. A long discussion took place on tactics and drills to be adopted for the future. Stones were used to emphasize positions and all were invited to have an input.

Entry into the buildings and dealing with booby traps was top on the list. It had brought it home to all of them just how lucky they had been bashing in the wired up door.

Bomber suggested that they use a method he had seen demonstrated at Warminster as an IJLB and Blaze and Doyle seemed to like the idea and said they would pass it up but he would do it through the ACI and not the unit as the ACI could go straight to the top for clearance.

The next day, an RE (Royal Engineer) Sgt. and an SAS (Special Air Service) trooper turned up with an assortment of wood, plastic explosive, and fuse cord. They all gathered round the pair keen to see what was going to happen.

The RE Sgt. joined two of the four-foot planks together with a couple of nails making a St. Andrews cross. At each end, he placed a wad of plastic explosive into which he inserted a round of gun cotton. Taking four lengths of detonator cord, he attached a detonator to each and placed the detonators into the gun cotton rounds. The fuses were attached to the center of the crossed boards and joined with another single piece of fuse which was the piece to light. The length of which gave you the timing before it all exploded. The Sgt. then demonstrated how to test the burn time of the fuse cord, no less than thirty seconds he emphasized.

Unfortunately, they could not test the effects with an explosion in their present location but he assured everyone that this would blow open any door and if placed against the wall of a house, it would blow a hole large enough to allow easy entry. It would eventually become known as a 'mouse hole charge'.

The Trooper took everyone through updated house clearing techniques and what to watch out for and then he introduced them to the *S* mine, a nasty piece of hardware developed by the Germans during the war. Later copied by the Soviet Block, it was an anti-personal mine set off by the pressure of someone stepping on it. The first detonation lifted it up into the air and the second blast blew shrapnel over a wide area, making it lethal for unprotected troops.

Bomber pondered the fact that although we have a new weapon at our disposal, so do they. Things were becoming very complicated.

No raids were conducted over the next two nights, the attempts at setting the AIC guys up with duff information and an ambush. The attempted murder of the head of AIC showed that the raids where effective in upsetting the dissidents, mainly the NLF, and it was considered important to keep the pressure on and show that the AIC could not be intimidated.

It was decided that all the teams would deploy and hit a group of houses in the Sheikh Othman area and that the new entry method had been cleared for use. They were after some leading members of the NLF and it was reported that in at least two of the locations, there would be a large catch of arms.

Timings for the raids would be changed to try and catch the dissidents off guard. Instead of going in between two and four in the morning, they would hit at a quarter to midnight.

As they left, the AIC Bomber felt relaxed. He had managed a nap in the afternoon and had slept like a baby. Now he was alert and felt in control of not just his body but his mind as well.

The teams took slightly different routes at a set speed so that they would all arrive at the targets at the same time. Bomber's team's target was more like a hovel and he wondered if they were at the wrong location but number one assured them it was correct. The building was single-story made of thick mud bricks and had a stout-looking door. A backyard surrounded by a six-foot fence made of wood and tin sheeting enclosed the back of the house. There was no gate.

A silent approach with the vehicles being left out of sight was adopted. Patrick carried the new explosive entry cross which was placed against the side wall of the building – no more taking chances on going in through the door.

Patrick lit the fuse and scurried back to the others, who were sheltering behind a wall some twenty yards away. When the explosion occurred, it was louder and more forceful than he had imagined it would be. They sprinted to the building where a hole had been blown in the wall. The width was almost that of the cross but the upper part of the wall had collapsed, meaning they did not even have to bend down to gain entry.

Inside was confusion. Any light that had been on had been blown out. Thick dust filled the air. Cries of "Room clear" came back to Bomber and now they could use their torches to begin examining the rooms.

In a back room, Sean had discovered two men who were on sleeping mats. They had been sleeping. Now they were completely dazed and disorientated from the explosion. They could have been father and son but number one confirmed that they looked like the ones on his list. They were handcuffed and taken to the vehicles.

Searching the two large rooms, they drove probes into the earth floor looking for soft spots, but it was Jos who let out a cry of triumph when under the crude table in the back room he found two pistols cleverly slotted into separate holsters that had been screwed to the wood. Anyone who had been sitting at the table could easily draw the pistols and shoot without even getting off the chair.

In the backyard, they found two four-foot long steel tubes, innocent enough by themselves but one end on each had been welded closed with a heavy steel plate. Shining his torch inside, Bomber could see that the inside of the plate had a protruding piece in the center.

"You know if they had some mortar bombs, I would swear these were mortar tubes," Patrick said thoughtfully.

"I think you're right," and called number one in to inspect the find. He agreed, laughing out loud and exclaimed, "This will slow the bastards down."

In one corner under some tarpaulin was a small welding kit and some more steel tubing.

Both finds were dragged out to the vehicles and jammed in. The only thing missing was some mortar bombs to make the evening complete. Bomber figured that this was a workshop, so the bombs would be stored elsewhere, maybe at one of the other target houses.

On returning to the AIC, they found out that mortar bombs had indeed been found at one of the other targets plus some weapons and ammunition.

This was their last raid. The AIC boys took a couple of days to question those arrested and evaluate the effect of the night's work on the NLF.

A new set of teams had arrived. Bomber and the rest were waiting for transport to take them back to barracks. They all felt disappointed to be going as they considered they had achieved a lot in a very short time working alongside the AIC. Bomber suspected that normal duties were going to be a little dull in comparison.

Just as they were about to climb aboard the trucks to leave, Bomber saw number one walking towards them. He smiled for the first time that Bomber could remember.

"Thanks, lads, for all your hard work. Keep your heads down and stay safe." They all gave him a cheer and comments such as, "Any time you need real soldiers to help you, let us know."

Bomber heard later that number one had been badly injured by a grenade tossed onto the balcony of his flats where he was sitting one evening. The culprit was not caught.

Chapter 19
Roll on Death De-Mob too Far Away!

"Only five more months of this and we will be flying home," Jos muttered quietly to Bomber. "All we have to do is stay alive."

There had been a few casualties recently amongst the security forces, two to an *S* mine which had been buried on a verge by a road where they had been patrolling. It had been set off by a child standing on it while playing there.

The child had been killed and three of his playmates badly injured. The security patrol had been well spread out; those injured had shrapnel wounds. The effect on the lads hearing about the children put them all in a dark mood.

Bomber thought that the NLF didn't care who they kill just as long as the terror effect was maximized to ensure control over the population and to make it more difficult for the security forces to operate against them.

Bomber stared out over the compound wall of the Sheikh Othman police station. Jos' words kept coming back to him, 'Stay alive. Stay alive'. They were on the roof with an LMG and it was pitch black, the only light being the millions of stars. All the house and huts around the station were in darkness. It was three o'clock in the morning, a dangerous time as it's when all sentries began to feel drowsy.

Bomber was not sure what made him notice but something in the alleyway directly opposite them attracted his attention and was beginning to make him jumpy.

"I think there is someone out there," he whispered to Jos.

"Point me," Jos whispered back, pulling the LMG tight into his shoulder.

"See the alley over there." Bomber indicated by pointing. "The one with the very dark shadow. Every now and again I think the shadow changes somehow. Look about ten yards or so in."

"Got it. Ring down and get the okay to blast it. Let's not wait to get taken out."

Just as Bomber lifted the field telephone, a voice rang out in clear English, "Don't shoot. Plain clothes patrol needs to come in."

Bomber relayed it to Doyle below in the control room and the next minute, the gates opened. Doyle's thick Londonderry voice cut through the night, "Double in and hold your hands in the air."

Four shadows sprinted across the road and into the compound. The heavy gate was slammed shut behind them.

The four were quickly surrounded, pushed against the wall, and frisked. One told Doyle he needed to get to a phone quick and to keep a watch out for anyone that might have been following them.

Bomber had been distracted by the activity in the compound but Jos had kept his eyes firmly on the alley that the patrol had emerged from.

"Look more shadows," he hissed.

Bomber tried to focus not looking directly into the alley but used his peripheral vision and sure enough the shadows moved, more of a ripple than anything else.

"Fuck it. Let's do this," Bomber swiveled the spotlight by his side lining it up on the alleyway. Ringing down to Doyle on the phone, he got Sean, and Bomber told him what they were going to do.

More movement. Bomber let go of the phone and flicked the switch and a beam of bright light stabbed the alleyway.

"Jesus Christ!" yelled Jos. Then he let rip with a ten round burst from the LMG.

Crouched in the alley was a group of men. All looked armed and they did not flee but started shooting back and Jos let them have it with three well-aimed bursts.

Bomber reloaded for him. Suddenly the spotlight disintegrated and Bomber heard himself curse as pain shot through his hand. The spotlight was ripped violently from his grasp. A burst of gunfire had come from a different direction, taking them by surprise. By now heads were coming through the hatch way and bodies crawled to firing positions on the roof.

Another sustained burst of fire cracked over the roof and Bomber guessed that it was intended to make them keep their heads down.

Two of the lads returned fire and that put an end to any more shooting from that direction. Suddenly all was quiet, no incoming fire after a minute or so. They could hear vehicles revving up and driving away.

Doyle had organized a fighting patrol which he was going to lead. Bomber was ordered down to the control room to man the radio. He also got given a reprimand from Doyle for using the spotlight.

"You know it's a target for every gun toting knob head around. Now the standby platoon is on its way. I am going to do a sweep of the alleyway." With that, he disappeared into the night.

The patrol did a sweep of the alley and for a block around the station. One body was found in the alley along with lots of blood and drag marks, indicating someone was wounded. Under the dead man's body was an AK47, scattered around were empty cartridges.

The field telephone rang and Bomber answered to hear to Sean telling him about gunfire to the south. Bomber relayed it to Company HQ. They acknowledged and asked for an update on the situation at the station which Bomber gave.

He later learned that the standby Platoon had run into the vehicles with the fleeing gunmen. When they had tried to block the road, a gunfight had erupted. One of the platoons was slightly wounded but two gunmen were killed and their weapons recovered.

The three on-duty policemen had removed themselves from the front of the building and were in one of the cells drinking mint tea. Bomber did not blame them. Poorly paid and unarmed, they had to live in the community with their families and try to survive. If the regime fell, they would undoubtedly be the subject of revenge, punishment or would be killed.

Bomber looked at his hand that had been holding the spotlight. It hurt and was swollen but there was no visible wound.

The lamp must have been struck by one of the bullets which ripped it from my hand, thought Bomber, *causing the damage.* Better not let Doyle see it or he will never let me live it down.

Doyle and the patrol returned dragging the body between them which they laid out in the compound and then covered it with a tarpaulin.

Later an ambulance, escorted by RMPs, turned up, collected the body and the AK47 and then disappeared at high speed.

The four-man patrol that had sort sanctuary in the station was drinking tea. They were reluctant to talk about what had happened apart from they had run into the large heavily armed group while on another mission. Knowing they could not win a firefight against so many dissidents, as they only had handguns with them, they made a run for the station, making it just in time.

Just before dawn two Land Rovers turned up and took them away, no-cap badges were seen, so the conjecture was they were sneaky beakies or SAS.

The Company Commander arrived unannounced late on the day after the shooting. Doyle briefed him, while Bomber sat at the operation table listening. The Company Commander congratulated Doyle on his handling of the events but informed Doyle that they would have to stay on an extra day before being relieved.

When he had left, Doyle said, "Well I am glad I'm in our nice cozy police station and not doing another dammed cordon and search."

On returning to barracks, Char wallah was there to meet them. He was now living in the barracks in one of the old garages made available by the QM. His shack which he shared with two others had been attacked by a group of men and burnt down. The three of them barely escaped with their lives but lost what belongings they had.

He explained the attackers were shouting anti-British slogans and calling them, "British arse lickers."

Later, the lads had a whip round and gave him some clothes and some cash. He was visibly moved by this and thanked everyone endlessly. Shaking hands, he promised he would always be there to serve tea until the end of time.

"Hope I'm not going to be here that bloody long," exclaimed Jos.

Sitting in the NAAFI that evening, taking small sips of their cold beers to make them last, they talked about the next four months left of the tour.

"Would we go back up country?" Sean asked.

"Would we get the bloody Flag Staff job again?" Jos speculated.

"I'm for HMS Sabre best food in Aden," John exclaimed.

"Well, all I can say is roll on death de-mob is too far away." With that, Jos stretched and said, "I'm off to my pit. Don't wake me unless the bunk is on fire because I will be dreaming about making love to a beautiful woman."

"She would have to be blind to make love to you," scoffed Patrick.

"I'll have you know back in Northern Ireland I have to beat the girls off with a stick and all due to my good looks and personality."

With that, he staggered off to cries of, 'pull the other one' and 'was that in your dreams as well?'

Bomber lay on his bed listening to a squadron of mosquitoes trying to find a way through his mossy net and reflected on the last eighteen months since leaving England and joining the regiment.

The ultra-realistic training that all the new boys did on arrival in Aden, which some could not cope with. The first experience of the relentless heat, hard physical training combined with the training staff making it more stressful by shooting live rounds overhead. Sleep deprivation and constant patrol drills. All this wore down even the most resilient of them but Bomber loved it, playing games in his head to keep going, using his stubborn streak to defy the pressure of being the youngest new boy. He knew the staff would jump on and exploit any sign of weakness. Being pushed straight onto an NCO's cadre on the recommendation of the training officer did not give him any time to recover physically. Fortunately, the cadre was less on beasting them and more on teaching. He had taken some stick from the older candidates on the course, but soon put an end to that, by showing them that his IJLB training put him well ahead and he finished top of the class. This meant that he would automatically be promoted but as he was still only seventeen.

The Commanding Officer had doubts, so a little test was devised for Bomber.

Dressed in trainers, shorts, and a vest standing in a boxing ring with a PTI talking to him while fitting him with boxing gloves. The PTI was a tall muscular L/Cpl.

As he tightened the gloves, he asked Bomber, "Have you boxed before?"

"Yes, a little at IJLB." This was a slight exaggeration to say boxing. They had all been taught the basic and then sparring which was a part of their physical training lessons.

"Right, that shit head over there," he indicated to Bomber a beefy-looking opponent in the opposite corner. "He is a lot heavy than you, and he fancies himself as an Energy Cooper, so keep moving, make him chase you, use your left. He will drop his left hand when he is ready to throw a right at you, so get in quick with your right over the top, got that?"

Bomber nodded and then the bell went.

The Commanding Officer, Bomber's Company Commander, the RSM, and a dozen other hangers on sat watching.

Beefy moved into the center of the ring and quickly swung a left and right. Bomber swayed back at the waist and shot a hard left jab at Beefy's nose and it contacted with a satisfying smack.

Beefy stopped startled. He paused for a second as blood trickled into his open mouth, so Bomber hit him twice more which seemed to galvanize him into action. Now he stalked Bomber, throwing hard left and right hooks which Bomber blocked with his arms and jab in return. Then to Bomber's relief, the bell went and he gratefully returned to his corner, his arms feeling numb from blocking the powerful punches.

The PTI was full of praise and told him to use his right after the left jab as he sponged Bomber with cold water.

The bell sounded for round two and Bomber walked straight into a punch that sat him on his back side. Bomber shook his head. Everything seemed to have slowed down. The referee was counting and Bomber could hear his PTI telling him to get up and move. Struggling to his feet, Bomber saw Beefy rushing in. Side stepping, he swung a right at Beefy which connected with the side of his head and sent Beefy reeling into the ropes. Bomber moved and Beefy chased, but now Beefy was angry at this shrimp, hitting him and making him look foolish. Bomber jab, and every time Beefy dropped his left guard to throw a right, Bomber hit him with his right.

Then a voice said, "Enough!" The referee stepped between them. The Commanding Officer who had spoken nodded to the Company Commander and then they all followed the Commanding Officer from the gymnasium.

The gym quickly emptied and Bomber stood with the PTI who was removing Bomber's gloves. Suddenly Beefy was there pushing at Bomber, "You shit, I will have you later just you see." That was as far as he got the PTI head butted him and Beefy fell to the canvas. As Beefy lay there, the PTI put his foot on his chest and said, "Try anything and I will come after you. Now fuck off and keep trying to convince yourself that you are a boxer."

Beefy struggled to his feet and disappeared to the changing room.

Later that day on Company orders appeared Bomber's promotion to L/Cpl.

That all seemed tame compared to his first encounter with the enemy and being shot at and shooting back, the first dead bodies and seeing the result of what you did at close quarters. Bomber was relieved that he had not had any repetition of those dreams lately. He wondered if he was getting hardened to the death, squalor, and the killing of human beings.

Bomber fell asleep with the little voice in his head whispering, 'You are alive. Don't worry about tomorrow. It will take care of itself.'

Chapter 20
Fighting Sappers

The dust hung in the air and Bomber sipped the warm water from his bottle, rinsing his mouth to try and clear the dust that had coated his throat.

The whole Platoon was on foot, spread out on the Dhala road not too far from the village of Al Milah. The Dammed were on point. They would move in pairs leapfrogging through, scanning for likely ambush spots or any signs that the road had been booby-trapped. The object of the patrolling was to stop the NLF from taking over control of this ancient route that went all the way to Mecca.

They had been on the road for three days. Patrolling by day and at night, they would harbor up in a strong defensive position with the hope the NLF would attack, but so far they had not taken the bait.

Each morning before dawn, they would stand too, then have breakfast and move out. Two Pioneers with mine sweepers worked with the lead section, followed by the rest of the Platoon. At the rear, the platoon truck with all their needs crawled along guarded by a Saladin armored car.

A day behind them, another platoon followed doing just the same. Any NLF activity after the first Platoon had past would be caught between the two.

Studying the road ahead, Bomber could see a team of Sappers doing some construction work. They were the Territorial Army Parachute Sappers. As they approached, Bomber could see they had a sentry out and he waved for them to stop as they drew close. A S/Sgt. came down to Bomber and asked if they had any spare water in the following truck? Their resupply had failed to show up yesterday and they were getting low. Bomber told him to speak to the Sgt. who was with the truck.

Leaving the Sappers, the Dammed carried on as point section. The two Pioneers swept the ground with their mine detectors just in front of Sean and John who were leading the way. The Pioneer in charge was a Cpl. called Trait, a very thin, sunburnt man from Norfolk. He raised his hand and Bomber and his section went to ground in all round defense. The Cpl. indicated they had found something. He stretched out flat on the ground, carefully clearing the soil and stones in front of him using a small trowel. He dug down a short way and then reached down into the hole.

Trait then got to his feet and instructed the other Pioneer to search the verges on either side of the road. Walking over to Bomber, he sat wearily down beside him and asked, "See anything to make you think we are walking into trouble?"

Bomber shook his head, "No, but I have been feeling uneasy since we left the Sappers."

"Know what you mean. This could be where they put in an objection to us being here." He nodded in the direction of where he had been digging. "Got a land mine double stacked, one on top of the other plus there's a wire buried going that way," he indicated uphill to the left trying not to be obvious. "So I will have to take a chance and cut it, so you need to get your lads further away."

Bomber heard footsteps coming up from behind him. Upon turning, he saw the Platoon Commander approaching. "Okay, tell this to the boss. I will move the lads further away into a better defensive position. What are you going to do with the mines?"

"Well, they are going to be detonated by whoever put them there remotely. So after I have cut the wire, I guess it will be me that blows them."

The Cpl. briefed Blaze while Bomber moved his section further away and into better fire positions. None of them needed to be told to put on their steel helmets which were being carried hooked on to their rear pouches.

Bomber heard Sean calling him, so went to his position. Sean pointed higher up the hillside to the left. "Some movement up there, possibly two men maybe more and they are going uphill now."

Bomber used the radio to brief Blaze who told him to sit tight. After a few minutes, he came to Bomber with one section and Bomber pointed where the men had been spotted.

"Right. We are going up to investigate you stay here and protect the Pioneers."

With that, Blaze set off up the hill with one section. Bomber watched with Sean as the section kept disappearing then reappearing through the scrub and rocks.

A shout from the Pioneer Cpl. signaled that he was blowing the mines.

A great roar ripped through the air and Bomber felt the life being sucked from his lungs and then a rush as the red hot air seemed to force its way back. Stones spattered around them and Bomber heard one or two clangs as stones landed on helmets.

The ever-alert Sean shook Bomber by the shoulder and pointed up the slope. Blaze and one section were returning. Stopping by Bomber, Blaze informed him that the wire ended at the point when the men had been spotted. No detonating device had been found but judging by the number of cigarette butts. There must have been about four of them hanging around there for some time.

Returning to the road, they found two section shoveling rocks and dirt into a crater that the explosion had created. It was obvious that two mines stacked on top of each other would have completely written off a truck and possibly destroyed a Saladin. Blaze reported back to Company HQ using the radio. He then called a Section Commanders *O* group.

He was about to start the briefing when a shout went up from the second Pioneer, who was checking the edge of the track with his mine sweeper. He had found an anti-personal mine. Trait went and joined him. After a cautious search, they found four in total which Trait put in a pile and attached some plastic explosive ready to blow them.

The destruction of the anti-personal mines was a damp squid compared to the ear-shattering roar of the anti-tank mines and hardly registering with the Platoon who had become hardened to such things.

Blaze continued with his briefing saying that they would push on to the nights position and that he would put two sections up front one either side of the road covering the pioneers. The

Saladin would also be moved forward to stay just behind the Pioneers. Bomber and his section would be in reserve which pleased Bomber as they had been on point all morning.

As they moved off, it was obvious to Bomber that the NLF were trying to establish some boundaries that if crossed would be punished. Having defeated the first boundary, thanks to a very brave Pioneer Cpl., Bomber considered the next line in the sand would be a far more aggressive affair.

Great care was taken by the Platoon Commander in organizing defensive fields of fire at the night camp. Trip flares were placed just about everywhere around their position. The truck was placed in the middle of the position with the Saladin. The Platoon Sgt. brought extra ammunition to each section and told them a hot stew would be ready shortly.

It would be a long night with half of the Platoon on watch and half-resting, waiting for an attack to come. When it came, it was not what any of them had expected.

They heard the explosions and machinegun fire echoing around the mountains a little before midnight. Listening carefully, Bomber could tell it came from back down the road they had traveled that day. They could now hear the sound of SLRs and LMGs firing in reply to the explosions that seemed to come at regular intervals between long bursts of heavy caliber machinegun fire.

"Whatever is happening, it was not just a few pot shots by a small band of NLF," Sean spoke in a loud whisper to Bomber.

"It's big and someone is in real trouble. Could be the Sappers or the rear Platoon," he replied.

Bomber could hear Blaze talking on the radio and next came the call for section commanders.

Five minutes later, they were on the road hot footing back towards the sound of the gunfire. Doyle and what there was of the Pl. HQ section, the Saladin, and truck was staying put. The Sappers were under attack by a large group of dissidents armed with RPGs and machineguns. The rear Platoon, that was a day behind, was also making the best speed towards the firing, hoping to catch the enemy between them.

It had taken over four hours after passing the Sappers' location to reach the night position walking at the pace the Pioneers set with their mine sweepers. That was in daylight and now they were moving in the dark not knowing if they too were walking into an ambush. Even dropping good patrolling drills and running most of the way, they would probably take two hours or more to get there. Bomber wondered if they would be quick enough to help the Sappers. As long as they could hear SLRs and LMG firing, they knew the Sappers were holding out.

Two hours later, they had reached a prominent bend in the road that had some trees that overhung the bend. Bomber and the Dammed were leading. Bomber stopped and signaled for all to halt.

Sniffing the air, Bomber caught a faint whiff of rancid tobacco smoke that had become so familiar to him. Or was it his imagination just working overtime?

Bomber signaled Sean to cover them with the LMG while they advanced in pairs intending to leapfrog through. Suddenly bursts of fire came from under the trees before Bomber could hit the ground. Sean had let loose the longest burst from the LMG that he had ever heard. It must have been a full mag as he heard Sean reload while the rest of the section laced the area with SLR fire.

Realizing that there was no more returning fire, Bomber called ceasefire. Watching and waiting, Bomber was aware of groaning coming from behind him. Bomber called out, "Is any one hit?"

The groaning stopped. "I'm not hit but I think I've broken my fucking arm," came a reply from John.

"See to him, Donnie. Sean, keep us covered." Bomber ordered Jos and Patrick to follow him and they circled right to give Sean a clear field of fire while they closed on the ambush position.

The position was cleared and Bomber called the others forward. Blaze came with them. After a quick discussion, they agreed that rather than an ambush they were probably just a couple of lookouts who were now off to warn the main group.

Donnie reported that John had broken his left arm when he had dived for cover. He had strapped it up and Blaze had ordered him to follow with the rear section. Blaze now wanted the pace increased as they could still hear explosions and machinegun fire and it was very close.

They now worked in pairs going forward and then kneeling to cover the next pair. Doing this at a jog gave some illusion of good patrolling and at the same time increased the speed they covered the ground.

Bomber didn't like it but if they were to help the Sappers, they had to keep moving and the sound of firing would cover the noise they made jogging on the stony ground.

At Patrick's insistence, Bomber stopped. They were getting to spread out. Bomber felt his lungs were on fire and his legs heavy with fatigue. A few minutes later, the others caught up and Jos who was tail end. Charlie gasped out that he had lost touch with the next section.

"Okay, let's wait for them to catch up." Sean stopped him before he could say anything else. "Listen."

They listened and realized that the firing had stopped. Bomber looked up and saw the night sky was getting lighter but dawn was still some way off.

Blaze staggered up and Jos called him to their position and he slumped down. The other section took cover on the other side of the road. Blazed gulped down water from his bottle and gasped, "The firing has stopped. Shit, I hope the bastards haven't overrun the position."

"Right. Let's go and keep going. No stopping."

They set off. The short rest had caused Bomber's muscles to stiffen and it took a while before he could move freely.

Hearing the others suffering, he realized that he had to slow the pace or lose his men to fatigue and dehydration. Suddenly, Bomber knew where they were. It was the straight section of road where the Sapper had stopped him asking about water. Their position was just a short distance further on.

Halting the section, he waited for Blaze to arrive. Listening to the groans coming from the guys, it was clear that they would not be able to shoot straight until they had rested and taken on water.

Bomber reached for his water bottle, shook it, and realized he was down to a just a few swallows. Each swallow felt like nectar as it went down.

Blazed organized the Platoon to move forward two sections up with him leading. One section was in reserve and they advanced along the road. The big danger now was being fired on by the Sappers thinking we were NLF. After about a hundred yards, Blazed stopped and cupping his hands like a trumpet around his mouth, he called out and identified himself.

No reply. *This did not bode well*, thought Bomber. Blazed tried again, after a pause a voice called out, "What's the Arsenal football team's nickname?"

"How the fuck do I know?" Blaze shouted back. "I'm a rugby man."

"It's the Gunners, sir," Bomber called out quickly, not wanting to be shot up by his own side.

"My Cpl. said it's the Gunners."

"Okay, come in."

By now, it was getting lighter and the Platoon spread out taking up fire position and listened to the Sappers as to where the NLF had been firing from. Looking around at were RPGs had landed, it must have been a hell of a fight and the Para Sappers had done extremely well to beat them off.

They had just settled in when the rear Platoon arrived. They too looked all in. Bomber realized they must have been pushed extremely hard as they would have been further away than his platoon.

The Sappers said they were running low on ammunition, when the enemy mounted a final strong attack with RPGs and machineguns. While others of them tried to reach their position on the left flank. Two of the Sappers were dead with at least five wounded. Donnie was helping with the wounded and had collected up just about the whole platoon's supply of field dressings.

Now there was the sound of trucks and Saladins coming from the South. Several ambulances also arrived and the wounded were loaded into them, including John who had passed out on reaching the Sappers' location.

A short while later, two Hawker Hunter aircraft flew over and later could be heard firing rockets and their cannons further on and higher up in the mountains.

Doyle had now arrived with the truck and Saladin. Blaze ordered the Platoon onto the back of the vehicles and Bomber found himself clinging on tightly to the Saladin all the way back to the night position. In daylight, the drive seemed to be over in minutes compared to the desperate nighttime run out. Bomber guessed Blaze considered the odds were against anyone ambushing us or the road having been mined with all the action on it last night.

With sentries, posted food and sleep were the priority. Bomber was woken by Doyle roughly shaking him and telling him to get himself and the section into gear as they were on the move.

Everyone was congregating at the truck were tea and biscuits were being quickly scoffed.

Bomber gulped his tea and listened to Blaze giving orders while taking large swallows of tea and demanding a refill for everyone before setting off. Bomber looked at his watch and realized that they had only had about four hours' rest. His body ached. Every muscle seemed to protest when he moved and his head felt fuzzy from lack of sleep.

There had been a report from the Hunter pilots that some of the NLF were holed up in caves not too far up the road in a position overlooking the road.

"Why the hell haven't the Hunters blasted them to the devil and back?" demanded Jos, "instead of us having to go up there?"

"Must be a good reason. You know how they love to fire off their rockets and cannons any chance they get," Bomber said without any real conviction.

"Oh, I know why. It's fucking tea time. There's no way they would miss that," Jos fired back.

Blaze led the Platoon up a side *wadi* until they could climb out onto a ridge that led to the area that the NLF were using to dominate the road. As they got to the top of the ridge, they took cover and scanned the area ahead. Several caves could be seen about two hundred feet below, a jagged peak that gave a clear view along the road and now through his binoculars, Bomber could make out figures moving around in the mouth of the caves. From this position, it became clear why the Hunters had not blasted them. The surrounding peaks and the position of the caves made it impossible for the Hunters to line up, fire, and be able to pull up without crashing into the mountain side.

Suddenly, the figures scurried into the caves like ants as the Saladin came into view on the road below. It then stopped at what Bomber would have guessed to be eight hundred yards. The plan being the Saladin would draw the NLF's attention while the Platoon made its way unseen left flanking, to the caves.

Eight hundred yards would be well out of range of any RPGs for a direct shot but not out of range of any heavy machineguns.

Using the radio, Blaze passed information to the Saladin Commander. A few seconds later, the Saladin's 76 mm gun opened up. A shell screamed towards the caves landing about fifty yards short. Blaze gave some more directions and then another shell crashed closer to the caves.

This was prompting an instant burst of machinegun fire from the caves followed by the flash of several RPGs and Bomber was surprised that they actually landed as close as a hundred yards of the Saladin. Perhaps they were getting the extra range due to the height advantage but at least the Saladin could pull back if they got to close.

Now they were on the move again, Blaze leading them in an arc to the left while the Saladin kept the NLF occupied. The terrain was difficult, jagged, and loose rock made a slip or fall likely for any one not concentrating on their footing. After almost twenty minutes of hard slog, they were a hundred and fifty yards from the caves. Bomber could clearly see figures moving out of the left-hand cave armed with RPGs trying to get within range of the Saladin. Blaze had spotted them and ordered one section to get in position and take them out.

In the next instant, a shell exploded in the mouth of the cave where the machineguns were firing from. There followed shouts of dismay from the RPG men who redoubled their efforts to get closer to the Saladin. As they abandoned any attempt at stealth, they were exposed to one section. The barrage of 7.62 mm bullets tore into them like a swarm of angry Bees.

A GPMG, LMG, and six SLR in trained hands can put down a huge amount of accurate firepower and one section did not waste any ammunition in less than a minute; the RPG men lay dead cut to ribbons.

Blaze set off again having told the Saladin Commander to cease fire on the caves, leapfrogging through, giving each other cover they approached the caves from the side. The left-hand cave looked empty, but Blazed signaled Bomber and his section to move closer and throw in some grenades.

Donnie and Patrick closed in while Bomber and the others trained their weapons on the entrance. Bomber saw them both throw in a grenade each and then ducked down out of line with the entrance. One high explosive sent out jagged fragments of muscle and bone-shattering metal. One white phosphorus grenade produced a large cloud of lung-choking smoke and burning phosphorus in all directions. There were no shouts, screams, or men running out of the cave, just swirling dust floating out into the daylight creating patterns in the air.

In the entrance to the next cave, Bomber could see a machinegun lying on its side, a large 12.6 mm on a tripod and what looked like a smaller caliber weapon. Several bundles lay close by. Bomber could only assume they were bodies.

Now Donnie and Patrick were creeping closer to this cave, ready to repeat the process with the grenades. Suddenly a burst of gunfire erupted from further back in the cave directed not at Donnie and Patrick but towards Bomber and the rest of the section. Sean who had the LMG with Jos was now working as his number two.

Bomber felt the sting of rock shattering and spattering his shoulders and back. Sean let rip with several three to five round bursts while shouting that Jos had been hit. As soon as Sean stopped firing, Donnie and Patrick rushed to the side of the cave and threw in the grenades. As the dust cleared, they ran in firing. A few seconds past and they both reappeared and signaled all-clear, Bomber saw Patrick vomiting and wondered if it was just the tension or had he had seen the results of the grenades on the gunman in the cave.

Jos was unconscious. A round had struck the side of his helmet cutting a grove almost through the metal. Blood trickled down the side of his face and Bomber turned him over, hoping his neck was not broken. The blood was coming from the side of his ear which had been cut by the chin strap when the helmet had been forced sideways by the impact.

Bomber poured water from his water bottle over Jos' face and he came to with a groan. "You are going to have one hell of a headache," Bomber told him. "But you are one lucky son of a gun."

"Just goes to show what lousy shots they are how could anyone miss a head as big as that?" Sean said, laughing with relief.

Jos struggled to sit up but sank back with a groan. Turning onto his side, he vomited, narrowly missing Sean who was quick enough to roll away.

Blaze ordered the caves to be searched. They found catches of water, food, and a lot of ammunition for both the machineguns and the RPGs. This was a clear change in tactics from the normal hit-and-disappear method. It had been a determined attack to take the Sappers' position and now they had been forming a strong defensive position to control the road.

Blazed had the weapons and ammunition stacked together and the Pioneer Cpl. who had been called forward to rig some plastic explosive to the pile ready to destroy them. Having retreated a safe distance, the pile was blown and some of the RPG rocket flew skywards and exploded, adding to the excitement.

That night, they all felt exhausted and Blaze ordered one hour stags in pairs to ensure that sentries could stay awake. Jos had been given some painkillers and was allowed to sleep through. Bomber could see the strain his Irish lads were under by just looking at their faces and guessed he must look the same. He certainly felt ragged. Bomber slept but someone kept replaying the cave scenes in his head over and over again. Finally it was his turn for sentry and it almost came as a relief to be with someone else who was awake and to watch the dark road for any sign of intruders.

After stand too, they had a breakfast of tinned beans and sausages and a large mug of tea. Blaze then called a section commanders briefing. He informed them that they were to remain in position until relieved by *B* Company, then they would be in reserve.

Everyone was happy that they would get a break to take stock. They were low on food and water and three section now only consisted of Bomber, Sean, Patrick, Donnie, and Jamie, having lost John with a broken arm and Jos who Donnie said had probably got concussion and needed to see the doctor. In fact, one section was the only full section in the Platoon with eight men.

At midday, the Company Commander arrived with all the paraphernalia of the Head Quarters. A little later, *B* Company pushed through and carried on up the road.

The Company C/Sgt. resupplied the platoon and even gave out some apples which were a rare treat. Making the most of the food and the rest, everyone was hoping that they would not have to move again that day.

Towards evening, there came the faint sound of gunfire from further up the road but it quickly died away and there was no call to stand too. The Company medic had checked Jos over and given him some more painkillers and pronounced him fit to return to duty. However, thinking he looked pale and shaky, Bomber asked Donnie to keep an eye on him.

While having a bad dream of being attacked by RPGs, he awoke to the sound of explosions and gunfire from further up the road where *B* Company would be.

Bomber nearly wet himself when a voice said close to his ear, "Big bad *B* getting it. Fancy a brew?" It was Donnie.

"Shit! Are you always making tea? Don't you sleep at all?"

"Just finished my stag, so putting a brew on for those having trouble sleeping."

"Listen," Bomber said, cocking his head to help hear clearly, "it's stopped."

"Yep, and I think it will be like this all the way up to the Radfan and we will be the donkeys that have to deal with it."

With that, Donnie disappeared and then reappeared within a few minutes with a hot mug of tea. As he handed it to Bomber, he said, "The C/Sgt. got hot stew at the back of the truck if you are hungry."

Bomber sipped his tea and wondered what they would be tasked with today. At the C/Sgt.'s truck, the Company chef had a thick stew and luxury of luxury's some bread. Bomber took two slices. The chef told him to make the most of it as its back to hard tack biscuits tomorrow.

After a mess tin full of the stew and the bread to mop up the gravy, he almost felt human again. It was now one hour before dawn. Bomber went and woke the rest of the section to get ready for stand too. Jos groaned but did not wake up. After several minutes of trying, Bomber gave up and went and got the company medic to look at him before taking up his own stand too position.

After stand too, the medic told Bomber that he had asked for a medevac helicopter to collect Jos as he was not at all happy with his condition.

Two hours after dawn, the helicopter arrived and Jos was loaded on and flown off to hospital in Aden. "The curse of the Dammed strikes again, eh!" said a voice from behind Bomber as he watched the helicopter gain altitude.

Turning, he saw the CSM looking a bit grim but also staring after the helicopter which was now just a dot in the blue sky.

Bomber nodded and replied, "Or it could be the luck of the Dammed as the bullet hit his helmet and not his skull."

The CSM nodded and then said, "The Company Commander is briefing the Platoon Commanders and I think you will find we are returning to Aden when relieved later today. So best get your lads organized." With that, he turned and walked away, his SLR looking like a toy in his large hands.

Later that day, the steady drone of helicopters could be heard until looking up. They could see a fleet of them heading up country.

Bomber thought he counted twenty which, if each held, a section of eight men that would be one hundred and sixty men, a reinforced company or so. The helicopters were flying high enough to be out of range of any heavy machinegun fire and once again Bomber was happy that his feet were on the ground and not in one of those flimsy machines.

Without any warning, the air was split with a scream as two Hunter jets roared overhead at low level following the line of the road and mountains. Bomber found himself instinctively ducking and then looked around sheepishly to see if he was the only one. He was relieved to see they had all ducked. The Hunters flew past several times during the morning and Bomber speculated that they must be hammering the NLF prior to the helicopters going in.

Just after midday, a convoy of trucks arrived. They loaded up and returned to Aden. Bomber and his lads were allocated one of the new Stalwart six-wheel cargo vehicles which could handle the rough terrain much better than the normal trucks, so they had a far more comfortable ride back to barracks.

Chapter 21
Oh No, Not you, Brown

The next six weeks passed with a monotonous repetition of patrols, guard duties, and cordon and searchers. Only one small riot and grenade dodging lifted the boredom for Bomber and the Regiment. It seemed all the best jobs were being given to the units arriving for a six-month tour of duty. These were arriving in greater numbers in the last few weeks and were being billeted in a makeshift camp near the airfield.

John had rejoined the section having had the plaster taken off of his arm. Jos had been flown back to England and apparently he was in a bad way. The Company Clerk promised to keep them updated on his condition.

At last, they were informed of when they would be leaving, what they would be doing and where. Six-week leave followed by reforming at Celle in Germany, to be equipped with the new armored personnel carriers, the four, three, twos as they were designated. Bomber had seen these vehicles demonstrated in Warminster in 1963. The fifteen-ton beast had tracks instead of wheels and could handle any terrain including swimming rivers. However, Bomber could not believe they ran on petrol instead of diesel. In the Second World War, the Germans called the Sherman Tanks Tommy Cookers as when they were hit the petrol incinerated the crew. Now the same mistake was being repeated with the new vehicles.

Bomber wondered what the Russians would call them if they got the chance to shoot at them.

The Company was formed up on the road outside of the Company offices. Tables and chairs had been placed on the pavement. Seated at them was the company clerk, the movement clerk, and the Pay Sergeant who had a large pile of money in front of him

One by one, names were called out. The individual marched to the table where he was given his flight details, passport, and finally his pay. Eventually Bomber was standing on his own and the clerks were clearing up the paperwork. Confused, Bomber turned to Doyle who was talking to the Company Sergeant Major. "What about me, Sergeant?"

Everyone stopped talking and clearing up and turned to look at him. *What the hell is going on?* wondered Bomber.

Doyle stared at him with a smile on his face. The CSM was grinning. It appeared to Bomber that they were both sharing a joke at his expense.

"Oh no, not you, Brown. You are going to Kenya. You have to report to Battalion Head Quarters. The Chief clerk will see you in twenty minutes."

Bomber was stunned and blurted out, "Kenya Sergeant, why am I going there?"

"Personnel training and development, Brown. You and two others. Don't worry, the Mau Mau war is over. It's a wonderful country. You'll enjoy it." Doyle burst out laughing and the others joined in.

Bloody hell, thought Bomber. *What now? Who the hell are the Mau Mau?*

At just over nineteen thousand feet, the view was stunning it completely took Bomber's breath away, what little he had left after the long climb to the summit of Kilimanjaro. Technically, he and the others from the Outward Bound School Loitoikitok Kenya had crossed the border into Tanzania as the summit of the long dormant volcano was on that side of the border.

The Outward Bound staff and students were the only people allowed to climb Kilimanjaro from the Kenya side. Sitting on the snow, Bomber felt elated and sick at the same time. Elated he had made the climb and sick suffering from the effect of altitude. The quick ascent made over two and a half days left, little time to acclimatize. Looking far across the plain below he could see the summit of Mount Kenya glinting white in the sunlight at just over seventeen thousand feet, it was the second highest on the continent. Bomber made a promise to himself that one day he would stand on that summit.

Bomber could not believe it had only been six short weeks since his flight from Aden to RAF Eastleigh, Narobi. The Argosy cargo plane, nicknamed the Whistling Wheelbarrow, had taken off from Aden with a cargo of explosives, ammunition, and thirty passengers. He had said a silent pray for a safe flight and landing in Kenya.

Since then, he had felt he had grown both physically and mentally. His mind had been open to a culture and country that he had not even dreamed of before, training with people from three different countries, Kenya, Uganda, and Tanzania under the guidance of the head of the School, a retired Parachute Regiment Major. It had been a wonderful experience.

The training at the Outward Bound School, situated on the wooded slopes of Kilimanjaro, was tough. At dawn, a cross country run finishing at the school's swimming pool. The water of which was fed straight from the streams that ran directly from Kilimanjaro's glaciers. The ice-cold water took the breath away but made everyone swim much faster.

Most of the Africans either could not swim or were poor swimmers. As children, they were taught that the rivers and lakes held terrors. Hippos, crocs, and snakes were best avoided for any recreation. Those from the coast appeared to lack this fear and seemed to enjoy the swimming pool sessions.

Bomber and the other two from the Regiment, Vicars and Sharkey, had been given the task of helping to teach the non-swimmers to stay on the surface of the water rather than on the bottom of the pool trying to walk. They had some success but the fear of the water was ingrained and Bomber didn't think any of them would be competing in the commonwealth games.

High in the trees, an Orangutan-designed rope course tested even the most daring of them. Team initiative test, unsupported treks across country watching lions stalking game, rhinos making mock charges at the team, giant crocs at the river ford. All wove a magic on him that he knew would stay with him for the rest of his days. Forgotten the dust, dirt, and death of the Radfan and Aden, at least for a short while, the coming weeks had pushed the horrors of the recent past even further back into the dark corners of his mind where they would lurk, waiting for the trigger that would call them back to haunt him. Little did Bomber know that trigger was not that far away!

Key

L/Cpl.   Lance Corporal second in command of an eight-man section.

Cpl.   Corporal commands a section of eight men.

SSgt.   Sergeant second in command of a Platoon of thirty-two men.

CQMS   Called Color Sgt. (C/Sgt.) looks after company stores and rations.

Pl Comd.   Platoon Commander of thirty-two men.

Lt.   Lieutenant, Normally a Platoon Commander.

Capt.   Captain normally second in command of a company.

Coy Comd.   Company Commander, commands a company of three rifle and one support.

CO   Commanding Officer, Lieutenant Colonel of a regiment.

PO   Political Officer, liaison with locals and military and much more.

Op Officer   Operations Officer normally in charge of selected operations.

PTI   Regimental Physical Training Instructor.

SLR	7.62 caliber self-loading rifle.
LMG	7.62 mm Light Machine Gun magazine-fed.
GPMG	7.62 mm General Purpose Machine Gun belt fed.
RPG	Rocket Propelled grenade.
Medivac/casevac	Casualty evacuation.
HQ	Head Quarters.
MTO	Motor Transport Officer.
FRA	Federal Regular Army.
Regt	Regiment.
NLF	National Liberation Front.
FLOSY	Front liberation of South Yemen.
MP	Military Policeman.
Donkey Walloper	Person from a cavalry regiment.
O group	Orders group for briefing commanders at any level.
Sanger	Improvised stone wall defensive position. Also Sangar or Sangu.
Rag Head	Term used to describe a local.
Stripes/tapes	Slang for the rank worn on the arm by Junior and senior NCOs.

Nick Names

Bomber	Anyone named Brown.
Chalky	Anyone named White.
Paddy	Any Irishman.
Micks	Any catholic Irishman, derogatory term.
Nobby	Anyone named Clark.